BATMAN
RISE OF SIN TZU

DEVIN KALILE GRAYSON AND **FLINT DILLE**
BASED ON THE GAME SCRIPT BY FLINT DILLE

BATMAN CREATED BY BOB KANE

ASPECT®

WARNER BOOKS

An AOL Time Warner Company

WARNER BOOKS EDITION

Cover design by Don Puckey
Cover illustration by Olivier Nicolas

Warner Books, Inc.
1271 Avenue of the Americas
New York, NY 10020

Visit our Web site at www.twbookmark.com

An AOL Time Warner Company

Printed in the United States of America

First Paperback Printing: November 2003

10 9 8 7 6 5 4 3 2 1

Shadow and Flame

The image of Batman's masked face flickers and then breaks down into visual static, replaced by what must be Sin Tzu's countenance, a frightening mask of mutable gold accented with a red and black Yin and Yang symbol on his forehead. There's something at once mesmerizing and threatening about him, like a beautifully colored poisonous snake you don't dare take your eyes from.

"The battle is fully joined, albeit its outcome is a certainty."

"First rule of war, Sin Tzu," Batman answers calmly. "There are no certainties."

The Marauders

The Scarecrow: He controls fear itself and can leave the strongest opponent, even Batman, paralyzed with abject, uncontrollable terror . . .

Clayface: This villain can transform his mutated body into nearly anyone or anything, including new weapons and attacks that Batman has never before encountered . . .

Bane: Brilliant, impossibly strong, and inhumanly cruel, he is a one-man mercenary apocalypse with venom coursing through his veins . . .

The Defenders

Nightwing: Dick Grayson's all grown up—and still doing what he does best—guarding Batman's back . . .

Robin: Batman's current protégé, Tim Drake, is a tough kid with an uncanny understanding of Gotham's mean streets . . .

Batgirl: Barbara Gordon is the wild card, a seasoned fighter with unique skills and instincts.

Join the Dark Knight's war to save Gotham City, with non-stop action in a thrilling adventure based on the exciting new video game from Ubi Soft.

BATMAN: Rise of Sin Tzu

CONTENTS

PROLOGUE

Sin Tzu
11:27 p.m.

At this moment, the conqueror of Gotham City sits cross-legged behind the bars of a cell marked "Sin Tzu," though no one will realize this for many hours. My strike will begin precisely at midnight. As I wait out the final half hour, I remember words I wrote long ago:

> *The great commander will always seize the highest*
> *ground, whether on the battlefield or whether in his*
> *mind. He must always see the battle as a vulture*
> *would see it, from high above . . . watching for the*
> *place of death, knowing that death spreads from*
> *death as fire spreads from fire . . .*

If one were to look down upon the streets of Gotham, at first glance one would hardly see what could make this grim, dark metropolis a more desirable battlefield than any other modern American city. Its architectural cacophony of skyscrapers, office buildings, apartments, parking lots, shopping malls, and bodegas is not unusual, particularly in the daylight hours.

But at night, the darkness has an uncanny depth. Which, I admit, makes Gotham City particularly intoxicating ... but that in and of itself is not uniquely attractive to me.

No, the allure of Gotham is in its defender. After dark, the citizens of Gotham brace themselves with stories of a bat-winged guardian hostile to the night's predators. A man so ultimately trained in mind and body as to be the perfect combatant. The perfect warrior.

The perfect opponent.

This city lives under his shadow.

Do you see, hiding like a cancer just to the left of the city's heart, the stunted and craggy mansion jutting out from beyond the sewage treatment plant? Do you notice the gothic stonework, its crooked towers, a mixture of rotting Victoriana and shining modern glass, rising above the soggy excuse for land called Mercey Island? This is Arkham Asylum, home for the criminally insane, a once-abandoned mansion as fragmented in design as the minds of the lunatics it houses.

Come inside its narrow, sloping stairwells and hear the shrieks and grunts of its inmates; their screams, whispers, maniacal laughing and demoralized sobbing. Choke on the smell of damp mold that never dries. Hear the incessant echo of a leak that no one can ever find to fix and the scuttling scrape of rats racing for shelter along mildewed baseboards.

Now open some doors, their paint cracking and their hinges loose. One reveals, covered with dirt and cobwebs, a torture chamber fit for the Inquisition. Behind the next, a gleaming, sterile room stocked with the best of modern pharmaceuticals. Past a third, a brick-halted hallway now mysteriously bereft of some forgotten purpose. Somewhere along the way, the layout of Arkham became a labyrinthine mystery. Its clean, modern rooms were grafted far too quickly onto the rotting foundation of the old Mercey Mansion, and, as with all botched operations, gangrene has set in.

Suppose one were now to take a tour of the official Arkham, the part that pretends to be modern science. And suppose one were to take the appropriate turns, past the therapy rooms, past the exercise yard, past the guards' gated lockers. Sooner or later, if one had the appropriate keys, one would enter the wing where Arkham Asylum's most famous and most lethal criminals reside: the Rogues Gallery. Past the divided man, the plant woman, the spindly creature who marks his kills upon his own body. Past the grunting thing. The crying thing. The thing too disgusted with itself to utter a sound. Past the crocodile and the man of ice and the puppet keeper.

Sooner or later, one would come to me.

I sit in darkness. It is chilly in my cell, or rather would be should I let myself feel the cold. The latest tray of untouched slop lies before the door. I have not eaten in two days. My guard has notified the dietician and the government worker assigned to my case. They are worried that I am on a hunger strike. Perhaps I overestimated the American intelligence agent in assuming he would realize how beneath my purpose such a sad protest would be. After mere months of study, he thinks he begins to understand me. This is amusing. The conceits of children always are.

They know nothing. Nothing of me and nothing of meditation. Denial of self is a pathetic, nerveless way to do battle. I have nothing to protest. My mind is set on conquest.

Down the hall, a madman cackles loudly at his own joke. Another voice is raised, and in honeyed tones tells him to shut up. A third voice promises exquisite torture to them both.

From far down the corridor a man blurts a riddle to no one in particular. I hear him without effort, despite the distance, much as I hear the scuttle of the roaches on the hospital kitchen's greasy flagstones and the steady flip of a coin along with muttered curses from the disfigured madman in a cell three doors down. The range of the senses is merely a question of concentration.

The man repeats his riddle in desperate glee. Sometimes, others give him an answer. Mostly they do not, despite the childlike ease of the clues he gives them. Eventually, he will reveal the answer to his nonexistent audience and snicker with delight over his own cleverness.

Many times I am able to solve the riddles without effort, despite the fact that they usually involve puns in English, a language that is not my first. But I rarely answer them out loud. There is no need to encourage him. More importantly, the discipline of holding knowledge close is of legendary value. A fool brags about what he knows; a wise man makes others guess.

The riddle is chanted a third time. How can you have four hands? The answer is disappointingly plain: By doubling your fists. Not by borrowing your cellmate's, as another inmate crudely replies. But no matter. The time for these simple games has ended. The great game is just moments from beginning.

The ultimate game—the game of war.

Focusing, I deafen myself to the riddling man and his abusive, captive audience. I remove them from my consciousness, breaking language down to its component sounds and then expunging these from my thoughts.

I must not be distracted. No outside contaminants may enter me now. The night is rising. My night.

It is time to set the wheels in motion.

I sink into myself, drawing energy from without, like a black hole, sucking it in, processing it, storing it, amplifying it, focusing it.

The power of Yanjin Alchemy is a very old one. Ancient, unstoppable, and all but forgotten. Energy flows from the physical world to the world of the mind and out again in deadly force. There is nothing in this world, or the next, that cannot feed the mind, and that the mind cannot, in turn, control. Or destroy.

As with most divine mysteries, these principles are shared today only in harmless, neutered form. Those meditative religions which come closest to keeping these truths alive have all but buried their rightful meaning under the ludicrously irrelevant concept of "compassion." For example, there is a practice yet taught of the meditative art of sending and taking. In very simple terms, one breathes in all the negativity of the world, all the pain, hate, suffering, and despair, and breathes out hope and light and, yes, *compassion*.

Today many mistake this practice as an exercise in the development of courage and a fearless heart. Nonsense. It is an exercise in power, instructions on how to tap into a battery, a well of energy that is never depleted. As long as there is consciousness there will be hate, jealousy, fear. "Compassion" is what masters teach their slaves to feel for their oppressors. "Turn the other cheek . . . carry it the extra mile . . ." Bah . . . It is a weakness, a liability, as is clearly indicated by the instructions to breathe it out and dispel it.

I made this point to a so-called "master" of the meditative arts I camped with once in Chulan. He tried to convince me that all of humanity—indeed, all of life—is one, that to love yourself is to love all others and that to harm any other is to harm yourself.

As he was making rice for us later that night over a low fire, I sat forward and slit his throat with a rock.

"Now I have two bowls of rice," I told him. "How am I harmed by harming you? It is obvious that my situation has improved."

He prayed for me with his last gurgling breath. Pitiable. I'd expected more from a philosophy that has, as its first noble truth, "Life is suffering."

Now I move past that suffering, into a vortex of strength. The shadows of the solid world recede. The inner light, the pure light of Mehta-Sua, expands to fill my inner eyes. The spirit voices chant their approval.

I inhale the scents of the asylum—sweat, chlorine, the exotic flowery aroma of rare orchids that emanates from the cell of the plant woman. This last is a threat. It charms, tempting me back to the humid jungle campaigns of my youth. It reminds me of my young innocence, when assassination with my bare hands was an exhilarating process. Then, the kill still had the spice of doubt. I was new to the Mehta-Sua. I had not yet fully mastered the channeling of mental and physical energy into deadly attacks. I roamed the world, seeking out ever larger challenges, honing the power of Yanjin Alchemy. Even as my authority grew, the possibility that I myself might face defeat was a delicious sensation.

By now, of course, there is never any question that I will accomplish the kill. But I have learned a larger lesson. Slaughtering bodies is merely a road to defeating the soul. Once the soul—of a person, a city, a country, a world—is defeated, victory is assured.

But these memories are a distraction. They lure me

from my true path. Another act of discipline and . . . they are gone. Acknowledged, and dismissed.

I return to a perfect state of readiness; quiet, empty. I see, smell, hear, and taste nothing.

I begin to focus on the here and now, the immediate. I place myself in space. I believe, according to the primitive Western calendar, that this is the dying season. Autumn. The air is crisp and cool. I am sure there is some foolish name for this day, this time. All that will change. After tonight, this day will always be remembered as the Rise of Sin Tzu.

My senses expand. I spread myself out across the city. Its inner movement becomes my breath. Its streets, my blood. I know it intimately.

I allow myself to hear two bells toll in the distance. One comes from the magnificent Gotham Cathedral, which looms high above the constructs of the City Hall district. The other, more modest, comes from the great Clock Tower a mere two miles from the cathedral. There— across town, a whistle blows. It announces the beginning of the night shift at the Oven Fresh Bakery. Eleven-thirty.

I hear the rhythmic footsteps of various Arkham guards. Mine, whose fluids wheeze past arteries clogged with brittle, hardened fat, will be crossing within view of my cell in five minutes and fourteen seconds . . . if he doesn't stop to drink water, relieve his bladder, or try to answer another insipid riddle.

An instant is an eternity. I descend back into my receptive state. Once again, I run my plan through mental fingers, as if it were a silken scarf, from major premise to finely woven detail. I return to words written over two thousand years ago:

*The victorious commander must know four things:
He must know himself. He must know his enemy. He
must know the time of his battle, and he must know
the place of his battle. If he knows all of these things,
victory is assured.*

At midnight the battle will begin. I will launch my first attack, and Gotham City will be valiantly defended. I know myself. I know the time of my battle. I know this place.

And, oh yes, I know my enemy.

The Batman. Gotham's general. Hunter and jailer of so many souls within this asylum. The ultimate strategist and warrior. From the moment I first read about him in a foreign newspaper, the spirits I serve called me to him. It has been many long years since I have felt such anticipation while developing a battle plan. Like me, the Batman is a creature of darkness. A creature of strategy. But without an equal to defy him, a general is nothing. As I have written:

*A great conqueror must have a worthy opponent and
a worthy prize.*

History has proved my worthiness in battle. Countries have wept blood as they begged for my mercy. When the time came to choose my next opponent, I knew that it would not be easy to find one deserving of my attention. Had the spirits not guided me to the Batman, I would be searching for one still.

Now I am here, ensconced in this city, challenging the Batman for Gotham City. Gotham, the Batman's lair.

This campaign is treacherous, even for me. The plans for the Batman's undoing have been long in the making. I have deceived the international police forces that think they have me contained. I have calmly accepted my long incarceration at Arkham. All for the love of war. For as I myself once wrote:

The art of war is deceit. First, you must attack your enemy when he least expects it, in a place where he feels strong, but is in fact weak, and with an army he feels he has already vanquished.

Gotham and the Batman. The womb and the child. The father and the son. Not unlike the symbol I myself wear embossed in the bones of my skull, of the yin and the yang, two opposing entities encircled together. Without one, the other means nothing. In Batman's Gotham, as poisoned as it is, he knows every whimper, every cry. He patrols its streets, winnowing out the criminal and the insane. A general of the night. He believes *he* controls the darkness. But this night, he is wrong.

I listen to the Batman's city as a doctor listens to a patient's heart and lungs, as a master knows the movements of his servants. All is normal. Traffic is light. A siren cries in the distance. The occasional horn sounds, but it is nothing like a few hours ago, when the masses blared and shrieked in pitched battle to gain yards and minutes in their gasoline-fueled maze.

Those are the sounds that are. Likewise, I turn my attention to the sounds that are not. There is no relentless grind of construction. The big machines are sleeping. The drudgery of petty commerce has ground to a halt in the Financial District. Now and again, I hear the distant buzz of an airplane leaving from or arriving at the Goodwin International Airport, but there are fewer now. No helicopters. The sound-that-isn't tells me that much of Gotham City sleeps.

A restless sleep. Gotham feels the fear of every large city. The fear is this: Safety is an illusion.

With every hushed breath the city waits nervously for attack. It fears terrorists, destruction by bomb, virus, or chemical. It fears ordinary night terrors of theft and violence brought about by outsiders or, worse, one another.

But Gotham City and its dark general both wait for the wrong kind of attack. How could they ever consider— even for a moment—that anyone could *conquer* it? Seize their terrain and hold it? Not sabotage the board, not skew the dice, but simply claim the game?

The great city of Gotham does not yet acknowledge herself as a citizenship under the guard of a military general. She does not know that the force that will conquer her is already seething inside her borders. The Batman does not see my army, massed beneath his very nose—a force of criminals and criminal madmen whom society has stripped from the herd of common humanity and mustered together in its prisons and asylums . . . bitter, angry, violent men who wait only for the call of a great commander to transform them into a potent legion. An entire army of deviants, whom I will let loose to do exactly as they have always wished—to wreak havoc on Gotham City and bring her to her knees.

The felons at Stonegate Prison. The violent madmen of Arkham Asylum. Those whom the Batman believes he has bested. These are my troops. They feel no love for Gotham. They are in my service now. They await my command.

It is the sheer audacity of my objective that ensures success.

For months, I have been here at Arkham, Yanjin

Alchemy allowing my orders to flow from my mind to the criminal masses like a satellite broadcasting to a million television sets. How eagerly their clouded, angry thoughts yielded to my own! How hungrily they consumed my mental commands! For the past several weeks, I have been painting in their minds, creating the urge, designing a night of rage, pillage, and chaos.

Of course, I cannot command prisoners like disciplined troops, nor will that be necessary. Consider this maxim, written hundreds of years before Hannibal or Alexander:

Commanding men is like channeling water. As water does not run uphill, men will not do those things that are not their inclinations. Water will always flow downhill. The great commander uses the natural tendencies of his troops to his own advantage.

Were this a conventional campaign, my choice of legions would be quite foolish. But this campaign is anything but. The prisoners and the mad are my skirmishers, my fodder: cheap, expendable, and able to create a crisis that the forces of the enemy cannot manage. As in ancient warfare, their job is to throw dust in the air, distracting and confusing my opposition. Once released from prison, they will spill out into the city like a flood.

And as with any flood, one must sometimes let the flow rage as it will. Beyond the grand plan of liberation, to release them into Gotham's tender streets, I did not specify what crimes to commit any more than you would direct a particular drop of water to stay in the center of a river or at the edge. Let them do as they please, so long as they spread chaos and mayhem. The aggregate of all of their actions is what I desire.

Think of the termite. Ugly and brutish, each termite possesses a very small brain, and yet en masse they can destroy cities of staggering size and complexity. Likewise, each criminal, stupid, bestial, and nondirected as he or she may be, will become part of an elaborate structure of chaos.

But these petty thieves, larcenists, and murderers are merely a segment of my army. I bring my own elite forces from without, summonable at a moment's thought. These troops, loyal to me and trained by the spirits I channel throughout the decades, merely await the word to serve their master.

Of these, there are two camps: my mortal ninjas, flawlessly trained in the arts of murder and deceit; and the Eternal Elite, automatons of Mehta-Sua, ancient warriors of stone, golems of remarkable power and grace.

And too, I have solicited and recruited some of Gotham's own, from here, in Arkham. Captains who bring with them their own troops. Of the many potential warriors—of the many within these walls who have faced the Batman, who loathe him and wish for his destruction—I have selected three whose inclinations best serve my objectives.

Unfortunately, it will not be possible to release all of Arkham's illustrious costumed madmen. In the interest of maintaining control of the field, I cannot afford to subject the flow of battle to the less predictable inmates of this asylum. The chaos I release upon Gotham tonight will be under my control; a broken dam of water that I can at least trust to rush downhill. There are those within these walls who could not even be trusted that far, and so these will become prisoners of war before the battle has even truly begun. I have written:

*The commander must pick his lieutenants well, both
for skill and for loyalty. For once the weapon is
forged, it must never be allowed to turn back on he
who wields it. Power must be delegated carefully. The
blood of commanders stabbed by their own
lieutenants would fill rivers and many victories have
turned to defeat in the hands of unsound
lieutenants . . .*

For instance, the laughing lunatic known as the Joker
and his clownish woman thrall, Harlequin, are too difficult to predict. In the case of the thrall, I find her to be er-
ratic even by the standards of lunatics. In the case of the
Joker, I find him highly psychotic even by the standards of
Arkham Asylum. He lives for chaos, and if released, could
easily turn the tide of battle in any number of undesirable
directions. He could end up aiding the Batman, amused by
his own creation of irony, or, more likely, engage his own
campaign, unleashing the sort of random attacks that
could upset my ability to retain this stronghold. He is a
variable that no skilled general would set loose in the theater of war. There is a difference between applied disorder
and absolute pandemonium.

The two are mad geniuses, truly, but unsound tools for
the waging of war. Even if they managed to fall in line
with my battle plan initially, they would pose a great threat
to me during the final claiming of this territory. My concentration must remain on the Batman during that crucial
phase. I cannot afford to be distracted by my own minions.

I rejected the notion of using the green-clad man who
weaves riddles for similar reasons. His pathological need to
present the Batman with clues masks a desire to tell the
truth. Curiously enough, though he is a criminal, he is incapable of fulfilling my maxim—*all warfare is deceit.* As

for the plant woman, her reliance on living materials makes her undependable where there are none at hand, and her wish to be away from the pungent flesh of humanity exceeds her wishes for revenge. Her ability to transform the very landscape of the battle, too, is a factor I cannot risk employing without the utter certainty that she could be controlled. I have had time here to observe her, and it is my opinion as a military strategist that she cannot.

But there are many other suitable captains within these walls. Each has his prowess; each serves his role. I have selected three to launch my attack, champions of terror, brutality, and rage. They will serve their purpose and sap the Batman of his strength. Separate him from his troops. Challenge the Batman's skills and force him to play by the rules I dictate. Battle is won and lost when initiative is won or lost. Victory is best achieved when you control the actions of your opponents.

I hear the footsteps of my guard. The time draws near. I must concentrate. I must send out my message to the inmates of Stonegate, encouraging them to now go forward with the plan I developed for them months ago. I close my eyes and I see them—not their paltry bodies, but the force of their human energy.

They hear me. They are responding. I feel a thousand furtive thoughts. Simple thoughts. Brutal thoughts. Their spirits surge and splash against the bars of their cells, waiting for the strike of midnight when I, the moon to their tide, shall set them free.

Back here in Arkham, a guard walks by my own cell. Effortlessly, I gather his mind like one more strand of rope into the cord of thousands I hold in my hands.

Though my guard walks normally, he controls neither his arms nor his legs. His face is blank and slack. As he reaches my chamber, I guide his hand to his key. Move it to the lock. Push and twist. Hear the tumblers move, the lock open. I swing his arm and hear a shrieking of metal. My cell is open. My guard stands outside the door, at my command.

Only four minutes to go now.

I walk through the Rogues' Gallery. In this higher state, the world shifts to my command. The spirit voices that guide me chant their approval. There is harmony. They are pleased.

I pass the laughing man . . . I turn. He sneers. Something in this cracked being is not quite human. In his own way, he is perhaps as worthy an adversary as the Batman. No matter. Perhaps another time. I activate the Yanjin. I project my energy and deflect his. The yin and yang of cosmic balance ebb and flow. The laughing stops. He is frozen in place.

Next, the harlequin girl who chirps double entendres . . . the riddling man, frozen in time and space between question and answer, now never to solve the last mocking riddle he shoots at me of the chicken crossing the road . . . and, finally, the two-faced man who often tells all of them to shut up is, himself, silenced . . .

I enter the passage that will take me to my hidden stronghold in Arkham.

The timepieces of Gotham tick away the last minutes of this day. In a short while, I will hear the bells of the cathedral and the Clock Tower chime again in the distance, and, on cue, like an instrument in a symphony, the alarms from Stonegate. And then the gunshots.

In mere moments, the Night of Sin will commence. Gotham will soon be mine.

The spirits within me shall be satisfied.

The Yanjin itself shall rejoice.

ONE

Alfred Pennyworth, Wayne Manor Butler
11:42 p.m.

It was a simple robbery, an accident of place and timing. The crime was perpetrated by a desperate felon either too scared or too incompetent to appropriate the petty cash and jewels he desired without use of lethal force. Utterly senseless. And yet that single act of cowardice and violence has reverberated through my life with a force attributable, as a rule, only to acts of God.

And perhaps divinity did have a hand in this, if for no other reason than that the murders of Thomas and Martha Wayne created a holy warrior.

Though, to be fair, there was a bat involved, as well.

It is a chilly fall night as I pull the Rolls-Royce up to the curb in front of the Mahan Opera House. The Opera House has long been one of my favorite buildings in Gotham City: a huge, sixteenth-century stone structure with a lovely vaulted ceiling, windows of exquisite glass quarrels, fluted columns, and a charming sculpted frieze. It is located directly off of Grand Street, neatly demarcating where the Financial District meets City Hall, and hinting at some of the city's more colorful four-hundred-year history.

Gotham is, as its name implies, a towering revelation of urbanity. Nestled in the East Coast, Gotham comprises a mere three hundred and twenty-seven square miles, and yet is home to well over eight million with a sustained three percent annual growth. Though attracting fewer tourists than cleaner and more approachable cities such as Metropolis and New York, Gotham is still considered the City of Cities—to say one is from Gotham is to be granted an instant badge of honor; we are the prototypical melting pot, the American Dream with scabs. True grit.

Though it includes three main and six minor islands between the Gotham and Sprang Rivers, most of the nation associates our city with South Gotham Island, the first settlement and still the hub of the municipality. From the narrow, meandering streets and alleyways of Old Gotham to the wide, busy avenues of Midtown and the Upper East Side, Gotham City is a twenty-four-hour town, a cornucopia of sights, sounds, smells, and textures. There is nothing this city doesn't have, save for patience, and nothing this city cannot accomplish, save for peace. The nation's poorest shuffle through the streets of the Bowery over debris-lined asphalt and shattered glass. The nation's wealthiest stroll through the tree-lined streets of Coventry, their imported Italian shoes clicking over six-inch squares of diamond-patterned Plaza Stone units in mercantile gray and ivory. Understandably, it is a city full of contradiction, incongruity, disagreements, and intrigue. Not to mention taxicabs.

Even the very founding of Gotham continues to be a subject of great debate. I can tell you with relative certainty, however, that the Wayne family, whom I have served loyally for most of my professional career, came to Gotham directly from Scotland in the seventeen hundreds. Currently, in the backseat of the car I chauffeur, the last remaining heir to that long distinguished lineage clears his throat and rustles a newspaper.

"You may wish to put away the reading material, Master Bruce," I tell him, glancing in the rearview mirror as his stony blue eyes rise to meet mine. "I'm afraid we've arrived."

Streetlights gleam off the hood of the car, which I myself polished by hand this morning. As I glide the auto to a stop, the valet, a young man of about twenty, rushes up to greet us. His outfit is ill-fitting and his smile too solicitous; no doubt he is a Gotham State student attempting to earn some extra spending cash parking cars for the insanely wealthy.

In the backseat of the Rolls, Bruce Wayne sighs and folds the evening edition of the *Gotham Gazette.* "Fifteen minutes, Alfred," he tells me, as the young valet opens his door. "And not a second longer. *Please.*"

"I understand, Master Bruce, and have synchronized our watches."

Bruce's eyes dart to the two long-stemmed red roses lying on the seat beside him, carefully wrapped by the florist in creamy brown butcher paper and a raffia bow. Though he is without a doubt Gotham's most eligible bachelor, Bruce Thomas Wayne will not be bestowing these flowers on any young lady tonight. Theirs is a much more somber destiny.

I suppose the same could be said for any young lady upon whom Master Bruce might wish to bequeath them.

As the young valet opens the back door, Bruce begins to unfold all six feet and two inches of himself from the automobile. Tonight he is attired in a black silk tuxedo, carefully tailored to flatter his figure without calling undue attention to his strength and musculature, a crisp white shirt underneath, and a silvery-blue tie and cummerbund

which I selected specifically to set off the unusually striking color of his eyes. His dark hair is worn short and carefully tousled and he is, as always, clean-shaven and
immaculately groomed. Even his eight-hundred-dollar
shoes are polished to a high sheen. All in all, I think it safe
to say that he will make every best-dressed list, prove the
social highlight of his host's evening, and, in general,
arouse frenzies of interest, jealousy, and intrigue, as is only
fitting for a beneficiary of his pedigree.

He is almost all the way out of the Rolls when he turns
to look at me over his shoulder, his brows furrowed in af-
fable confusion.

"What is this thing about, again?"

"The annual fund-raiser for the Gotham City Rainforest Endowment, sir."

"Gotham has a rainforest?" I hear him ask with wonder, as the valet gently supports his elbow and helps him
to the curb. I cannot be certain whether this display of
confusion is for the benefit of said valet, for my personal
amusement, or for himself, as an exercise in self-
transmogrification.

This is rather difficult to explain, but the rich, conspicuously handsome, cultured dilettante now heading up the
steps of the Opera House is, fundamentally, a fraud. Were
you to follow him now into the fund-raiser, perhaps to toast
him with champagne or simply to invite him to your club
for a game of racquetball later in the week, you would leave
with the impression that the heir to the Wayne fortune is
dazzling, decadent, and dumb as a doorpost.

He would make sure of it.

The truth of the matter is more complicated—is, in
fact, legend. The truth of the matter is that the gentleman
now pretending not to know how many zeroes to add to
his donation check will, in a matter of hours or even min-

utes, don armor from head to toe, hide himself beneath cape and cowl, and spend the rest of the night fiercely protecting Gotham City with an intelligence, drive, and discipline few could comprehend, let alone emulate.

The truth of the matter is that Bruce Wayne is really the Batman.

Many people spend the entirety of their lives searching for a sense of purpose, a true vocation or calling. Personally, I have never experienced the anxiety of that quest, nor the luxury of it. I thought my world was ending when, at the age of twenty-six, I was summoned from the stage of the Lyceum Theatre in London to my father's sickbed in America. Engaged then in a thrilling run of *King Lear* as Edmund, bastard son of Gloucester—one of the greatest parts I was ever to play, as it turned out—I was none too pleased to be called away, even for something as grave as the passing of my sire.

I was even less pleased when the promise he extracted from me on his deathbed turned out to entail a lifelong sacrifice, as opposed to a brief favor or pithy errand.

In the grand tradition of fathers before him (indeed, including his own), Efrem Pennyworth wanted his son to take over the family business. I was to immediately give up any thoughts of a future on the stage and instead turn my attention to more domestic matters. Specifically, those domestic matters concerning the Wayne family of Gotham City.

I had already been educated in the ways of the manservant and had shown a particular aptitude for cooking, in which I was encouraged. While I had attended the classes purely to prove to my father that I was not, in fact, cut out for the job, I foiled my own campaign by earning high marks at every turn. There was a degree of fastidiousness in my nature that I was unable to repress; I simply could not tolerate seeing a thing done wrong, much less to be the one involved in wrongdoing. There are really only so many ways to fold a napkin, after all, and one should not possess silver if one is not prepared to see to its proper care. It is utterly foolhardy to put a chambermaid on formal dining service unless your only other option is a stable boy, and, to this very day I cannot understand the breach in social etiquette that allows certain individuals to fail to respond to RSVPs.

Before I knew it, I was certified by the Ivor Spencer International School for Butler Administrators/Personal Assistants and Estate Managers.

Which is why, of course, I immediately joined the Royal Air Force.

My military service felt in many ways like a continuation of butler school. Only in the RAF, I concentrated on learning the arts of attack, defense, and medical restoration as opposed to estate management, housekeeping, and entertaining. I have never been a violent man by nature and do not entirely approve of Master Bruce's insistence on putting himself perpetually in the face of danger, or, indeed, taking the law into his own hands, but I did appreciate the . . . science of fighting, if you will. That is, though the thought of taking another man's life interests me not at all, the thought that one could do so with merely a precisely aimed index finger interests me greatly. Mankind's physiology is truly a wonder.

And so it was with an eye towards efficiency and a greater comprehension of the human condition that I absorbed everything my superior officers had to teach. I specialized as a field medic, and hope it is not unseemly to assert that I served my country well. Rumors that I was then drafted into the British Secret Intelligence Service, operating there well beyond my military tour of duty, are, of course, unsubstantiated. The records will clearly show that I left the RAF to pursue a career on the stage.

In any case, I thought any expectation of my becoming a butler was over and done when my father summoned me. I took over as the Wayne family manservant with a mixture of dazed remorse and fatalistic self-pity.

As time went on, however, I grew more comfortable in my position. Indeed, by the time Thomas and Martha brought home their baby boy from the hospital, I was content with what I then considered to be my fate.

I was wrong.

My destiny was written in bullets and blood eight years later, when my employers were shot to death in a Gotham City alleyway. They left behind a single legacy, their son. It is to his care and well-being that I have pledged my life.

It is to his destiny that I have surrendered mine.

Truthfully, I cannot imagine being more proud of him, and yet I grieve sometimes for the life he has lost. If the Waynes had lived, who would their son be today? Would he have become a hero in some other fashion, some other manner, or was Gotham City bound to pay for her guardian in blood?

Bruce was six when he saw the bat.

His family home, Wayne Manor—a grand estate by any measure—was built high on a mighty cliff in the Bristol district, at precisely the point where the Gotham River meets the Atlantic (of which the formal dining room boasts a magnificent view). Beneath the house runs a series of caves, occupied primarily by *Eptesicus fuscus*, better known as the big brown bat. Dashing through the fields behind our stables, young Master Bruce once found himself quite literally falling through the earth. He landed about ten feet down in one of the caves and discovered, before his father could assist him back out again, that he was not alone. He later told us that the bat had shuffled out of the darkness towards him, hissing and scarred, as if it had survived many terrible fights.

It was the only time as a child, with the exception of the aftermath of his parents' murder, of course, that I can remember seeing him afraid.

It is difficult for me not to regard that creature as some kind of harbinger, much like another bat, much later, that smashed through the study window while Master Bruce contemplated ways of intimidating the criminal element he hunted. I would have insisted it was an apparition had I not personally spent half an hour cleaning up the broken glass.

How is it that fate, so elusive to so many, presents itself to others in such unambiguous signs and lucid avatars? Master Bruce is a firm believer in self-determination, but it has always seemed to me that the forces at work in his life exceed the inspiration of even a rarefied genius such as his. I never worry—well, never overly much, at any rate . . . about Bruce himself. My fear is that those forces that guide him may one day prove fickle.

I pull a small silver pocket watch from my vest pocket and glance at the time. Master Bruce has been inside for four and half minutes. I find myself wishing that there were an opera this evening. These streets could use the sweet strains of a plaintive aria to sooth them. Or perhaps it is my nerves that could use the soothing.

Bruce was only eight when his parents were killed. He was with them on that dreadful night when, walking home from the theater—they had just been to see *The Mark of Zorro*, a film he has never again permitted himself to watch—they were held up at gunpoint in an alley then known as Park Row.

I am not certain as to the exact particulars of what transpired. Though a witness to it all, Master Bruce has never spoken of that night in detail.

It seems most probable to me that Thomas Wayne resisted. He was shot at point-blank range, as was his lovely wife, Bruce's mother, Martha. When the police found him, young Master Bruce was standing utterly still in the alleyway, deeply in shock. His mother's pearls were scattered by his feet and the soles of his shoes were wet with his father's pooling blood.

Bruce's young life had been spared, and yet I felt him slipping away. For years, he moved through his days like a somnambulist, silent and locked away in some remote corner of his own broken heart. I went through the motions of daily life with him, trying to keep some sense of stability and birthright alive in the large family manor he had inherited, and in which I remained employed as his butler, but I feared that his will had been irredeemably broken.

And then something inside of him changed.

One morning he came down to breakfast with his jaw set and a new, steely intensity in his eyes. He expressed a sudden feverish interest in his education, began to arrange travel, began a systematic process of self-governing reinvention. Eventually he left home altogether, striding out the heavy mahogany door with unflinching resolve.

Some instinct told me to wait. I polished the hardwood floors and unused silver of Wayne Manor for nearly ten years, occasionally receiving brief, perfunctory phone calls from places as far away as Europe, India, and Japan. I held the dust at bay, hoping, I suppose, that Master Bruce would return home healed, having shed some of his childhood grief.

Instead, he came home darker than ever. He came

home devoted to vengeance, the night already quite in love with him.

By the time he donned the cape and cowl, I understood that I was living with a man at war. He chose his costume to strike fear into the hearts of the criminals he stalks, though by now many of them are known to experience spontaneous incontinence based on his reputation alone. Batman is terrifying, demonic. I can imagine no adversary more daunting. It is not just his physical aptitude or his faultless detective skills that make him so formidable. Batman possesses remarkable resolve.

It is not humanly possible for one man to protect an entire city. Every night crimes are committed that he cannot attend, lives are lost that he cannot save. Batman knows this. And every night, he goes out anyway.

The very thought exhausts me to my bones.

Another glance at my watch verifies that it is time to rescue my employer from the hell of caviar and Cartier in which he currently finds himself. I step carefully out of the Rolls and make my way up the wide stone steps of the Opera House. A quick word with the doorman grants me instant access to the building, which tonight is brightly lit by crystal chandeliers and filled to the brim with socialites, philanthropists, and bon vivants of every ilk. The dresses of the ladies shine in satin rainbows of crimson, emerald, and peacock blue while the men are a traditional sea of black and white.

They all stroll about the circular entrance hall, balancing drinks served in real crystal and small paper plates of food. I am shocked to notice a young woman, properly attired in white shirt, black slacks, and apron, offering around a silver tray of room-temperature tapenade on garlic crostini while, on a nearby buffet table, a platter of baked brie with sun-dried tomatoes goes cold.

I am about to ask to speak with the catering manager when I hear my employer's boisterous laugh a few feet away.

I elbow through the crowd until I see him, predictably sandwiched between the Rainforest Endowment treasurer and a supermodel. He beams as I approach.

"Hey, Alfred!" he shouts out over the din of laughter, clinking glasses, and a hired string quartet. He gestures to the young lady. "This is Eureka!"

"Ulrika," the model corrects him in a thick Swedish accent.

"All-right-a!" Bruce laughs.

I clear my throat.

"Terribly sorry to interrupt you, Master Bruce, but I just received word that your presence has been requested at the Sultan's soiree across town."

"Eureka," Bruce says, unfazed, body turned towards the supermodel but hand gesturing towards me, "this is my butler, Alfred Pennyworth." He leans in closer to the young woman and, dropping his voice, huskily stage-whispers, "He's nearly as much of a peach as you are."

"Charmed," Ulrika says tightly, between clenched teeth miraculously devoid of the shining red gloss that covers the rest of her mouth. I am left with the impression that she prefers not to be on a first-name basis with the help.

A quick glance around the room confirms that Master Bruce has, as usual, made a wise choice of evening companions. Ulrika is stunning: nearly as tall as Bruce himself, her long blonde hair pulled severely back from her high forehead and cheekbones before being left to coil coyly around one shoulder, her other marvelously sculpted shoulder left bare by the tight scarlet gown into which she has poured herself. The feline cast of her smoky eyes reminds me of another young woman in the opposite circumstances—that is, one for whom Bruce has actual feelings, but who, accordingly, could not hope to wrap herself around his arm in public.

But Miss Ulrika is from out of town, and therefore unlikely to converse with available Gotham maidens as to Mr. Wayne's dating history. We wouldn't want her learning, after all, that the city's most notorious playboy manages to develop a headache before midnight during nearly every social engagement, or that on those nights when he does not, he nonetheless finds he must retire early—and alone—in preparation for a corporate conference call the next day.

Ah, yes, business. Perhaps one uses the term "dilettante" to describe Master Bruce a tad misleadingly. Master Bruce is, in fact, the CEO of Wayne Enterprises, one of the largest and most respected business conglomerates in Gotham, along with LexCorp and Multigon. Wayne Enterprises—which includes subsidiaries such as Wayne Tech, Wayne Chemical Refinery, the Wayne Foundation, and Wayne Medical—employs over three hundred and forty thousand employees locally and is involved in everything from technological research to social philanthropy.

And yet despite the company's reputation for cutting-edge business models, innovative product construction, and highly ethical hiring and environmental policies, Wayne Enterprises' CEO is widely regarded as a dense, if decorative, figurehead. The business's success is generally attributed to the genius of V.P. of Operations Lucius Fox, who is, indeed, one of the greatest minds in business and an invaluable resource to Master Bruce.

Even Mr. Fox himself is not entirely sure what to make of his occasionally brilliant but often laughably thick employer. Which, I assure you, is just as Master

Bruce intends it. One must operate with a tremendous degree of discretion when one is secretly using company resources to fund a one-man war against crime, including, but not limited to, the creation of state-of-the-art crime-fighting equipment such as Batarangs, knockout gas, and the Batmobile.

I worry that it must sometimes be unpleasant for Master Bruce to risk tarnishing his father's reputation with his own farce of incompetence. Though admittedly there is no sign of that now as he extracts himself from Miss Ulrika's studiously phlegmatic embrace.

"I'll call you!" he shouts to her cheerfully as he begins to follow me back through the crowd towards the main door. Miss Ulrika says nothing, but a quick glance over my shoulder confirms that her eyes remain hungrily focused on his retreating back.

"Shall I add her to the Rolodex?" I inquire dryly, holding the door for him as he fetches his coat.

He doesn't get a foot past coat check before being besieged by three charming, if somewhat superficial, young ladies, all intent on delaying his escape.

"Brucie, you never called me!" chides the smallest of the bunch. She is in an appealing gown of pink satin and cannot stop beaming at Master Bruce to save her life.

"Bambie!" he smiles back.

"Bunny," she corrects with a mock pout.

"Bootsie," he says apologetically, "forgive me. I thought of you the whole time I was in the Alps."

"The Alps?" she asks, a look of confusion clouding her otherwise spring-fresh face.

"Yeah, you know—I was remembering that time we went skiing together!"

"That was me," interjects one of her companions, this one a bosomy redhead in a yellow dress of tulle. Master

Bruce looks suitably confused, prompting a nervous giggle from Miss Bunny.

"Oh, Brucie, really, you're too much!"

"And yet never quite enough . . ." mutters the red-head. I disguise an upward twitch of my mouth with a quick, discreet, and, of course, hand-covered cough.

"I don't think I've ever been skiing," muses Miss Bunny.

"We'll have to go, then!" Master Bruce asserts, waving and all but pushing me out the door ahead of him. "Nice to see you again, Bambie, Joanie!"

"Bunny!"

"Jodie!"

"I thought you said Selina would be here tonight," he hisses into my ear as soon as I shut the door behind us, catching me off guard. Selina Kyle, better known as Cat-woman, is *l'objet d'affection* to whom I alluded earlier.

"I believe I mentioned only that this seemed the sort of event Miss Kyle might be interested in attending. As you well know, she is not in the habit of appearing on confirmed guest lists."

"Neither am I," Bruce mumbles darkly, shouldering on his coat and glancing up at the cloudy, moonless sky. As he follows me down to the car I am momentarily distracted by a delusional fantasy of a happily-ever-after for Gotham's Dark Knight, replete with wedding bells, the pitter-patter of little feet . . . By the time I am closing the backseat door behind him, though, my mind is clearing. The bride would be wearing skintight latex and carrying a bullwhip. The groom would no doubt wait at the altar with a bitter frown and handcuffs. And the children . . .

. . . Well, I suppose there *are* children, in a matter of speaking. First and most prominently, young Master

Dick, who came to Master Bruce and me at the age of eight after the tragic murder of *his* parents.

My idea of incorporating him into our home was to provide him with clean sheets, three hot meals a day, and all the parental adoration I was never permitted to lavish on Master Bruce.

Master Dick's idea of integrating himself into our daily lives was to force us, as much as he could, into the recognizable configuration of a family, filling our days with his natural affability, cheer, and affection, not to mention a truly stunning array of questions and endless curiosity.

And Master Bruce's idea of assimilating him into our routine was to dress him up in a mask, cape, and short green trunks, enlist him into his holy war, and train him as an assistant crime-fighter, or "sidekick." Thus was the legend of Robin, the Boy Wonder, born.

I have never completely forgiven Master Bruce for so ruining Master Dick's chances at a normal life. But then, Master Dick has never quite forgiven me for not allowing him to begin the whole enterprise earlier. I suppose that even I must concede that if there is such a thing as a "natural" for this kind of work, Master Dick fits the bill wholeheartedly.

And, too, like a real son, he eventually grew up and left us.

Master Bruce surprised me greatly by enlisting another young orphan, Master Timothy Drake, into the role of Robin, and Master Dick surprised me not at all by returning, with a new costume and moniker of his own (he now goes by "Nightwing"), to Gotham and to Master Bruce's aid.

Recently, too, a young woman has asserted herself into the boys' club. She asks to be referred to as "Batgirl," but Master Bruce knows her to be Barbara Gordon, daughter of his best friend, Gotham City's Police Commissioner.

I really cannot overemphasize the importance of these allies in Batman's life. His is a dark and driven existence, and, whether working as de facto captains in his antiwar army or simply providing him with perspective and companionship, these young men, the young lady, Commissioner Gordon, and myself are, in some sense, all that Batman has.

Unless you count Gotham herself, which is as real and vital to Batman as we are.

Master Bruce is silent as I drive north up the Aparo Expressway towards Burnley. The long-stemmed red roses are now clutched in one of his large hands and his mood is foreboding.

This is a difficult night for him, the most difficult night of the year.

This is the anniversary of the Waynes' murders.

Earlier this evening, Master Bruce visited the graveyard behind Wayne Manor, leaving flowers there before the large granite tombstone that reads: "Thomas and Martha Wayne, in Loving Memory." He does not consider his mourning ritual complete, however, until he has also left flowers at the very spot where they were brutally gunned down, almost thirty years ago now. And of course, once this mission is accomplished, he will not take the night off.

Batman never takes the night off. Never.

Despite the debt she owes him, Gotham City has not come to a consensus on her Dark Knight Detective. To many, he is nothing more than an urban legend, a tale contrived to frighten young hoodlums and ne'er-do-wells. Even among the believers there is dissent; some claim that

Batman himself is responsible for the methods and motivations of the very villains he fights.

This is an interesting argument, and one I sometimes find difficult to refute. Many of the more fanatical delinquents he engages with do seem to be somehow . . . inspired by him. They join him in masquerade, taunt him and set up schemes solely for his consideration and response. Would their criminal insanity have found less lethal expression had they not sought to pit themselves against their own, personal huntsman?

"Alfred, police scanner, please." Master Bruce's voice, as it comes from the backseat, has transformed again, dropping a full octave and taking on a gravelly, menacing quality I associate with his alter ego. Indeed, the Batman costume is in a briefcase in the trunk, and will be fished out presently.

I oblige the request, despite my stated preference for Brahms, and muse on the fact that although Bruce Wayne can hardly bring himself to remember her name, Batman could tell you exactly where Miss Ulrika resides, when she arrived in Gotham, and when she is expected to leave, in addition to giving you detailed information on her age, height, weight, distinguishing features, medical history, and any relevant criminal records. I wonder which of the two men she would truly prefer?

At last we reach Park Row, better known as Crime Alley. Master Bruce steps out of the car and disappears with the roses into the shadows of the alley while I go around to the back of the Rolls to fetch the Batsuit.

I remember feeling a vague wave of horror the first time I saw the Batman guise. It is, I suppose, a calculated effect. The costume is made primarily of a dark gray weave of bulletproof Kevlar and fire-resistant Nomex. A large black bat is spread across Batman's massive chest, his feet clad in black boots, his hands gloved in spiky black gauntlets, the entire effect completed by a combination cape and cowl. The cape is a dark, swirling, armored shadow that drapes from his shoulder to his ankles. The black cowl, complete with two pointed bat ears on top, covers his throat and two-thirds of his face. The only bright color is a yellow utility belt worn around his waist, and any criminal knows that this is not to be mistaken for a pleasant accessory.

I am frowning over the costume as Master Bruce emerges from the alleyway, hands now empty, face stricken with sorrow and grief. I swallow as I see him, my heart going out to this gentleman whom I have known since his infancy, this kind and decent human being who would sooner cut off his own arm than hurt a fly.

How do I explain, then, the transformation that occurs as he takes the costume out of my hands, disappears back into the shadows, and then reappears as a demon of vengeance, handing me an empty tuxedo and preparing to unleash himself onto the night?

With his heart already full of pain, Batman will spend the rest of the evening fighting for Gotham's safety, whether that includes citywide patrols and the apprehension of petty criminals, or a grand, eccentric battle with any one of the endless parade of costumed villains who haunt our nights here, such as the notorious Joker, Crown Prince of Crime, or the twisted Riddler, a social terrorist with a bizarre sense of fair play.

Perhaps I will explain this fracture simply by holding the connection between the two myself, no matter how divorced they may seem. Yes, it is true that Bruce Wayne is really chiefly a disguise for Batman, an act he plays to divert suspicion. But it is also true that Batman was born of

Bruce Wayne's anguish and so, like all things in Gotham City, must be assumed to carry inherent contradictions.

As he swings off into the darkness on a grapnel line, I must also assume that Batman carries Bruce Wayne's heart: a terrific vulnerability, and also an incalculable asset.

I do hope the night is kind to him.

TWO

Freddy Galen, Stonegate Inmate
11:59 p.m.

I'm ready. It's almost time, it's gonna happen here, now, and I'm ready. I'm so totally ready.

I just hope I don't see the Batman.

That's what I'm thinkin' as I press against the bars of my cell, waitin'. I don't think I've ever heard the prison this frickin' quiet. The guards, seconds from being relieved at shift change, have stopped pacin' and are all standin' on the Broadway as close to their locker room as they can get. "The Broadway" is what we call the first floor of the tier—the wide strip we come and go on, marching to and from the yard. No doubt they's dreamin' 'bout what they gonna do when they get home; honeys ta kiss, dinners ta eat, nice private toilets where ain't nobody botherin' them 'til they's done with the sports section.

Meanwhile, me and one thousand four hundred and eighty-eight other inmates, we're holdin' our breaths. Most of us are watchin' the big clock over the common area, but a few look to be strainin' their ears to hear the Clock Tower out across the Rip in Old Gotham.

My cellie's on his bunk, starin' at the floor, breathin'

hard through his nose. We just passed count and so far everything's goin' accordin' ta plan.

Not our plan, though. This other guy, Sin Tzu, is orchestratin' the whole kettle of fish from Arkham. Normally, we wouldn't pay no never-mind to no dint from the Ding Wing, but this Sin Tzu guy's different. I ain't never actually met him but I—I feel like I know him, you know what I mean? The first time I heard this plan from Sean McNally out in the yard, I knew it was a winner. It sounds crazy, I know, but I felt like this Sin Tzu guy must really care about us—me, 'specially. I just get this feelin' that he believes in me.

Now that I think about it, maybe I have met him. I feel like I know the sound of his voice, and plus which, there ain't no way he coulda worked this all out if he hadn't been on the inside at some point. I mean, he's even got it so when we leave we go out through separate tunnels. Makes it harder for the guards to follow us, sure, but more important, it keeps us from stickin' each other.

Anyway, no matter what he thinks a us, believe you me he knows this prison. Sin Tzu's a frickin' genius is all there is to it. And this thing, this plan . . . I don't see how it can go wrong.

"I just hope I don't see the Batman," I say out loud. Jimmy looks up at me from the bottom bunk with a scowl.

"Don't even say that, Galen. Think positive. And shuddup, will ya? You're makin' me nuts."

"I'm just sayin'," I say, and then I do what Jimmy says 'n' I shut up. Not 'cause Jimmy said to, mind you, but because it's close now, real close.

I've been here at Stonegate for three years now, which ain't nothin' compared to some of the old-timers. Stonegate's a maximum-security prison meant to house maybe eight hundred felons. Of course, like every other prison in the nation, we's overloaded, and although we'd love to help out with the population count by plannin' an escape or two, Stonegate has a rep for being the hardest jail in the country ta break out of. We're out on a tiny island, see, right in the middle of the Gotham Harbor, separated from Gotham's South Island by a real nasty channel of water known as "the Rip." You try to swim from Stonegate ta the Tricorner Yards, say, and the Rip's gonna sink you faster than if you was wearin' cement shoes. Ain't nobody—*nobody*—ever swam the Rip and survived.

I just wish I could meet the sadistic bastards who put this place up. I'd like to see if theys can float.

'Cause of the water, too, it's always cold and foggy here, even in the middle of the summer when it's eighty-nine degrees over in Port Adams. And inside, Stonegate is always friggin' damp, an' it stinks of sweat, piss, and chlorine bleach cleansers. The cement floors are always cold, and the bars are even colder.

But lemme tell you, it was a haven when I first got here. I mean, compared ta the places I was imaginin' the Batman might take me, well . . . I didn't care if I couldn't get out, long as I knew he couldn't get in.

Truth is, I shouldn't even be in here. Nah, don't laugh, I'm serious. The burglary was Sean's idea, I was just along for the ride. Normally, I don't go in for that stuff—I mean, yeah, I'll roll a suit every now and then or maybe shoplift a little, just the stuff you've gotta do to get by in the Bow (that's what we call the Bowery, where I'm from, you know), but I don't even got my own gun, I had to borrow one a Sean's.

Anyway, that week my mother, Lord love 'er, had kicked me outta the house again and Tommy Haley had slashed two of the tires on the Camaro I was fixin' up for Dave Callahan, so I really needed the cash. And I figured

I'd be doin' Sean a favor to boot. Sean's kinda like the leader of our little group. I mean, we ain't no gang or nothin', but we've all known each other since grade school and everything and Sean, he's always been the glue that holds us all together—like the smartest and the best-looking and a favorite with all the nuns in school, not to mention the guy who could always score beers even when we was fifteen and the guy who would always ask his girls if they had friends or sisters for the rest of us.

So he's got a place all cased out, Von's Video on the corner of Bowman and Ninety-third. We've got Dylan Fitz behind the wheel of Sean's Thunderbird with the motor runnin' and we just walk right into Von's waving our guns and shoutin' for everybody to get down. Sean told me not to say nothin' much, but I get kinda caught up in the adrenaline and everything when we first get in there, so I'm actually doing a really good job of gettin' everyone who ain't behind the counter onto their stomachs on the itchy green cut-pile carpet. It's kinda a rush, really, how people listen to you when you got a gun.

Sean's workin' the employees, gettin' them to open the cash registers and safe and I'm takin' wallets offa the customers. Everything's goin' just like Sean said it would until all of a sudden the lights cut out, just like that, plummeting us into total complete frickin' darkness.

"Freddy, what the hell!?" Sean yells back to me. I'm in the Romance section pullin' a couple Jacksons outta some lady's purse.

"I didn't do it!" I yell back. And then I hear a snap and what kinda sounds like Sean moaning. And then a loud thud, like a body hittin' the floor. "Sean?"

I drop the purse and the money and start pointing my gun every which way, squintin' in the dark though I can't see nothin', not a goddamned thing.

"Sean?" I ask again, this time real quiet-like. My voice is dryin' up in my throat. I keep thinkin' I see a shadow movin'—a shadow that's somehow darker than the dark. Shakin' a little, I spin around and point the gun behind me, and then it's not in my hands anymore. It's just . . . gone.

I'm still tryin' to figure out how my hands got empty when I see these two eyes—white slits narrowing, like eyes you'd see on a devil or in a nightmare or something. "Sean?" I whisper. Though I know it ain't Sean.

Something barrels out at me from the darkness at a hundred miles an hour, and next thing I know, gloved fingers are curling around my neck and lifting my feet off the floor. Then a voice comes out of the dark—a growl, really—low and filled with hot coals and glass shards.

"You're not the thief who helped Sean knock off the mini-mart on One-hundred-and-twenty-third last week. What was *HIS* name?"

"K-Kevin . . ." I gasp, tryin' to speak through the claws I swear I feel sinkin' into my gullet. It's all I can do to keep from peeing right there. "Kevin McNally. S-Sean's cousin."

And then he lets go of me, and my knees are too weak to help when my feet hit the floor again, so I crumple down to my butt like my legs are made of jelly. A cop light flashes outside, red then blue.

And that's when I really see him.

He's at least eight feet tall, and his head is actually the head of a bat, with spiky ears and everything. He turns towards the flashing light and I can see that he has wings, too, and a giant bat clingin' to his chest like some kinda freakish pet. And then he disappears, and I mean like vanishes, right into thin air, like they say Dracula can do. By the time the cops turned the lights back on, I *had* peed, right there on the itchy green cut-pile carpet.

I got six years, and Sean got ten. The Batman even got Fitz out in the car and Kevin right in the middle of his date with Brenda McGillicuddy.

Anyhow. That's history. Right now the big hand's lined up against the little one on the big clock they got out on the Broadway, the guards move towards their lockers, and though it's only the faintest echo from here, out there in the city, we can just barely hear that big Clock Tower countin' down.

BONG.

Jimmy jumps up from the bunk and joins me by the cell door.

BONG.

I pat my jumpsuit pockets, double-checkin' the essentials.

BONG.

Lighter? Check.

BONG.

Shank? Check.

BONG.

Photo of Mary Cotter from back before when she got married? Check.

BONG.

Down on the Broadway, Castillo unlocks Sean's box. This Sin guy must've paid him a pretty penny. Castillo's been the warden's pet CO for as long as I can remember, but now he's helpin' us along like he's just one a the boys. He ain't even makin' those stupid jokes he usually makes. He just looks kinda glazed.

BONG

Sean slips outta his box, quiet as smoke.

BONG.

Castillo moves up to keep six—keep watch, that is—

squintin' down the hall as the second shift begins to move in.

BONG.

Sean reaches the fuse box . . .

BONG.

. . . and cuts the lights.

BONG.

Castillo backs inta Sean's cell, where he thinks he's gonna ride out the riot.

BONG.

Scan finds the master switch and with one loud clankin' sound, our cell doors slide open, and we're all shoutin' and shovin' and racin' for the yard in one big breakin' tidal wave of freaked-out, hopeful, mad-as-hell, desperate, dirty men.

This is gonna work. This is gonna happen.

I just hope I don't see the Batman.

Jimmy stops by the guardroom, skippin' in place to keep his energy up, ready to dish out some payback. I come up behind him and look over his shoulder—I don't wanna hurt nobody, but I got money on who takes down which guard first.

Thing is, though, the room's empty. No guards nowhere. They's just gone.

"Come on," I urge, smackin' Jimmy on the side of the arm. Everyone's shoutin'.

"Let's go, let's go!"

"Guard post two going down!"

"Move, move, move!"

"Call in SWAT!"

Sounds like there're still some guards outside in the towers, though, 'cause I hear shooting comin' from the yard. Between that an' all the yellin' an' the alarms now goin' full blast, it sounds like a goddamn combat zone. I guess it is a combat zone. I just hope I don't see the Batman.

I make it to the yard as fast as my state-issue shoes will carry me and all I can make out is little frenzies of orange jumpsuits crowdin' around different pieces of the fence line. Sean told me and the gang to meet up at the southeast corner of the fence, so that's where I head. The gang is just me and Sean and Jimmy and Kevin and Fitz and all the guys from the neighborhood. We're Irish and we're Catholic and so we kinda stick together, but we ain't a proper prison gang like the Aryan Brotherhood or the Filipino Ferrets or anythin'. We don't even got tats. I mean, yeah, Sean and Kevin both have some ink, and once Sean got in, Fitz got a "13½" on his arm (that's, like, the sum total of twelve jurors, one judge, and one half of a chance of gettin' off), but we don't all have the same tats is what I mean.

I look over my shoulder while Fitz finishes cuttin' through the fence with the wire clippers Sin Tzu somehow left buried and waitin' right there by the fence. The electrical wires ain't a problem no more now that the lights are out, and I see Nation, Hobz, and Reiso climbing guard tower three like they been trainin' to do it their whole lives. The tower's takin' shots, though, and I don't wanna wait to see who falls.

As I shove my way up to the fence I feel like I gotta pee, real bad. That's when Fitz steps back with a grin and I see the hole.

Can I just say God bless America? This is capitalism in action, am I right? Supply and demand, and like, we demand to get the hell outta here and Sin supplies. It is a beautiful frickin' night. I start dreamin' 'bout what I'm gonna do first: find a honey ta kiss, grab a hot dinner, find a nice private toilet where ain't nobody gonna be botherin' me 'til I get done with the sports section. You know what would really hit the spot? One of them steaks you can get at O'Neils, with that big pile of mashed potatoes on the side, smothered in gravy. Yeah, that and a nice tumbler fulla scotch. And a pack. And real coffee. Oh, man, I can taste it already.

Some of the guys have been talkin' 'bout revenge, but I don't feel that way. You know, they got their lists of people they think set them up, everyone from cousins to jurors to cops who testified against them. Not my thing, though. I mean, don't get me wrong, I can't stay another day in this godforsaken hole, and I could practically kill Sean for draggin' me inta that video store.

But the other thing is that I been in Gotham my whole life, and I know how it goes. They're certain people that just been born ta be locked up. If we hadn't gotten caught at the video store, it woulda been somethin' else. America ain't got no use for us—we're a dime a dozen. I got a cousin over in Burnley what became a cop, my sister Tara's got two kids and ain't never been in no trouble, and my ma, of course, is a saint, but damn near everyone else in my family's seen the inside of the joint.

If I'm mad at anyone, I'm mad at Gotham. I wanna get some money in my pocket, some food in my stomach, and then show this town what a real frickin' criminal can do.

'Cause that is what happens when you send punk-ass delinquents to jail, you know. We become proper frickin' lawbreakers.

Now I'm pushing my way through the hole—we're goin' kinda single-file-like, since it's a little low, and you gotta crouch or you'll rip your back up on the fence. And there, just thirty feet ahead, are some boats lined up to take us across the Rip. Like I said earlier, Stonegate's built a little like Alcatraz, what with it being on an island and all. There's a land bridge, too, and that's what most of the big prison gangs are usin', but Sean volunteered us to be one of the little groups that takes a boat.

"Hey!" Kevin catches up with me and Jimmy from behind, and we head down the slope to the boat together. "Look," he says, pointin' straight up at the sky. "No moon. Bet Sin Tzu picked this night special just 'cause a that."

"You better believe it," says Jimmy. "There ain't nothin' he said so far that hasn't been on the up and up. I mean, look at this!"

Jimmy motions to the waitin' boat, which Sean is already standing in.

"You talked to him? To Sin Tzu?" I ask Jimmy. "I mean, yourself?"

"Yeah, sure," says Jimmy. And then he shivers 'n' rubs his arms as the harbor spray kisses his skin. I'm cold too, but I'm lovin' it. It's freedom-cold, not turnkeys-in-a-pissy-mood-cuttin'-our-heat cold. "Well, I mean, no, not directly, but . . ." Jimmy looks confused for a sec and then turns to Sean.

"You talked to him, right, Seanie?"

"Just get in the boat," says Sean, though he's grinnin'.

"Whatcha gonna do first?" I ask Jimmy as he helps me climb on board. Sean's already pulling at the motor.

"It's all about the money, Freddy."

"I hear ya." Gotta good point there. Gonna need funds. Maybe I'll revise my plan a little—roll a few civilians and *then* head over to O'Neils.

"Forget that!" says Fitz, scowling. "Money later. First, I wanna spill some blood. I got some serious payback comin'."

"You and me both, brother," Sean agrees, guiding our boat out into the Rip. Water laps against the sides. It's just the five of us on this thing, and as we start out, a strange tension settles over us. It's wicked dark, and we're caught between two worlds here. Somethin' goes wrong, we're all back where we started, but worse. We make it to that other shore, though, comin' right in by Port Adams and the Financial District. Well, all we gotta do is lose the orange and we're free men. Free.

"He's got a plan, though, right? For the Batman, I mean, this Sin guy, he's got a plan?"

The minute the name "Batman" escapes past my big fat mouth, Fitz, up by the stern, almost jumps overboard. It ain't fair, us havin' a personal bogeyman like this. Those of us who've seen the Bat—well, we don't never wanna see him again.

"I swear to God, Galen," Jimmy says to me through clenched teeth. "You don't stop with the Batman crap, I'm gonna throw you right over."

"He does though, right?" asks Fitz, teeth chattering as he clutches the railing for dear life. "The Sin guy, he has a plan for him, right?"

"Of course he has a frickin' plan!" Jimmy explodes. "If the Bat weren't under control, don'tcha think he'd *be* here by now?"

Jimmy means this to be reassuring, but Fitz and me, we start looking around with real wide eyes. You don't see him comin' is part of the thing.

Jimmy grunts at us and turns away, shakin' his head. He got brought in by the GCPD. He just don't know.

I offer Fitz a little smile and he exhales slowly, like he's been holdin' his breath for an hour.

"Screw Sin Tzu, and screw the Batman," says Sean, glaring out across the water.

"Amen," says Kevin, crackin' his knuckles.

"I'm serious, you two are major wusses." Sean laughs.

"I hope I *do* see the frickin' Batman. I ain't spent three years in Stonegate gettin' soft, ya know. I'm ready for my rematch, thank you very much."

"I ain't even hopin'!" brags Kev. "I'm goin' after him. First thing, I step outta this boat and the hunt is on! I'm gonna skin the Bat alive! I'm gonna make him sorry he ever heard the name Kevin McNally. I'm gonna make that spook pay!"

"Yeah, you and about fourteen hundred other inmates," Fitz mumbles.

"Hey, you ladies do whatever you want." Sean again. "We all gotta split up when we hit shore anyway. Sin Tzu was real clear on that. He's happy to help us all out, but what he needs in return is for all of us to be on our worst behavior. You know what I'm sayin'? He wants major chaos, all right? Coming from every part of the city. Keep the PD jumpin', that's what he wants, and that's what's gonna keep us out."

"Sure sounds like a nice change from the old lay-low routine," says Jimmy. "I can think of six or seven people right off the top a my head I think I'd like to visit tonight, if ya know what I mean."

Kevin shares a lewd smile with Jimmy. I hesitate a second and then jump right in.

"But what about the Batman? Seriously, what's Sin Tzu doing about the Batman?"

All eyes turn towards Sean, who smiles as he guns the boat's motor. "You let Sin Tzu worry 'bout that, 'kay? We do our part, he'll do his."

Fitz mumbles something into his jumper sleeve.

"What's that, Dyl?" asks Jimmy.

"Robin," Fitz says a little louder. His voice is trembling. "No one ever says anything about Robin! That kid kicked my *teeth* in!"

Sean reaches down and pats Fitz on the shoulder. "You just do what you do best," he says, and Dylan Fitz relaxes a little against the hull. "That's all Sin Tzu's askin'. By tomorrow morning, the Batman, Robin, the GCPD—none of it'll be a problem."

Sean's voice has a calming effect on me, too, and when I close my eyes, I swear I can hear Sin Tzu's. And really, ta be fair, so far so good, right? So maybe I will stop worryin' 'bout all that right now. One day I'll look back on this night and I'll think about how frickin' scared I was and I'll laugh.

My mood's really improvin' as we hit the shore. Sean helps us all outta the boat and then we all clasp a hand on one another's shoulders by way of goodbye, and then we scatter into the night like bats returning to the—scratch that. Like rats or bugs or somethin'.

Anyway, we all split up.

Except that the city is flooded, and I mean just flooded with us. Everywhere I look there's an orange jumpsuit and a crime in progress. It kinda starts to feel like a party, if you don't think too hard 'bout what everybody else is doin'.

Yeah, like a party—'cept the kind where you stick to your own dark corner and mix your own drinks.

I look up at the sky again and take a deep breath. Holy Saint Mary, I am free. Free! I love this big, ugly city so much I wanna rip it apart with my bare hands and smear its blood and its smell all over my face. I wanna be in it, in the action, rollin' in it, stinkin' of it, everywhere, everything! It's like the worst kinda blood lust, a hunger, starvation. It's like that crazy way you feel when you first fall in love and you know it's just chemicals and crap that'll wear off if ya take it easy and 'sides you wanna savor it so you tell yourself you'll take it slow but you can't wait, you know, you just can't frickin' wait to grab that honey and lay her down and cover her with yer sweat, mark her, make her yours, and before you know it—bam!—it's over and yer tryin' to catch yer breath and realizin' she's not so hot after all, maybe, but what the hey, you are, you're the man, so bring it on, nothin' matters anyway, give that chick a kiss.

Yeah, I'm elated, and then my stomach growls and I realize there ain't no canteen breakfast comin' my way in seven hours 'cause I'm fendin' for myself now. And I admit, that makes me a little bit nervous, and being nervous on my first night out makes me a little bit mad.

I remember what Jimmy said and start thinkin' 'bout how to make me some commissary. I wanna hurt someone while I do it, too. Just ta make sure, you know, ta make sure I'm really free.

Standing over someone you've knocked down onta the ground and then walkin' away with their money, yeah, that's how you know you're free.

I start walkin' up through the Financial District, figurin' I'll head northwest into Old Gotham, and the scene is surreal, you know, just totally off. It's like a movie set someone's filled up with convicts. Ain't usually much of nobody in the Central Business District this time a night, so you've got Industrial Boulevard, for example, totally empty 'cept for three yellow cabs and fourteen guys in bright orange jumpsuits, kicking over *Gotham Gazette* stands and breakin' windows everywhere just for the hell of it. Some jerk has broken into the sixty-stories-high Von Gruenwald Tower and is busy yellin' somethin' 'bout his accountant and throwin' business papers outta the thirty-sixth-floor window like some kinda ticker tape parade. The Gotham Stock Exchange–Bruford Tower complex is on fire, alarms are blaring from the Crystal Palace/America's Mall complex, and two guys from the Aryan Brotherhood are kickin' the crap outta a coupla armed rent-a-cops from the Port Adams Plaza.

I'm thinkin' about stealin' some clothes before I cross Commerce Street, knowing that the Gotham City Police Department Headquarters are right there at the Moench Row intersection, but Commerce is such a carnival scene when I get there, I end up not even botherin'. Four guys from the third tier have turned over a cop car in the middle of the street—with two cops still in it and civilian cars and cabs laying on their horns and brakes as they try to skid around it—and this has set off a sort of riot mentality, includin' at least four active carjackings, a seven-car pileup in the left lane, and a violent in-progress mugging. I figure if I move fast, nobody'll even notice me, and I might make it inta the heart of Old Gotham before that parta the city's at war, too.

I ain't even gone six blocks when it gets totally quiet. All that chaos is behind me. For now, anyways.

And in another three blocks, right near Crime Alley, I fall in love.

There's this old dude all done up chauffeur-style, closing the trunk of the sweetest black 1961 Rolls-Royce Phantom V limo you ever did see—I can tell this baby's all original, with a shining cream top, that enormous 3,683-millimeter wheel base, black leather interior in the front, creamy beige in back, walnut cocktail cabinet with TV on the dash, the works. Looks like someone spit-polished it, too, lovingly waxing it for hours 'til it shined like a disco ball.

Now *that* would start to make up for three years in Stonegate.

The guy's got a prissy little pencil-thin mustache hovering oh so properly over a bland frown, and sunken cheeks that probably make him look tired even when he's not. His eyes are alert, but he's low-lidded, adding to the overall drowsy effect. He ain't asleep on the job, though—guy's standing so straight you could use him as a yardstick. And like I said, he's all done up chauffeur-style, complete with the double-breasted waistcoat, stiff black boots, and eight-point cap.

Now, I ain't dumb or nothin', I know the car ain't his, but the kind of rich dudes who have chauffeurs still give tips in fifty-dollar bills and expect their servants to grab 'em things like expensive smokes and liquor. So I'm willin' to bet that Mr. Rolls-Royce here has some pocket lettuce worth pilferin' plus there might be a nice long coat in the back that'll cover my jumper.

And oh, sweet Jesus, that car . . .

I watch him from across the street for a minute and don't see anything to dissuade me. Can't even figure out what the hell he's doin' there—unless his boss is slummin' it in Crime Alley, I can't think of a single event down here that'd warrant this kind of display. And the place is deserted, just absolutely quiet. He's the only sign of human life on the street, so I move in fast and direct-like, just walking quickly across the narrow street 'n' right up to him.

"Hey, Jeeves!" I say, to make him turn towards me.

He raises like one quarter of one eyebrow but otherwise don't move a friggin' muscle, so I figure I'll just take him out fast and get this over with. I raise my right to clock 'im, and then he grabs my arm and the world flips upside down and I'm on my back on the pavement.

What the hell's goin' on here!?

I roll back up onto my feet and stand up in front of him, panting a little bit from the shock as much as from the exertion. "Wanna play rough, do ya?" I ask him, and I think, though I ain't totally sure, that he smiles. He can frickin' laugh in my face, ain't gonna stop me from beatin' him silly and takin' that car.

I step in for a left hook—this has taken Manny Vincent down in the showers more 'n' once, you know—and Jeeves here just steps off to one side so fast I don't even got no time to reposition myself.

"I'm afraid your attire is entirely inappropriate for this side of town," he says to me in some phony British accent thing.

To which I say, "Huh?"

I look down and smooth out the jumpsuit. "Oh, yeah, the prison rags." I smirk. "Well, this is the best I got right now."

"I do know of a place at which that apparel would be quite fitting."

"Yeah, on the other side of the Rip, right? I don't think so, Jeeves." I lunge at him, just going for a full-body tackle this time, planning to slam him over the car hood, loath though I am to risk denting the baby. His back does touch the Rolls, but then I feel his foot in my gut and I go flyin' over him *and* the hood and land on my backside on the pavement. I must be way the hell outta practice!

I see a beer bottle lyin' empty in the gutter, and I grab it as I get back up and toss it at him as fast as I can. Finally, a freakin' reaction! He jumps to one side, away from the shattering shards, and I lunge at him again, this time knocking him off balance so that we're wrestling on the sidewalk by the Phantom.

Some weird-lookin' cell phone type thing falls out of his inside jacket pocket and as I glance at it outta the corner of my eye, he sticks two fingers under my jaw and into my throat so suddenly I can't breathe or nothin'. I shove him off and roll away, scooping up the little piece of tech and shoving it in my hip pocket 'fore I book down the street as fast as I can go. What the hell are they teaching chauffeurs these days, anyways!?

That guy musta been a goddamn secret agent or somethin'. Honestly, if I'm that spry when I'm his age, I ain't gonna have no complaints.

I don't stop runnin' for four blocks and then I duck into an alley to catch my breath and check my neck just to make sure I ain't bleedin' or nothing. My mood's really goin' downhill 'til I remember the doodad I lifted offa ninja-Jeeves.

I reach into my pocket and pull it out and look it over. I don't know . . . some kinda mini TV maybe? Didn't know they made 'em that small. It kinda flips open if you push this button, must do *somethin'* . . .

Well, I don't need to know what it does to pawn it. I start heading for Felker's Firearms—he's been known to do some pawning on the side—but right when I tuck it away again something really frickin' weird happens.

The Batman's voice comes outta my pocket.

"Alfred, is everything all right?"

Okay, fine, so I jump. I spin around in the alley and I ain't ashamed to tell ya, I'm ready to burst inta tears. Better than pissing myself, which I also almost do. I'm startin' to have serious questions about my bladder control. I better see a doctor when I get some bank.

It takes me a minute to realize that the voice came from that electronic gizmo, and I pull the thing outta my pocket with shaking hands. Okay, now I'm askin' for real—what the jimney jack *IS* this thing?

Well, what you don't know can't hurt you quite so bad, right? So I hurl the frickin' thing as hard as I can, out towards the street. And that's when a real ninja shows up outta nowhere and catches it, just like that.

"Thank you," he says real calm-like, standing nearly as straight as that Jeeves guy. He's got an accent too, kinda Asian-like. And then he lifts his head without lookin' like he's movin' at all and looks at me—no, past me . . . holy crap! There's two more of 'em now, standin' behind me, covered in black from head to toe, only their eyes at all visible, kinda Oriental-lookin' but not like no Gotham gang I ever seen.

And each and every one of 'em with a red-and-black yin-yang symbol thing embroidered on their hoods.

"Whaddya want?" I ask the first guy. He's been examining the thingamabob real careful-like and now he looks up at me with narrow eyes.

"You're one of the Batman's soldiers?" he asks, pronouncing the words real precise, like English ain't what he usually uses.

I start ta laugh. "Who *me!?* You got the wrong guy, Mac, sorry."

Spooky passes his hand over his hip and the gizmo disappears, like inta some kinda secret pocket or somethin'. Then he does one of those Bruce Lee/Jackie Chan moves, standin' sideways with one arm extended and one pulled back, both palms facing forward like he's about to kick my butt, but he just nods at the other two behind me.

They both suddenly step forward in one synchronized movement, and somehow each of them ends up with one of my arms. "Hey! Come on, now! The Batman don't know me from Adam!"

There's a rustle behind me and then either Tweedlespook or Tweedlespookier slips a burlap bag over my head.

"You're makin' a big mistake!" I holler. But they ignore me. I hear a van drive up and screech to a halt just in fronta the alley. No way, screw this, I ain't going for a ride with no ninjas, not on my first night out!

I kick forward as hard as I can, hopin' Spooky's still in fronta me, but I don't make contact with nothin'. I'm strugglin' to try to throw off the other two when what can only be the side of Spooky's gloved hand comes smashing into my stomach, doubling me over and making me feel sure I'm about to vomit. It's like that feelin' you get when you exercise too hard, plus you've eaten way too much chili, plus someone hits you in the stomach with a lead ball.

Next thing I know, my hands are tied, and with the bag still over my head so I can't see nothin', I'm on my knees in the back of the van and off we go. And really for at least fifteen minutes, all I can think about is how bad my stomach hurts from that one karate chop.

Obviously, I'm tryin' to figure out what went wrong here. These guys ain't correctional officers or GCPD, I'm pretty sure a that. Maybe *they* work for the Batman, and I shoulda said I do, too? Naw, that don't make no sense. I seen the guys what work with the Bat and they're always kinda flashy and wearin' armor 'n' all. No, these guys are somethin' else all over again, and I don't know what ta do about it 'cept go along and hope for the best.

The van stops after about thirty minutes—we're all the way on the other side of town, or maybe outta Gotham altogether. The back doors open and someone climbs in and pulls me out. I still can't see nothin' but the inside of the bag over my head, plus which I can still feel my stomach throbbing, so I don't struggle too much.

We walk down a linoleum hall—I can hear it squeakin' under my shoes—and go through a bunch of doors and finally stop. I hear Spooky Number One just in fronta me and to my right.

He starts to say something in Chinese or somethin' and then I hear someone snap his fingers and he starts over again, in English. I guess his boss wants to make sure I'm gettin' all this loud 'n' clear.

"We found one of the Batman's soldiers," he says. "He was carrying this."

Right at that same time, someone behind me rips the bag off from over my head and the fluorescent light slams into my eyeballs. I blink and squint up and then my jaw hits my chest.

This guy standin' in fronta me? He's gold. I mean, all gold, like plated, like someone dipped him in the frickin' stuff and let it dry. 'Cept for his hair, which is long and black, and pulled back tightly, and his eyebrows, which arch up all pointy-like. And he's got that same crazy black-and-red tat on his forehead that looks like that yin-yang sign the Oriental gangs're always inkin' on themselves.

I've just barely taken all that in when I notice his hands—or should I say claws? I don't know if they was deformed to begin with or something went wrong when someone dunked him in gold or what, but it's like his fingers don't end where they oughta and instead change into these clawlike things that can't be good for nothin' but shreddin'.

"Is this true?" he asks me. He's holdin' the gizmo now and he's also got a weird accent I can't place. I can't stop starin' at his claws. He's frowning severely and he's got these wicked high cheekbones and totally white, narrow eyes you can't see into or nothin', like . . . like the Batman's! "Are you a soldier of the Bat?"

I shake my head, tryin' ta find my voice. "The Batman put me away," I finally squeak. Who the hell is this guy and where are we and what does he want with me?

I am definitely, definitely gonna piss myself now. I

wanta stop lookin' at him but I can't take my eyes away. He's terrifying. And hypnotizing. And he makes the hair on the backa my neck stand up. Something's really wrong with him, like he's there but he ain't. Like negative space in a picture, you know—the shadow insteada the thing. "I, uh, I got the doohickey off some chauffeur guy in Old Gotham. I don't know where he got it."

"The hailing frequency was open," says Spooky Number One, like that proves somethin'.

The gold guy nods. Jesus, he's even wearing armor of some kind. Gold and black. And I can't stop staring at his eyes, like I'm falling into them, like they're suckin' all the life outta me.

"We've already isolated and broken into the bandwidth they're communicating on," he says to Spooky Number One. "But it could prove useful, at least psychologically, to have an actual communicator."

What're they talkin' about? The bandwidth *who's* communicating on? What does any of this hafta do with me? Maybe I oughta pretend like I'm in on somethin', so they think I'm useful and they don't kill me. Or . . . or maybe they really did make a mistake and I'm not who they want so they'll just . . . just . . .

Jesus, Mary, and Joseph, this is really not a good thing here. Any way I cut this I'm dead, I'm just totally dead.

Spooky Number One bows, like he's done somethin' major. "I serve at your pleasure, Sin Tzu," he says.

Sin Tzu? SIN TZU!

Oh my God, I was so scared! I start laughin' now, exhaling. Well, that sure answers my question about whether or not I ever met him before, right? No way I woulda forgot this guy! Damn, no wonder the plan worked so well, this guy's obviously a major player, a genius even! I am seriously impressed. I mean, truly, what presence! And ninjas and everythin' even. Nice. Sin Tzu's the real thing, all right. Whoo, am I relieved!

"You Sin Tzu?" I say, still laughing with relief. "It's a real pleasure to meet ya, sir. I'm Freddy Galen, one of the guys you busted outta Stonegate tonight—you know, from Sean McNally's team."

I smile wider but he just keeps starin' at me with those depthless white eyes, so I continue. No way he doesn't remember Sean, everybody always loves Sean.

"Me 'n' the boys, we'd all just like to say thanks. 'Specially my bunkie, Jimmy—he was doin' Buck Rogers time! That's what we call it when your parole date's so far inta the next century you can't even imagine it, you know?"

I turn to grin at Spooky Number One, but he ain't smilin' neither. "Yeah, so uh, so he was real happy to get outta there, I tell you what."

The laugh finally dies on my lips, though I try to keep up a smile. Somethin' ain't right. Sin is lookin' right through me, and he ain't smilin' back.

Spooky Number One has straightened up and Sin speaks his next words right to him.

"However," he says, pickin' up from what he said last like I didn't say nothin' in between, "I doubt this cringing, idiotic menial is working under a general as great as the Batman. I would expect our enemy's soldiers to be far more loyal and astute."

Spooky Number One nods. How'd we get back to the Batman stuff? I thought we had that all cleared up . . .

"Yeah, I—I told ya," I stammer, "I don't work for the Batman, that's—that's funny, really, you know." I try a little laugh again but it dries up in my throat. "That'd be like you workin' for, I dunno, like who's your worst nightmare? Like the cops or somethin', right?"

"What would you like me to do with him, sir?" asks

Spooky Number One. Behind me, Tweedlespookier grabs my arm again like he's about ta take me somewhere.

Sin Tzu waves a hand real dismissive-like, already turning away, his attention on the chauffeur's communicawhatevah. "Kill him," he says, absolutely calm, like he says it all the time.

Whoa now, hold up! How did this all get so frickin' outta hand!? "W-wait a minute," I say to Sin, "you're jokin', right?"

Tweedlespooky starts pullin' me outta the room as Spooky Number One turns to me with a slight smile and a glint in his eyes.

"Sin, man! Buddy! Listen! I ain't no problem to ya, I'm inta this, honest!"

Tweedlespookier starts dragging me to the door as I struggle and shout after Sin Tzu, who's got his back to me now, wicked indifferent.

"Whatever you're tryin' ta do here—take over Gotham, right?—yeah, I know this city pretty good. Maybe I could help, you know . . . maps or somethin' or . . . Sin? Sin! Mr. Tzu?"

Tweedlespookier tosses me the resta the way outta the door while Spooky Number One pulls out some kinda sword from a sheath on his belt. The fluorescent light glints offa the blade.

Naw, this ain't happening. Aw, man, please, I ain't ready for this . . . I just ain't ready!

I wanna see the Batman! He don't let nobody die. He's always on top of his game. So maybe he's already here. Maybe he's about to jump outta one of these corners and just beat the livin' daylights outta these guys and then— and then Sin Tzu'll tear him apart with those horrible, dead, gold claws and still come after me when he's done and rip my heart outta my chest without even blinking an' . . .

Please, God, how can there be somethin' scarier than the Batman?!

THREE

Jonathan Crane/The Scarecrow
12:27 A.M.

My name is Professor Jonathan Crane, and I am the master of fear. It took me a long time to figure out why I, myself, had been sent to Arkham Asylum for the Criminally Insane, but I finally realized it must be due to my counterphobia—that is, a preference by a phobic for fearful situations.

That, or they're still going on about my fear gas being dangerous and illegal.

Within the stony walls of Arkham Asylum, they call me the Scarecrow. That's a slight improvement over "Ichabod," my childhood nickname based on my resemblance to the fictional character Ichabod Crane. By "resemblance" my foolish young tormentors meant chiefly that I was scrawny and bookish and painfully shy.

But I thought Ichabod was a rather wonderful character. He would have been a proper hero had he but overcome his fear.

Fear, you must understand, is more than a mere obstacle. Fear is a teacher, the first one you ever had. It's hard-wired into our brains, part of our chemical makeup just like the sensation of pain and the urge to procreate. It is foolish to dismiss fear as a mere emotion, or, worse yet, as an uncontrolled and transitory reflex.

Fear is a religion.

Not the one we preach—the one about the Golden Rule—but the one we live, day-to-day, dollar-to-dollar. The unspoken conviction that there's not enough of anything in this world, and that no one's got your back. The utter moral certainty that you've got no choice but to watch out for *numero uno*, because it's a dog-eat-dog world out there, and only the fittest survive.

Fear of starvation is what first prompted you to smile at your mother. Fear of social ostracism is what first made you desperate to please your father. Humans are gregarious, group-oriented animals by nature. Instinctively, we know that we cannot survive on our own. More than anything, we fear isolation and social exclusion. Fear of failure, you see, is fear of social embarrassment—you might get laughed at. But fear of success is fear of social ascendancy—you might be perceived as a threat and expelled from your group.

I suppose I'm a pretty good example of that myself.

None of this is conscious, of course. We don't wake up thinking about these things, or discuss them at dinner parties. But we know the fear in our guts, all of us.

And, ah, how these times embrace it! Today our government feeds us on fear. It's our national diet. Cereal and a spoonful of fear! Beer and a fear chaser! Hamburgers with an order of supersized fear on the side!

And really, why shouldn't we be afraid? In case you haven't heard, life is terminal. Cigarettes will kill you. So will your cell phone. Your microwave, the power lines, the squirming germs that raw meat leaves behind on your kitchen counter and the chemical cleaners you neutralize them with . . . all potentially lethal. Your car is a deadly weapon, alcohol a quiet killer. Too much fat, too much sugar, too much exercise or not enough . . . Don't lick the lead-based paint on your windowsills, don't lick the back of that postage stamp, and don't lick any strangers, oh, that can take you down quickly, indeed! Don't drink the water and don't drink less than eight glasses a day. Hold your breath in traffic, off-gas your furniture, stock up on duct tape! Don't talk to strangers, and if you're female, don't go home—you're more likely to be a victim of domestic violence than of burglary, mugging, or any other type of physical assault combined. Your environment is toxic, your natural resources are dwindling, your days are numbered, but whatever you do, don't panic! The stress, don't you know, will kill ya.

Why, for the last few years, even intelligence has become suspect and untrustworthy. Intellectuals have agendas, after all, and their agendas will seek to destroy the core of wholesome goodness we pretend to hide behind our prejudice and greed. At the very least, they'll make fun of us. We don't just suspect or believe this. We *fear* it.

And fear, you must believe me, runs ever so much deeper than faith. Which is why it makes such a powerful weapon.

Yes, fear is a religion, and I . . . I am its avatar.

I have learned to synthesize the compound that triggers fear in the human brain. You would not believe the elegance of this organ we hide in our skull, the ultimate receptor. It speaks a language of chemical threads and electrical impulses, producing its own hormonal neurotransmitters that it has cleverly designed to break down soon after their release.

I have invented nothing, really. All I can claim credit

for is beefing up some of those neurotransmitters to make them hit harder and last longer. I can administer it as a serum, but I prefer gas—there's nothing like blasting someone in the face with a billow of green smog to really get their adrenaline going, even before the chemicals take effect. People are just inherently afraid of green smog.

Fear isn't green, of course, but I add food coloring. Legends, after all, are made by the details.

Not that I expect the world will make much of my legacy. "Nothing to fear but fear itself"? Ridiculous. We *are* afraid of fear.

Sin Tzu understands this.

In all my time at Arkham, there has been only one man intelligent enough to comprehend the significance of my studies, to wish to build upon them in new and stimulating ways. Indeed, I must credit the genius of tonight's plan to Arkham's newest resident, the mysterious Sin Tzu.

He approached me in the rec room several months ago while I was quietly minding my own business, sitting in an old Victorian chair of ragged, worn Jacquard, once a vibrant red but now so faded and stained as to seem perfectly in keeping with the rest of the institutional furniture. I was reading a dog-eared copy of Poe when a chilly shadow fell across the chair. I squinted up to see him standing over me with a sort of regal bearing, appearing not at all afraid of my gruesome rags, Old West Tombstone-style undertaker's hat, skull mask, or even the noose I wear around my neck.

Dr. Jeremiah Arkham is an interesting man—he allows those of us who enter his facility "in costume," as he says, to remain so clothed, hoping that it will shed light on our individual pathologies.

Sin Tzu's lack of response to my appearance was disappointing, but intriguing.

He himself was terrifying without being macabre: gleaming gold skin accented by long dark hair and a sort of exotic cast to his features. He stared at me with opaque, narrowed, soulless eyes of white, a red-and-black tattoo seeming to swirl in the center of his forehead.

I'd never seen him in the rec room before. I looked to the guards, but they were staring blankly into space, their minds apparently elsewhere. The entire time I spoke with Sin Tzu, they moved not a muscle.

Perhaps they were afraid of him.

Eventually, the stranger spoke in a cool, cultured voice. "They call you the Scarecrow, do they not?"

I flashed him a ghastly grin and nodded my agreement.

"They tell me you are an expert in the ways of fear."

I rose out of my chair and stood eye to eye with him, smiling at his frown. No stench of sweat rose from within his clothing, so I circled him slowly, letting one of my chemical-tainted hands trail lightly around the breadth of his shoulders, listening for any changes in his breathing, watching for unbidden spasms of muscle tension. He remained utterly tranquil.

Interesting.

"I am," I said at last, cocking my head and squinting my eyes at him as I came to stand once again before him.

"I want to ask you, what do you imagine might be the psychological effect on the Batman were we to release all the inmates of Stonegate Prison into the streets of Gotham one night?"

"Fear response, of course," I answered evenly, attempting to hide my excitement. All the inmates in

Stonegate? Every one of the more than fourteen hundred of them?

"Ah, from the Mowrer-Miller theory." He nodded, and then recited, "A covert and unobservable response to a threatening or noxious situation that is nonetheless assumed to function as a stimulus for production of measurable physiological changes in the body."

I could not hide a beam of delight.

"In addition to perceptible overt behavioral changes, yes. You've done some reading." I paused, and sank slowly back into my chair, thinking. "Emptying Stonegate would not be enough, though, to stop the Batman for long. His response to terror is very systematic. He would simply round up said criminals one by one, even if it took him a week without food or sleep."

"I agree," said Sin Tzu, thereby convincing me of his intelligence. "Which is why that would only be phase one of the campaign."

I lifted my eyes to him again, intrigued. It's not often one gets to enjoy a civilized conversation in the asylum.

"And what would constitute phase two?" I asked, letting my fingers toy with the rough rope of the noose around my throat.

"You," said Sin Tzu evenly.

And so began a three-hour conversation.

I confess I glazed over a bit while he was describing the particulars to me. I was too busy analyzing his particular neuroses. He strikes me as a sort of self-taught master of free-floating anxiety. Which, of course, is only an accurate assessment if there is, indeed, no specific situation or reasonable danger to which to attribute anxiety. In his case, this is probably a dicey assertion.

He also mentioned voices once or twice. There's nothing like a schizophrenic mastermind to get the party going.

In any case, I was back on board when he disclosed some sort of marvelous hypnotic abilities in his possession that could be used to send a guard to my cell with a neatly packed plastique pipe bomb. At a predesignated time on the next moonless night, all I had to do was set the explosive against the wall, trigger it, stand back as far away from it as possible, and then, subsequent to the explosion, dash out of the resulting hole and make my way to the D'Angelo Sewage Treatment Plant. There a band of handpicked psychos would be awaiting my commands, themselves having been freed within moments of my own escape.

I praised the simple brilliance of his plan. It struck me as an excellent way to gauge the effects of extreme stress on the Batman's psyche. It would produce marvelous levels of testable fear and could be conducted on the kind of scale my experiments demanded.

That is when he confessed that my approval meant more to him than I could know. It turned out that he needed me. I was to serve as a sort of captain for him, he playing the part of the brave general planning the attack.

Mm. I revised my opinion of Sin Tzu's complex. Atelophobia, perhaps—fear of imperfection.

It is possible, too, that Sin Tzu suffers from some queer delusion of grandeur. After all, not just any amateur scientist can follow my analysis. I am—was—a professor of psychology at Gotham State University, from which I earned a doctorate in neurobiology with a minor in clinical neuropsychology and an M.D. in psychiatry and biomedical sciences. The majority of my studies remain unpublished and I do not anticipate layman comprehension.

We discussed my mission at great length until I became sure of two things: first, that he was entirely serious and could be counted on to uphold his end of the bargain, setting me free; and second, that he was shamelessly playing to my ego. But no matter. His proposal was the basis for research I could not resist, and at the core of it was the channeled force of fear itself. And who am I, at this stage in my career, to turn down those willing to sponsor my work?

My studies, of fundamental importance to the consideration of human physiology, are always criticized as being unethical. Unethical—ha! Notice that no one ever accuses them of being bad science.

That conversation was both the first and the last I had with Sin Tzu. Curiously, I never again saw him in the rec room, nor in the commissary, nor in any other open area of the asylum. But I had no doubt that our pact was sealed.

And in fact the escape from Arkham is going without a hitch. The guard comes to my cell exactly at midnight, vacant-eyed and acquiescent, and delivers the pipe bomb as if it were a cup of chamomile tea. I set up the explosives as instructed, at times certain that I'm hearing another creepy voice inside my own skull guiding me as I fret over certain particulars.

And then there is a magnificent explosion, the sound of tumbling rocks as the wall comes down, and off I run into the night.

It's enchanting.

Fear in the air everywhere, like a smell or a song drifting on the cool night air, punctuated by pipe-bomb explosions and screams. I catch snatches of it as I run: fear of being caught, fear of being hurt, fear of losing jobs—"Oh, man, this is *not* happening! Not on my shift, Lord, please!" sings one of the guards in a soaring baritone solo—fear of the outside world, fear of the dark, fear of the dogs, fear of the guns, fear of the blasts, fear feeding on itself and soaring into sweet, high melodies of terror before falling back into a quiet, steady baseline of doubt.

I pay no attention to the other "troops" and "captains" escaping with me. I am too busy moving swiftly through the darkness to rendezvous with my Sin Tzu selected Scaries, anxious to begin my part of the grand research project Sin Tzu has planned for the evening.

The night is pitch-black and moonless, and yet, within moments of our escape, the Gotham sky is ablaze with a harvest-colored searchlight. I stop in my tracks to savor the slow wave of alarm that washes over my fellow escaping inmates as they register the cookie-cutter blackness at the center of the *O* beaming up into the dark.

There, spread across the sky, with wings as wide as eight city blocks on either side, is the shadow of the bat. The Bat-signal has been lit. We are no longer fleeing into the dark privacy of night. Now we flee directly into the Batman's waiting arms.

I feel it too, a shiver. Worry. Dread.

Oh, the Batman is no joke. He fades in and out of shadows like a specter and then connects with a fist of steel. He's diabolically clever and completely without mercy. He tastes like an overamped designer drug. In his presence, your senses reel. He's everywhere at once—in your face, in your head, in the pit of your stomach.

And then he's gone and there is nothing but solitary confinement, hospital tapioca, and lithium. You don't know the Monday morning blues until you've been incarcerated by the Batman.

I might have slipped into a self-indulgent panic had I not remembered my objective.

I find my Scaries waiting for me, as Sin Tzu had promised, at the D'Angelo Sewage Treatment Plant, the only neighbor Arkham Asylum has on Mercey Island. There are over a dozen of them, some still clothed in mint green hospital gowns, but many marvelously stuffed—muscle-bound and brutish—into Halloween-themed costumes.

"Is fear illegal?" I ask my Scaries, after I, at last, round them up. Though they were waiting exactly where Sin Tzu had said they would be, they seemed not entirely prepared for my appearance. Seven of them ran, screaming, from me the first three times I tried to approach them.

Fortunately, they ran in ineffective circles, shrieking and waving their arms like children, and even more fortunately, the fear gas bombs Sin Tzu had promised to have waiting for me were also in place. Finally, I was forced to use anti-fear gas on them, which calmed them into a nice bug-eyed, tongue-lolling shuffle that I think will be perfect for our mission. Two of them cannot stop drooling, which I imagine might add to our overall effect once we hit the streets of Gotham.

I try again.

"These chemicals are produced by the human brain, and they are to be outlawed?"

None of my Scaries seem to have strong opinions on the matter. Several of them stare blankly back at me, shifting absently from foot to foot, as others sneer and crack their knuckles, waiting for me to point them towards our research subjects. I frown at them for a moment, and then sigh.

"Who wants to go to the city?" I ask.

This gets a rousing response, complete with "me, me, me!"'s and lots of jumping up and down. I appoint a few lieutenants, distribute a few fear gas grenades, herd them into the back of a white paddy wagon—the last of Sin Tzu's gifts to me—and close them in before hopping into the front and following Renfield Avenue all the way off of

Mercey Island and straight down to Old Gotham, just as Sin Tzu's map indicated.

Please believe me when I confess that I am a terrifying driver.

I pull the van over on Moench, three blocks from City Hall, and let my Scaries out of the back. During the ride, a few of them have acquired minor injuries such as bruised elbows and cut knees. They're looking more and more appalling by the minute, and I realize that this was probably calculated on the part of Sin Tzu. He truly is a man of vision, and, once again, I must give him a great deal of credit for the orchestration of tonight's experiment. The gas is mine—as is the specific targeting of Commissioner Gordon for the focal point of my experiment—but the simultaneous prison and asylum breakouts and the bold omission of a control group, those were his ideas.

I find him inspired.

It couldn't be done without the gas, though, and let us pause for a moment to consider the brilliance of my choice in subjects.

In his own boring, sedate way, Gotham City Police Commissioner James Gordon is almost as bad as the Batman. He's consumed with petty concerns such as the desire for everyone in Gotham to be able to "sleep soundly at night, confident and unafraid," and "walk their neighborhoods without fear of crime or criminal activity."

Forgive me, but is this or is this not a city? If that's how he feels, why doesn't he go join the police force in Smallville, Kansas?

He has foiled as many of my experiments as the Batman has, but that is not why I picked him to be my target tonight. Sin Tzu was very clear about needing to deploy his captains strategically, and was concerned with getting the

Dark Knight's attention as quickly as possible. And as much as I despise Gordon's old-school policies, pedestrian ideas, and bushy white mustache, none of these are responsible for his nomination as tonight's first victim. No, I picked Commissioner James Gordon for far better a motive.

The Commissioner is both easily accessed and highly important. Not only is he a beloved elected city official, he is also someone for whom the Batman has, in the past, shown personal concern. Yes, I picked Commissioner James Gordon because he is the Batman's best friend.

The Scaries get a little out of hand the moment I release them onto the streets, but that is acceptable, is even part of the plan. One of them—I can't remember his name but I believe he was in for eating his auto mechanic after murdering him with a blowtorch—forgot or misunderstood my warnings about staying downwind of the fear gas I was spraying on random civilians and ended up crawling up the double yellow line of Renfield Avenue screaming about the drive axle boots on his '66 Mustang.

I had forgotten how frightening car repairs could be.

I continue towards City Hall, a steady march, my ghoulish Scaries skipping and scraping along behind me, while the thugs of the bunch keep their eyes peeled for danger. It is truly a glorious night. In addition to my hair-raising band of mad, messy mischief makers, there is a wild game of cops and robbers in effect, the robbers neatly costumed in orange-colored penitentiary uniforms, the cops scared out of their wits long before I blast them with my gas.

It doesn't take me but a minute to find a nice shoot-out involving three police officers firing from behind a bullet-riddled squad car at three Stonegate escapees who have acquired automatic weapons. The ex-prisoners angrily discharge their deafening guns from the dark porches and doorways of a series of narrow apartment buildings, creating an old-fashioned standoff.

I play with fight-or-flight response for a moment, moving in and out of the shadows to gas the cops with fear gas and then the robbers with anti-fear gas, before reversing and mixing up the two until I find each individual's most aggressive stance. Interestingly enough, the cops seem to do better—that is, react more violently—on the anti-fear stimulus, which inspires them to increasingly bolder acts of offensive fighting, while the Stonegate prisoners are motivated by the fear gas into heinous acts of hostility and carnage.

I leave the six of them in the middle of the street, beating each other senseless, no longer satisfied with the indistinct, remote violence of their guns, and continue forward with my mission. I tell three of my loonier Scaries that the two policemen guarding City Hall have pockets full of gold and lollipops, and sneak the others through the main door while the cops try to restrain the eager hands of the inmates suddenly besieging them.

Once we have access to the building, we swing by the court evidence rooms to pick up gas masks for my accomplices. Heartened by the protective gear, the Scaries become increasingly raucous, randomly attacking the various city officials unlucky enough to be working so late. Under the effects of my gas, said officials hurry to cower behind file cabinets and hide under desks, creating a wonderful game of hide-and-seek for my demented, barefoot, gown-clad Scaries, while my beefier appointed lieutenants take up defensive positions in eager anticipation of the opportunity to fight the Batman.

I ignore these festivities. Sin Tzu has assured me that

the man I want to see will have set up an emergency office post on the third floor.

I run up the metal fire-exit steps without incident and gas two officers and a civilian aide in the third-floor hallway. The civilian aide goes immediately to her hands and knees on the carpet, clearly experiencing environmental distortion and nausea.

Ten feet past her, I can hear Commissioner Gordon's voice emanating from his office, tense and urgent.

"I don't know," he's saying, "I can't raise the warden. The tactical squad is on the way—"

I smile as I step into his doorway and wait until he raises his eyes to meet mine. Commissioner Gordon is in his late fifties, with a thick head of white hair complemented by that ridiculous, overly generous white mustache. His eyebrows rise up from behind his glasses and, a man of action to the end, he swiftly moves to pull his gun.

"Stop right there!" he cries.

I watch his intelligent brown eyes register panic half a second before I lose the specifics of his face in a lovely green cloud of fear gas.

He continues to fight, lunging across his desk as if planning to restrain me with his bare hands, but is finally overcome by the steady stream of aerial fear I pump at him. To his credit, I will admit that I wouldn't have thought to need this much on an elephant.

"Oh, my," he gasps, and then, small and tinny from a little device in his ear, I hear the voice I long to hear, the only voice that makes my blood run cold.

"What is it, Commissioner?"

Wanting to get closer to the voice on the other end of the earpiece—he would know soon, he would say my name—I leap onto the Commissioner's desk, tilting my head to one side as I crouch before him, papers scattering around me.

"No," the Commissioner sobs, eyes already dilated and filling with hallucinations I can only guess at, "no . . . not the . . . noose . . ."

I lean in closer still, pressing my ear against Gordon's as he trembles and fails to make himself move back and away from me.

"The noose," comes the Batman's voice from the earpiece. "The hanged man . . . Scarecrow, Jim! It's fear gas. Hold your breath. I'm on my way."

Oh, yes, ladies and gentlemen. Hold your breath.

He's on his way.

The Commissioner is heavier than I had imagined and he babbles like an overcaffeinated psychotherapist as I grab him by the armpits and drag him from his makeshift office into the elevator, across the cold tile floor of the lobby—still filled with cowering law enforcement fodder and my eager Scaries—and over towards Gotham's imposing courtroom. Several of my selected captains follow, apparently abiding by Sin Tzu's orders to protect me.

I have to pause as we pass the now broken glass doors at the front of City Hall, affording us a glimpse outside. The Commissioner and I watch a car skid into a lamppost as the driver narrowly avoids T-boning a small band of marauders still radiant in their bright orange Stonegate prison jumpers. They are beautiful creatures of spite and malice no doubt married to chaos from the time they were snot-nosed hoodlums . . . pure, organic acolytes of fear.

One of them is playing kick the can down the center divide with a full-sized trash bin while another manically brandishes a large baseball bat he has lit on fire, thrusting it into the faces of alarmed passersby. The third simply fires a police-issue handgun into the air at random intervals, howling like a college frat boy.

The Commissioner shudders uncontrollably at my feet, broken and sobbing. I breathe deeply, drawing the cold, polluted air into my lungs before I remember.

Hold your breath.

He's on his way.

I'm panting by the time I lug Gordon up the polished wooden steps of the courthouse, and am glad for the interruption of his communicator, which startles him into a small yelp as it comes to life with a sudden buzzing urgency. I reach down and open the frequency. The Batman's impassive, masked face fills the small monitor, but I can hear the concern in his voice.

"Jim?"

I grab the Commissioner by the back of his hair and yank his head up so that his face will fill the Batman's screen.

"It's over, Batman!" he gasps. "They control the city!"

"Jim," comes the Batman's dark, carefully modulated, voice. "Keep it together."

I kick him then, Gordon that is, in the kidney, just for the fun of it. He gasps in pain and fear, which I must attribute to my gas. I've seen him kicked before, and normally he shows no reaction at all.

"Scarecrow!" the Batman shouts. It is partly a curse and partly a demand.

I laugh and pull the Commissioner away from the communicator so that I can peer directly into the Dark Knight's glowering face. His face, not his eyes.

He doesn't have eyes.

"This is an amazing night," I tell him. "I'm not sure who's more afraid—the citizenry or the convicts. All of us here in Western culture, we're secretly terrified of freedom, don't you think?"

The Batman's non-eyes narrow.

"Surely a night like this scares you, Batman, just a little? Maybe you experience a brief arrhythmia when you think of what I could do to your Commissioner friend now, or feel a trickle of sweat run down the back of your cowl as you fail to keep your mind from adding up the total figure of inmates currently flooding the streets? You can't stop us all, you know."

"Right now, I'm only concerned with stopping *you*, Crane."

Crane. His attempt at unnerving me, reminding me that he knows my real name. I'll admit that it affects me, but only for a moment.

I frown as I drag Commissioner Gordon the rest of the way up the stairs and into the empty courthouse, wondering idly if it's always open or if some petty criminal has forced the lock before my arrival. I stop at the feet of Justice, gazing up towards her blindfolded eyes as Gordon continues to whimper and quake on the floor. The statue—a particularly romantic and fanciful representation of Lady Justice by any aesthetic evaluation—towers over the judicial bench at a nice, understated height of thirty feet. I guess the Gotham magistracy felt they needed a subtle reminder as to the general definition of their jobs in between accepting bribes. The scales she holds out in one slender hand are not actually balanced, despite both being empty, an artistic choice that distracted me to no end during my first trial in Gotham City.

Justice is blind. Love is blind. But fear sees clearly.

Not that seeing clearly does you any particular good in this world.

I grind my back teeth together and snatch up the

communicator again. My intention is to enlighten the Batman as to the full scale of my current experiment, but suddenly my ears fill with the screeching howl of shattering glass coming from behind and above me. I turn to face a downpour of shards and a sudden awareness of icy fresh air pouring through a rude absence of window just above the entryway doors.

At my feet, Gordon gives in to a fresh paroxysm of terror. I press my eyes closed and try to steady my breathing so as to fully appreciate the physiological effects of what is to come next. When I open them again, he is there in front of me, as I had known he would be, a final spray of shattered glass glistening off of his swirling cape.

The Batman.

I taste aluminum between my teeth and I swallow involuntarily. My mouth and throat go dry. My breathing catches high in my chest and my heartbeat accelerates. A cold sweat breaks out across my top lip half a second before my armpits dampen and my palms go clammy. A sudden uncomfortable tightening in the urethra is instantly answered by a loosening in my bowels. My body is ready to purge, to flee. I can smell the secretions of endorphin and hormones seeping from my skin. In front of me, he is pungent, acrid. He's been fighting. My legs begin to shake and it feels as though every nerve in my body rises to ripple and prickle subcutaneously.

For one insane instant I consider dosing myself with a quick blast of fear gas, just to string the glorious tension out across every fiber of my being. But before I can reach into my pocket for an aerosol, a scorching pain explodes across my jaw. My feet leave the ground and I open my eyes to see the Batman's gloved fist retreating from me in a declining arc.

I have only just realized that it's me who is moving

rather than him when the back of my head slams into Justice's cheek.

Arguments rage through the asylum cafeteria as to whether or not the Batman is human. We've all seen him do things we had previously assumed to be impossible. Now, after being sent flying backwards in a twenty-foot-high arc by a single uppercut, I cannot easily dismiss the possibility that the Batman is, in fact, a radioactive, super-powered, bionic, undead, chemically enhanced alien.

But that is dismissing the force of fear. A man capable of channeling his adrenaline could, in moments of extreme stress, easily send another, lighter man off to challenge the tyranny of gravity. As the Batman has just done.

Though my mouth is filling with blood and I can feel the bruising spread across the back of my skull, I taste a moment of supreme satisfaction.

I have scared him.

It is this thought that fills my head as the noose around my collar catches on the fulcrum of Justice's scales. It jerks at my neck, cutting off breath. The world blurs. So the Gotham courts would hang me after all!

I kick my feet in a futile effort to free myself and then am overcome by an unfamiliar feeling of peace.

Far below me, I can see the Batman turning his frowning attention from Gordon, upon whom he has just forced some sort of oxygen mask, up to the gruesome shadow I cast on the clean stone walls of the courtroom. As far as I know, they have never been splattered with blood.

"The reaper," I choke, trying to tell the Batman that everything is all right. "Maybe . . . this time . . . the reaper will come."

"No," the Batman says quietly from the ground. "Not this time."

I struggle for breath, lose the fight, and let my eyes close. When they flutter open again, the Batman is balanced above me, crouching as he uses one of his awful silver Batarangs to cut the rope that holds me.

I feel a rush of air and fall unceremoniously to the ground. Within seconds the Batman is on the ground behind me, pinching my wrists with his cold steel handcuffs. Nearby, the Commissioner rises unsteadily to his feet, pulling off the rebreather Batman had fastened over his mouth and nose.

That's another thing I hate about the Batman. He carries his own anti-fear gas.

"Jim?" the Batman asks. "Are you all right?"

The Commissioner nods slowly, still looking more lost than not. "I'm fine now," he asserts quietly, rubbing the back of his neck. A flashing red light outside bathes his face in a passing flush of distress. I watch him with narrowed eyes.

Outside, the night is still frenzied with sirens, gunshots, car alarms, screams. My Scaries run half-naked through the streets, following the whims of their dementia. The eastern skyline is ablaze.

The Batman is already moving swiftly away from us. "Take him to Arkham," he says, gesturing to me without even turning around.

"We can't," the Commissioner answers quickly. Impressive, really, how swiftly he has regained his wits. "It's been sealed from the inside. The tactical squad has it surrounded, but . . ."

Commissioner Gordon's voice trails off and we both watch the back of the Batman's cape as he pauses. Then the Dark Knight turns to me slowly, his mouth in a hard, thin line.

"You know who's behind this, don't you?"

I look up into the white slits where the Batman's eyes should be, and I smile. His attention darts to the Commissioner, who averts his own gaze to the floor. I see the Batman's non-eyes narrow.

Oh, Batman, my friend, my grand experiment has been a success. I taste your fear.

And if you think you're scared now, wait until you meet Sin Tzu . . .

FOUR

Robin/Tim Drake
1:03 A.M.

Robin, status report?"

Batman's voice comes over my comm link, a dark growl that freaks me out every single time I hear it until I remember that he knows I'm on his side.

He doesn't talk like that in the day, when he's Bruce Wayne, and that always mellows me out, you know? I always forget that the sun's gonna go down and I'm gonna find myself wearing a mask and red tights and red-and-black chest armor in a Kevlar/Nomex weave with a little "R" over my heart, and some guy twice my size is gonna be trying to kill me and just when I think I might live to see fourteen, this voice is gonna come at me out of a comm link in my belt, this totally scary, scratchy, unbelievably threatening voice, and he's gonna ask me for a status report or something and I'm not supposed to freak.

Okay, so don't freak. Take a deep breath, Tim, and answer the man's question. He wants a status report.

On what, I wonder? I mean, which part?

That I'm in the middle of a fight with two of the bazillions of muscle-bound thugs wearing Day-Glo orange

Stonegate Prison jumpers that are tooling around Gotham? That one of them's wielding a chain and both of them want me dead? That I've had a rock or something in my left boot for the past forty minutes and it's driving me totally nuts?

Or maybe he wants something more general, like the status of the whole city, which, as far as I can tell, has totally and completely wigged out.

Last time I heard from Batman, he said something about going after Scarecrow, and last time I heard about Scarecrow, he was in Arkham Asylum for the Criminally Insane, so you do the math—it all adds up to murderous nut jobs out on the loose. And obviously, someone picked up Stonegate Prison and shook all the inmates out of it and onto the streets of Gotham like some crazy game of Pick-up Sticks (or some game of Crazy Pick-up Sticks?).

Covering one mile tonight from Bristol down to Burnley, I stopped seven break-ins, four muggings, two attempted burglaries, and one simple beating. I realized pretty soon that, sorry, folks, the stores were on their own. Priorities dictate that physical assaults on another person take precedence, and that was pretty much *all* it looked like I was gonna have time to cover. There's stuff on fire, and sirens going off everywhere, and so many car alarms blaring that they almost drone out the whoops and hollers of the escaped prisoners rioting down Dillon Ave.

"Robin?"

Oops. I should have answered him by now, huh? The guy with the chain swings it at my head and I backflip over his buddy, causing the chain to hit his buddy instead of me, while I leapfrog over Chain Dude to buy myself a second and open my comm.

I wince as I hear the chain make contact against Buddy's skull. Buddy goes down.

"Hey, Batman! My status is of the kicking butt and taking names variety."

"Disengage and return hail."

"Whoa, wait! Diss who and re-what?"

There's silence on the other end of the line and that's way not good. Means something bad came up or, worse yet, I'm annoying the hell out of him. Trust me, you don't want to annoy Batman.

"Finish your fight and call me back. On the secure line, Robin."

"Ten-four. I'm all over that like brown on brown rice."

He clicks off, which is better than dead silence, and Chain Dude, who seems content to let his buddy rest against the brick alley wall for a while, moves to close the distance between us.

Nothin' like having someone try to kill you to get the blood flowing.

Not that I wasn't already pretty hyped. Anytime I get the call from Batman saying I'm needed, I'm in overdrive likethisandevenfaster. Of course, I'm pretty much always in overdrive. Batman says I'll grow out of it. Like that's a good thing.

Chain Dude swings again, aiming right for my face. I drop onto my back a tenth of a second before the chain has a chance to take off the top of my head and am pleased to see Chain Dude follow through on the swing and lose his center of balance.

Piker. First thing you learn is that without balance, you've already lost the fight.

And, sure enough, the step he has to take to keep from falling forward puts his left ankle at a perfect forty-five-degree angle from my right calf if I just roll this way a little, allowing me to sweep-kick his legs out from under him without even bothering to get all the way back up.

Nice thing about sweep kicks, too, is that if you do them right, the person you're kicking tends to fall backwards and away from you. Which is highly desirable when, like me, you weigh maybe ninety pounds soaking wet and tend to mix it up with guys pushing three g.

Now Chain Dude's on his back, but I could really use him on his stomach. I jump to a crouch right by his left side, quickly kicking his chain away, and, just like I hope he will, he rolls for me, angry, trying to grab my ankle. I spring straight up into the air and come down fast on his back the second his belly touches cement. Now I can do the cuffing hands and legs together bit with one hand tied behind my back.

You might think that's just an expression, but no. When you work with Batman and you say something like "I could do that blindfolded," or "I could do that with one hand tied behind my back," you don't just mean that you're pretty good at it. What you mean is that Batman made you do it fifty times in a row blindfolded *and* with one hand tied behind your back.

I don't even bother to call these guys in. The cops'll either find them pretty soon—the bright orange Stonegate jumpsuits'll stand out like a beacon to any passing officer—or they won't, in which case they're too busy for second-rate criminals like these two.

And so am I. Once they're both cuffed up good and tight, I hop up over to an isolated trash bin, crouch on top, and call Batman back. Uh . . . I mean, I disengage and return hail.

"Hey, Batman? I've got a question for you . . ."

"Robin, go ahead."

"Aren't *all* of our lines secure?"

"I'm not sure. Alfred didn't answer my last hail. It's

possible that one of our communicators is out in the open. Are you alone?"

I look to my left and then to my right. "Deep down, aren't we all?"

Silence. I'm about to remind Batman of his own assurances that I'll grow out of this, when he continues, his voice completely and totally without emotion.

"As I'm sure you've noticed by now, the chaos tonight isn't limited to any one section of the city. Complaints coming in through the police scanners range from the Financial District all the way up to Amusement Mile."

"Yeah, I could barely get out of Bristol. And I took the bridge this time instead of the tubes."

The Gotham County R.R. Tubes run, more or less on time, between the Bristol suburb, where Wayne Manor is located, and Amusement Mile, which is essentially the northernmost point of the city. Batman has a special tunnel rigged in the tubes that we can use to get in and out of the city without being seen—you know, like when we're in the Batmobile or something. But when he called me in tonight, it sounded like a little show of strength wouldn't be amiss. So I took one of the Bat-bikes across the Robert Kane bridge, which also links Bristol and the city, even though I'm not really supposed to be driving yet. I figured I'd slip that in now when Batman's in the middle of a complicated directive, so it might seem like a kinda low priority.

"By now, it seems unlikely that the Stonegate inmates are heading towards a specific rally point," he continues. "That suggests that their release was merely a distraction, and that something even worse is on the way. However, we can't abandon Gotham while we wait for the next strike."

"I've been sorta concentrating on actual assaults, you know, as opposed to burglaries and stuff."

"Good. I need you to continue incorporating that precise level of civic defense into a specific mission objective."

I grew up pretty much on the streets. First with my dad, Stephen "Shifty" Drake, who was a small-time crook and schemer, and then, when Dad went and got himself killed, by myself. I learned math on the racetracks, chemistry in a meth lab, and reading at the post office, making sure my dad and his friends weren't on the Most Wanted sheets. Point being, smartass though I certainly am, I'm not the world's most edumacated guy. And Batman, you know, is.

So sometimes he says stuff and it's almost like it's in another language. But I'll tell you something else. I always understand him when he needs me to. He could give me orders in Mandarin and I'd follow. It's something about how intense he is—it's like his will carries through no matter what he does or doesn't say.

I give him grief sometimes, but I'd do anything he told me to. He makes me wanna try harder, even when I'm trying my hardest. Maybe especially then.

"In addition to not responding to summons by communicator, Alfred has failed to access either the cave or the manor in over an hour," Batman continues. "I need a report on his whereabouts."

"Okay."

"I also need Nightwing to get to Stonegate and check on the status of the guards there. I suspect they've been left alive, but they'll need assistance."

"Okay."

"It . . . would not be prudent to mention Alfred's status to Nightwing. He'll . . . worry."

"Ooookay."

"Any questions?"

"No, sir."

"Oh, and Robin?"

"Yeah?"

"We'll discuss the bike in the morning."

Drats. Almost thought I got that by him. Oh well. If I haven't learned by now that you can't pull one over on Batman, I guess I never will.

Okay, so it's off to find the butler. Even I get the irony implicit in Gotham's most selfless man sending me on a mission that just reeks of nepotism—nearly fifteen hundred inmates on the loose, several patients from Arkham, and a couple million citizens in danger, and I'm looking for one particular guy. What's more, this one particular guy is probably amongst the top one percent in the city in terms of being able to take care of himself. Tell you the truth, I wouldn't want to be the unlucky escapee that thinks this skinny British dude is easy pickin's. I suspect that poor convict'll be regretting his decision for weeks.

Still, there're several good reasons to find Alfred:

1) He *is* about the most capable guy in Gotham, and would be an invaluable resource whenever and wherever he's found.

2) He's one of only a handful of people who know Batman's secret identity, so he has to be protected.

3) Finally and most importantly, he's the closest thing to a father Batman has, and if Batman's worried about his dad, even he might not be able to fight as effectively. And from what I'm seeing, Batman's the only one in the world who has a chance of saving Gotham. So if he's even a little bit distracted, the results could be really, really ugly for this entire city.

So, I *have* to find Alfred.

But first, I gotta call the only guy in the city who'd be more worried about Alfred than Batman.

"Nightwing? It's Robin, you copy?"

Nightwing's voice comes over my comm link, as expressive and full of life as Batman's was detached. "Hey, kid! Enjoying the circus?"

Okay, lemme see if I can break this down for you. If Alfred, who raised Batman—well, Bruce, I guess I mean—after Bruce's parents died, is kinda like Batman's dad, then Nightwing, who Batman raised after Nightwing's parents died, is kinda like Batman's son. Only Alfred was still there taking care of Batman while Batman was raising Nightwing—who, by the way, was actually Robin at the time—making Alfred kinda like Nightwing's mom. And now that Batman has taken me in as the new Robin to replace Nightwing, who doesn't wanna be Robin anymore, Nightwing (who used to be Robin) could kinda be considered my brother, except that I'm too new to all of this to be really part of the family in the same kinda way. I mean, I only wish I had a brother as cool as Dick. Who's Nightwing. Formerly Robin, the first.

Get it?

Well, okay, all you really need to know is this: You try to hurt Nightwing, you answer to Batman. You try to hurt Alfred, you answer to Batman and Nightwing. You try to hurt me, and you answer to Batman, Nightwing, and Alfred.

And usually if you try to hurt Batman you're just really frickin' sorry, but I don't want to think about that too much tonight.

"Thrill a minute!" I tell Nightwing. You know, Dick. Formerly Robin. You'll get it eventually. "Hey, listen, I just talked to Batman, and he wants you to go to Stonegate and check on the prison guards."

"Already on my way. Figured we'd need somewhere to put everyone once we catch them again. Where're you?"

"Haven't cleared Burnley yet. He's got me on some recon."

"Anything you can handle?" The concern in Nightwing's voice is evident, and somehow not the least bit condescending.

I worried at first that he might be, I don't know, kinda weird around me once I took over the Robin thing, but he's been anything but. When I ask him about it—not directly, you know, but just kinda checking in about stuff—he grins and tells me I'm doing him a bigger favor than I can imagine. When I ask him what he means by that, he always says, "Just watch his back out there, okay? As long as you watch his back, I'll watch yours."

"Nah, pretty routine. I'm good. You go take back the prison."

"Ten-four. But you get in a jam, don't be afraid to call."

I'm about to click off when I suddenly remember to ask him what I forgot to ask Batman. "Oh, hey, Nightwing?"

"Yeah?"

"What do you think's going on? I mean, tonight. How would there be a breakout at Stonegate and a breakout at Arkham on the same night? Isn't that kinda . . . weird?"

On the other end of the comm link, I can hear Dick exhale before he speaks again, his voice more serious now.

"It's supervillain-level weird," he tells me. "When things get this bad, I'm afraid it almost always means you should expect something even worse."

"Like killer-robot-ninja evil-overlord-from-outer-space worse? Or just random-maniac-targeting-Gotham-for-personal-revenge worse?"

"Yes."

Now I'm kinda sorry I asked.

"Keep your eyes open out there, okay?" Nightwing adds.

"Always."

"Stay safe!" he says, the smile back in his voice again.

"Stay dangerous!" I say back.

And now I'm off to find Mr. Alfred Pennyworth.

I pass by a half dozen Stonegate escapees flooding out of a jewelry store. Normally, I'd take 'em all down, but tonight they get a free pass. I've got my marching orders, and it's clear that Batman doesn't want us wasting energy on anything that isn't an imminent danger kinda threat.

One of the thieves notices me and wets himself as I run across an adjacent rooftop. I recognize him as Mark Filcher, a minor thug I took down last year. I make a mental note to look him up when this is all over. I don't have the reputation Batman has, so it's good to nurture the mooks who are scared of me. Hopefully a little tender loving care will help my rep to grow and pretty soon I'll be giving nightmares to criminals everywhere.

Yeah. Right.

That's when I notice the way those three guys are walking. They don't so much look like pals out for a stroll—at one o'clock in the morning—as jackals on the prowl. These guys don't have on orange Stonegate jumpsuits, so maybe they grabbed regular clothes somewhere, or maybe they just haven't been convicted of anything yet. Doesn't matter—it's clear they're hunting prey.

The only question is, have they seen any yet?

A quick scan of the block up ahead makes it obvious—the old guy with the cane doesn't know it yet, but he's suddenly developed a really short life expectancy. He's a decent size, but he has to be pushing eighty, and that cane isn't just for show. Unless I'm really mistaken—and

I'm not—this elderly gentleman is no Alfred. This guy is in deep trouble.

It goes through my head for just a second how much my life has changed. When my dad was on the street—after he stole money from Two-Face, one of Gotham's most notorious costumed criminals—I watched out for trouble just as hard as I do now. But then I was looking to avoid it, not stop it. Then Dad freaked, took off, and left me to hide from Two-Face by myself. I managed it for about a year. But eventually Two-Face caught me, figuring he'd hold me hostage until he found out where Dad had gone with his money, and I thought about Batman and Robin—who I'd heard about, of course, and totally thought were the coolest things ever—and tried to be brave.

But I was also thinking that if I could only get away from Two-Face, I'd learn to be even more careful and even more invisible and never stick my neck out for anything again. And then Two-Face found out that my dad was already dead—got killed by some gangsters in Central City—which made me, you know, *expendable*.

I was sure I'd never live to see high school. But then Batman came in and saved me.

Saved me literally, from Two-Face, but also, you know, deeper than that, too. I have a good home now, thanks to Batman, and I go to school, and I train with him to be a crime-fighter. And whenever he needs help, that's my job—I go out and I help Batman. Even saved his life once or twice. (Yeah, okay, he's saved mine a whole lot more than once or twice, but still. That's pretty cool.) And now here I am on the Gotham streets again, watching for trouble, but then jumping right into the middle of it to break it up.

Anyway, Batman doesn't need a partner who lets an old guy get beat up by a gang of low-life street punks.

I move closer, but decide to wait just a bit—I have to pick and choose my fights tonight, and there's always the chance that this cheerful trio is gonna get distracted by a liquor store or something.

But no such luck. It took until they were almost within striking distance before Grandpa finally noticed them, his hearing aid giving me a clue as to why he hadn't heard them sooner.

Nobody spoke. One of my jackal buddies very slowly removed a very large knife he'd had hidden on his person somewhere. The old man began to back up. He wasn't looking where he was going, though, so he ended up backing into an alley. The other two jackals smiled—he'd just made their already easy job even easier.

Or so they thought. Actually, he didn't know it, but Grandpa had really just made *my* job that much easier. Batman's big on the don't-let-anyone-get-a-close-look-at-you approach.

They're just moving in for the kill when I throw my Batarang. The attached line wraps around the wrist of the guy holding the knife five times before he even notices it. I use the railing from the second-floor fire escape as a fulcrum and drop with all my weight.

Even from thirty feet away I can hear the guy's wrist snap, followed by his scream of pain.

I'm in the shadows, though, so they can't see who or what is at the end of the rope. That's good for me. Keeps the others off balance, scared, and anything I can do to make three grown men scared of my thirteen-year-old punk-ass self, I'm gonna have to try to do.

My pal with the broken wrist keeps screaming, probably because he's now dangling from that broken wrist, his toes just barely touching the ground. That's *gotta* hurt. Part of the whole "crime does not pay" thing, I guess. I promise myself I'll cut him down just as soon as I take care of his buddies.

His screams are bouncing off the alley walls, echoing over and over again. It's freaking the other two jackals out even more than they already were. I'm briefly tempted to get fancy with them, build on that rep I mentioned, but I think better of it. I don't have time to showboat tonight, no matter what kind of dividends it might pay later.

So I simply jump down from the fire escape. My landing pad may outweigh me by over a hundred pounds and be a foot taller, but that's the neat thing about gravity— after falling ten feet, I plant my boots on his shoulders and he goes straight down, his knees popping like firecrackers. He sucks in his breath, hard, as he hits the pavement, and I know he won't be threatening anyone else tonight.

That leaves my last jackal. He's freaked out, all right, but deals with it by running straight at me, a pair of brass knuckles in hand. Apparently he's not aware that they're illegal in Gotham.

I jump straight up, catching the bottom of the fire escape and swinging my legs up and forward. My buddy's momentum carries him right underneath me, at which point I swing my legs down and back, pushing him forward.

He slams face-first into the brick wall at full speed and rebounds nearly as fast.

I drop back down to the pavement and then scramble back up onto the fire escape to cut the guy with the broken wrist loose. Then I jump off the landing for the last time and spray-paint all three jackals with Day-Glo yellow so the cops can easily identify them later.

And then, still bouncing a little from the adrenaline, I go talk to their victim.

He stares at me with eyes that look like they're about to fall out. I smile and hold up a hand. "Are you all right?" I ask.

He doesn't say a word, so I try again. "Sir, are you okay?" I ask once more, louder this time.

Nothing. "Are you hurt at all?" I ask, still louder.

"What?" he yells back. Finally.

I take a breath. "Are . . . you . . . all right?" I yell.

He takes a step back as an annoyed expression crosses his face. "You don't have to yell at me," he yells. "I just got mugged, you know."

I turn away from him to roll my eyes, being fairly aware of said mugging, which, if you wanna be technical about it, didn't actually happen. I know Batman would want me to be nice to this guy, though, so when I'm done smirking to myself, I carefully get my voice to a level he seems to find acceptable and suggest he accompany me to Leslie Thompkins' clinic, which isn't far away.

I know Dr. Thompkins will be open and doing a sparkling business on a night like tonight. She's lived in Crime Alley since back when it was called Park Row— which would be, specifically, before Batman's parents got shot to death there—and she apparently used to be a colleague of Batman's dad, Thomas, who was a doctor too.

In between studying my snap kicks and evades, I've picked up a thing or two about the Bat-family back-story. Thomas and Martha Wayne, Batman's parents, are more present than any other dead people I know. In fact, the whole reason he's Batman is because of a vow he made to them, after they were dead.

My dad once vividly inspired me to promise myself

that I'd never drink Wild Turkey for breakfast, but that's about it.

Anyway, in the way that Alfred is kinda like Batman's surrogate dad, I guess Leslie is a little like his surrogate mom. She was the first to arrive on the scene when eight-year-old Bruce Wayne's parents were killed in her neighborhood, and she's watched over Bruce—and Park Row—ever since. For the past fifteen years or so she's run a free health clinic, and she's also a pacifist, which is kinda neat, since I don't think hardly anybody else in Batman's inner circle is.

The trip to her clinic isn't terribly eventful. Just another half dozen mugging attempts, three more assaults, and one case of attempted arson. I guess the guy figured what with all the chaos going on, he'd make some cash out of his failing business by burning the joint down and collecting on the insurance. I think I helped him see the error of his ways—rob the place if you want, was my attitude, but don't even *think* about starting a fire that might take this whole city down. You want to be an idiot, I'm fine with that. You want to be a dangerous idiot, not so much.

We had almost gotten to Dr. Thompkins' door when the old man decided he didn't need a bodyguard anymore; he harrumphed at me and stalked off to join the line of injured people needing help. The queue was practically around the block, the whole scene like something out of a war movie, with people in white lab coats rushing around, trying to determine who most desperately needed help and would bleed out before much longer, and who could wait an excruciating few hours to have a broken arm or leg set. My elderly buddy clearly was not in desperate need, but he surprised me by immediately aiding the workers in assessing the various levels of injury.

I'm about to split when a movement catches my attention. The way one of the workers is going about his business is immediately recognizable, to me at least. I look closer and, sure enough, there, helping tend to the wounded with the skill of one long practiced in the art of battlefield injuries, is the guy I'm looking for: Alfred Pennyworth, manservant to billionaire Bruce Wayne and Batman's most trusted and important ally.

He's wearing one of the only two outfits I've ever seen him in—this one being a chauffeur's getup with a long black coat, tightly fitting cap, and pointy shoes, the other being a butler-type tuxedo, always perfectly ironed. Or "pressed," as he would say.

Alfred must sense me, too, because he looks up and around, slowly turning his head until he's looking right at me. I know there's no way he can possibly see me—I slipped back into the shadows immediately after Grandpa took off, and one of the first things Batman teaches you is how to disappear and stay disappeared. So there was just no chance Alfred could really be seeing me.

Except that he sure seems to be. I step forward a tiny bit and raise a hand, as in "hi." Alfred quickly goes back to work, dressing the cut on a little boy's arm. He gives the kid a smile, says a few words which make the boy laugh slightly, surreptitiously passes him a lollipop, and then casually strolls around the corner.

I meet him in the alleyway behind the Dumpster. Alfred's picked the spot well; there's no chance anyone'll overhear us here, or stumble upon us before we hear him coming.

I marvel again at how this skinny, uptight British dude has to be the second or third most capable guy I've ever met; only Batman and Nightwing are more amazing, and, of course, they've learned a lot of what they know from Alfred.

I realize something else too: I was a lot more worried about Alfred than I'd known.

He looks at me and says, in that flat English drawl of his, "Well, young Master Timothy, I see you've broken curfew once again. And on a school night, no less. Am I correct in believing you have a test in social studies tomorrow—or I suppose I should say, today? In just over seven hours, in fact."

I suddenly have a lump in my throat and Alfred gets a bit blurry and the next thing I know he reaches out and hugs me in this very proper, very safe, reassuring kinda way. I won't say I cry, exactly, because after all, I'm thirteen years old. But there are times when it's really nice to be with someone who loves you like a son, especially when your real parents are dead.

And after all, I am only thirteen. I'm sure by the time I'm fourteen I'll never get choked up like this again.

Alfred gently wipes some water off my face with a spotless handkerchief that smells faintly of sandalwood. "Undoubtedly you misplaced your 'kerchief whilst saving a damsel in distress, rather than simply having gone off without one again," he says wryly. He says stuff like that to Batman, too, which is amazing. He's the only person in the universe who can get away with scolding Batman.

Alfred quickly fills me in on how *his* night's been going. Turns out he'd been attacked and lost his communicator in the brawl. Although an elephant could tap dance on Alfred's foot and he'd never show a moment's distress, I could tell he was extremely unhappy about what he saw as an almost unforgivable error on his part.

"You *should* be upset with yourself," I assure him. "When someone twice your size and half your age mugs you and all you manage to do is beat the snot out of him, yeah, you *should* be upset."

He smiles. "Mm. Touché. A small dose of one's own medicine does occasionally do a body good, does it not? Very well, young Boy Wonder, your point is well taken."

I take out my own communicator and get in touch with the boss. "Good news—our package has been located safe and sound. We're at Leslie's clinic."

Batman doesn't hesitate or give any sign that he's happy to hear it—not any sign anyone else would pick up on, anyway, but both Alfred and I can hear that he exhales just slightly. And when you can run the Gotham Marathon in two hours and barely break a sweat, a tiny little puff of air can speak volumes.

"Fine," is all he actually says.

"Oh, and you were right about the communicator. It's in the field somewhere. Long story. The butler got targeted for a roll by some Stonegate—"

"Understood," he interrupts. "Coordinate your efforts with Nightwing."

Alfred and I smile at each other. "I love it when he gets all warm and fuzzy." I grin.

"Indeed," Alfred agrees. "I feel it safe to say he has a few things on his mind this evening. And now, if you'll excuse me, I really should get back to helping Dr. Thompkins. I know you will not, in reality, but please pretend for my sake that you'll be careful out there. I have seen the worst this city has to offer, yet even I am rather surprised by the depths to which some individuals have stooped tonight."

He looks me in the eye. "Pray do not give any one of them an extra-special notch on their belts."

And with that, he's gone. I call Nightwing, who answers immediately, his masked face filling my communicator monitor. "How many and where?"

"None and relax. How's your prison?"

Nightwing grins in that way he's got that makes me hope so damn much I grow up to be just like him—not that I'd ever tell him that, of course. It occurs to me briefly that maybe I'm more like Batman than I think.

"Ah, you know—a little lonely in here tonight," Nightwing says, at which point I can see him lean to one side, and then hear his booted foot kick in a metal door. The muffled shouts of gagged prison guards greet him, and he appears in the monitor again, crouching by one and untying him as he smiles at me once more. "But not a complete ghost town. Any news?"

I manage to tell him that Alfred was found without mentioning that Alfred was lost, and he nods with a slight frown of confusion, no doubt wise to me. We are both amused by the knowledge that even if anyone were to overhear us, they would undoubtedly figure that "the butler" was code for something completely different.

Sometimes hiding in plain sight really is the best plan.

It sounded like he almost had Stonegate prison under control again—he told me that whoever had emptied it out had been thorough. There were only four convicts still there, all of them too scared to even try to face the outside world, but willing, at least initially, to give Nightwing a run for his money. As usual, he sounded happy about the opportunity to fight.

Nightwing was worried about the rest of the city, though. The closer he had gotten to Stonegate, the more convicts he'd seen flooding the streets of Gotham.

Since he was down at the south end of the city—Stonegate is actually on an island in Gotham's south bay—and I was way uptown, he suggested we work our way towards each other. "Last one there's the bird that laid the rotten egg," he grins. He knows I hate that stupid holiday rhyme about Robin, even if they did sing it about him first.

"You'll be eating my dust, old man," I say in my best tough-guy voice.

"Go easy on me, willya?" he begs. "My social security doesn't kick in for two years yet."

I laugh. "I'll see if I can't spare you a tiny bit of mercy. Burchett Center sound like a fair place to rendezvous?"

"See you there!" he agrees and breaks the connection. I wonder for a second if it was a mistake to disclose an actual location, since Batman made it clear that we may be being monitored, but I dismiss the thought as quickly as it comes to me. Batman told me to coordinate with Nightwing, and he didn't say not to use the communicators, and he probably has some way crafty reasoning behind the whole thing that I'm not even gonna give myself a headache trying to figure out.

I start running south at full speed, slowing down only to smack the occasional Stonegate escapee in the back of the head; it's surprising how many of them go down for the count from only one punch. A few other incidents cause me to lose more time, and after the fifteenth mugging and the ninth attempted assault I lose count.

It doesn't take me long before I realize I'm not gonna be hooking up with Nightwing anytime soon. He might get the bragging rights, but that's a contest I can afford to lose. This night, this city, isn't.

I don't know who's behind all this—I can't even conceive of someone wanting to do something like this, on this scale—but I know I have the opportunity to make a serious difference, to watch for trouble and stick my neck out as far as it'll go. Better these mooks try to kill me than someone else. Because no matter how big or sick or dangerous they are, they're not gonna succeed.

The night is in me now. They don't have a chance.

That's what I think about as I move south from Burnley, picking and choosing my fights from among the Stonegate escapees. I'm more and more realizing they're really just a distraction from something even worse, meant to tie up Batman's resources. That's me, one of Batman's resources. And if my boss tells me to take care of all fifteen hundred Stonegate convicts tonight, then that's what I'm gonna do.

'Cause I know Batman's out there, taking care of the Something Even Worse.

Whatever that might be.

FIVE

Sin Tzu
1:15 A.M.

As I have written:

> *The wise general does not allow himself to become distracted by small events. He must always keep his eye to his overall plan. This is to say that the wise general must use his mind like an eagle, flying above the field of battle.*

I am at the highest point of Arkham, atop a pendulous, creaking wooden tower. The crumbling scrollwork of the balcony is embellished with bats. To one such as I, who has received the wisdom of the ages from the spirits of the Chulan Caves, Gotham's history is but the merest belch between courses in the universe's grand feast. But it seems bats have been rooted deep in the city's psyche for the length of its short existence. I am surprised that small carved robins do not adorn the woodwork as well. The Batman's loyal little tumbling lieutenant is quite as essential to Gotham as his master.

Behind me, two of my own best warriors stand, as unmoving as stone, to guard my back. I must keep all of my senses tuned, must use all my skills to part the fog of war.

I had no need to climb this tower. My Yanjin Alchemy allows me to see Gotham quite clearly even from within Arkham's walls. My chosen fortress, deep within a forgotten complex in the madhouse, is an excellent place to center myself and send my mind's questing fingers outward. Yet a true commander never loses the thrill of beholding conquest.

From my vantage point, individual gunfights reveal themselves in sparks and flashes. The areas where my forces run rampant are marked by the orange, throbbing glow of fires. Police positions can be easily identified by the flashing of blue lights. The hurrying fire trucks, streaming along Gotham's streets, strobe with red.

The sounds of battle chorus and crescendo. The bells toll, once. The clear chimes play softly under the gunshots and rise slightly above the crackling of the infernos that now burn throughout the city. They sing counterpoint to the shattering of glass and the buzzing of small alarms, the mechanical wail of buildings being looted. I hear their clear tones through the incessant howl of sirens and honking of horns.

And too, the scent of the air is intoxicating. Even should the spirits take my eyes, the Mehta-Sua would allow me to track a battle from smell alone. I inhale burning petroleum, burning buildings, the whiff of gunpowder, an occasional sting of tear gas. It all adds up to the fragrant stink of war.

On the emergency band of the radio, the Governor has called out the National Guard. The President is expected to call in the military, but it will be too late. By the time they can become a viable force, I will have secured my conquest. They will be forced to negotiate. An entreaty for negotiation is tantamount to surrender. As I wrote:

One must learn to read the signs of victory, for victory comes in many forms.

The battle for Gotham rages. The battle that I, Sin Tzu, have orchestrated and unleashed.

And how fares the Batman? I tempt myself with the possibility of meditation, using Mehta-Sua to become one with the conflict and locating the Batman at its heart. But no. I resist. For I know how the Batman is faring: exactly as I wish him to.

My first captain, the Scarecrow, has fallen, as anticipated. Though he has been neutralized, I am pleased. I never believed that Scarecrow could hold City Hall, for he is not a defender. His mission was to disrupt Gotham City's command and control center during a vital moment at the beginning of the conflict, and successfully draw the Batman into combat at the time and place of my choosing. My goal was to spread fear to City Hall at the precise moment when my opponents needed to focus their intelligence. As I have written:

Fear is the friend of he who can inflict it and the enemy of he who falls under its spell.

Scarecrow's shock attack rendered Commissioner Gordon temporarily ineffective, thereby forcing Gordon's policing troops into a position of vulnerability. For soldiers who lose their center and chain of command quickly become a mob—a mob that is as likely to inflict casualties upon themselves as upon their enemies. By creating so vivid an opening volley, Scarecrow bought my anarchy forces valuable time to disperse inside the city and wreak general havoc. I have created a crisis for my enemies that they are unable to manage.

And the Batman has revealed his primary flaw: compassion.

I should have known.

The Batman did not kill the Scarecrow. Indeed, even his police allies below kill only when left with no other choice. Only a foolish commander would fail to destroy an opponent he has vanquished. For if that opponent is not killed, he will return again, not only enraged by his previous defeat, but also educated by it.

Even more peculiarly, the Batman did not even allow Scarecrow to kill himself. How could the Batman have refused this opportunity? His own hands would have been clean of the death, and a formidable enemy would have been eliminated forever. I fail to understand why one so intelligent in other ways would be so foolish in this regard. But then, compassion is a virus spreading throughout this era. Perhaps I should not be surprised that the Batman has been infected.

I have learned something most valuable. This will be the key to the Batman's defeat.

The spirit voices assent. They are very near. They too scent the blood in the air. I chose my first captain wisely; I have crafted each mission to maximize the strength of my captains without exposing their weaknesses. My other chosen champions will be used with exactly the same precision. The spirits hum their approval. A glorious unity affirms my bond to them. I am at the height of my power.

Now to send the Batman into the waiting arms of his next opponent.

In my hands, I hold a communicator which allows me to listen in to the Batman and his most important allies. If used properly it is the key to victory; if misused, it could become the key to my defeat. If the Batman knows it has fallen into my hands, he will adjust his words accordingly and might well lead me into a trap. But if he does not know, I will discern all.

I have written:

> *The most valuable asset a commander can have in time of battle is information, especially secret information. This should be treated as the treasure it is.*

But I have also written:

> *The most dangerous liability a commander can possess is a belief in information. Especially information that is intentionally deceptive. The great commander must always be able to separate what is true from what is not.*

I resist the urge to press a single button and summon my foe, demand his attention, see his distraction and his anger firsthand. That particular pleasure must wait. With this same device I am able to speak directly to the police frequency. I will hail them, tell them of a strange figure seen entering Gotham Chemical. A figure that they will immediately know. A villain that only the Batman can defeat.

I raise the device. My hands have long since abandoned their human shape for the long, tapered claws of a higher being, better suited for dispelling the energy of Yanjin. But before I press a single button, the spirits have hold of me with a vengeance. Their swimming, buzzing blur fills my senses. I am taken by surprise. For once, I question them. Now? The fight has just begun!

They insist, angered that I would resist their pull. We are one, the spirits and I, and their temporary disapproval fills me with nausea and weakness. I yield, and the battle before me dims. There is something they want to show me. I have no choice.

They take me back to the beginning.

I will never know my real name, nor that of my parents. I was abandoned by the side of the road while still in swaddling clothes. My parents were most likely refugees in one of the numerous wars that ravaged my country. Possibly they were killed for their jewelry as they fled, and their precious son was overlooked in the carnage. Or perhaps I simply became too heavy for my exhausted kin to carry a step farther and was dropped, without regret, like so much waste.

Understand that in my culture to not know your heritage is a burning shame. Family is paramount. Without ancestry, without a past, better that I should have died by that roadside than live completely without human ties, completely alone.

But unlike many infants, I survived. The spirits were already guiding the path of my life, though I did not know it then. They directed the footsteps of the mystics of Unglong, who found me on the road and, attracted by my aura—already strong—took me into their cult to raise me as their own.

I do not remember any other children. I was reared by men for whom human kindness was considered a weakness. They were not restrained by compassion. The only purpose a child might serve for them would be as a provider of labor, and later assistance and care were they to reach a healthy old age. For these were not holy men as you might know them. They were a band of priests who descended from the Thugee, or Assassin, cult. They traveled the highways, robbing from the rich and giving the money to the poor—they themselves, of course, being considered among the poor. Such cults were common in the times before the Red Revolutions; this philosophy exists even today, among organized crime groups, computer hackers, and their ilk.

From the moment I could walk, I was taught to spot weakness and strike at it. To sense wealth and scheme how to steal it. I learned to live with deprivation, to see danger as a normal state of affairs and triumph over fear.

I thrived on it.

Children should be exposed to great risk at a young age and learn to survive in an environment of want and worry. It thins out the weak and the unlucky. More, it gives one a proper perspective on the life of a conqueror, who must live without fear of death, and offers him a great advantage over one who is still afraid. Mastery of fear is the common trait that all great conquerors possess.

My greatness was, in part, forged by my experiences as a young child, when it was my job to lure enemies into traps. I remember with particular clarity one occasion when we were pursued by hired thugs who strove to arrest us. Our head priest, Shenkir, believed that a local prince named JohNee had hired these men to track and kill us in retaliation for our having recently kidnapped and ransomed his son. I felt great loathing for Shenkir. He was a weak man who was bound by archaic notions of honor. (Have I not written that *The code of honor is the province of fools, but the appearance of honor is the possession of the wise*? This I learned from the downfall of Shenkir.)

We had no choice but to ambush JohNee's men. I was

sent out as bait. On my way to the marketplace to buy provisions for our band, I would be conspicuously dressed as I had been the night we kidnapped JohNee's son. I was sure to be spotted, and I was. When I was followed, I led the unsuspecting men to where the thugees lay in wait.

The thugees descended on the unwary hunters and slaughtered them to a man. Each was meticulously strangled, so their clothes would not be stained with blood. In the melee, Shenkir was killed. I knew that Shenkir's brother, Dakur, had arranged the murder so that he himself could lead the cult—for I myself killed Shenkir at Dakur's signal.

One must sacrifice what one loves if that attachment threatens victory. Dakur murdered his brother, whom he loved, because Shenkir was an incompetent leader. It was wise of him to do so in such a way that no guilt could be traced to him.

I knew, from the eyes of the other members of our cult, that all knew the true cause and nature of Shenkir's death. After all, was not deceit our life? But they knew as well that it was for the greater good of the cult that the truth not be exposed. Why pursue truth if the lie is more useful? Loyal troops will accept any crime if they believe it to be for the cause.

I know. I arranged several other deaths for Dakur as well before finally killing him myself, on the thirteenth anniversary of my rescue by the cult, in the darkness of the caves.

But that was later.

Once our pursuers were killed, and our dead were burned, we exchanged our clothing for that of the bounty hunters and took the bodies, dressed as our band, to Prince JohNee for our reward. JohNee was not a dimwitted man, but even he could not escape death at our hands once he realized what we had done. Later, we sold his head to a rival prince for a large sum.

It was the best time of my young life.

Of course, not all of our escapades were so glorious. We were not always able to avoid ignobly hiding until some threat had passed. I found this inactivity torture, until one such occasion when, pursued by soldiers of the imperialists, we fled into the caves of Chulan.

The moment I felt the cool, wet air of the caves, a part of my inner being rejoiced. Unlike my fellow thugees, I did not fear the dark, the damp, or the flitting cave creatures that brushed past us. I felt as if something were calling me, pulling me forward into the depths. I knew that something waited there. Something powerful. Something old. It had a secret.

And it wanted to share it with me.

As the soldiers pursued us, we headed deeper and deeper into the caves. At last, the soldiers' voices receded into dim, empty echoes. Still we continued forward. The thugees followed my impatient footsteps, the bobbing light of my small torch. I drove them onward until the tiny, cramped passageways suddenly ceased.

We were in an immense underground chamber. I could feel that the space continued impossibly far past each of my outstretched hands, and high above my head. Without thinking, I raised my torch to the side of the entrance and a chain of oiled lights blazed around the perimeter of the huge cavern. My fellow priests gasped.

We were not in a cave. We were in a tomb.

Hundreds of large terra-cotta soldiers, carved as meticulously as life, stood in even rows, still carrying the fearsome weapons of an earlier era, guarding the treasure of an ancient warlord. The Eternal Elite.

At first, the thugs were terrified, awestruck at what we

had found. But they soon realized that we had come upon a fortune greater than their wildest imaginings. With a greed that overcame fright, they fell to looting and pillaging the tomb, cracking open the beautiful ancient casks and chased boxes, reveling in the handfuls of precious stones and golden animals they found inside.

They were fools. The true treasure eluded them. But it sang to me. Voices were buzzing in my head. They had flared into full life the moment my torch had lit the chamber. For a single moment, I fought, fearing insanity; but then I knew. These voices were my voice. These thoughts were my thoughts. What had been many were now one. Thousands of years of writings, teachings, and campaigns became mine. The voices of countless warriors, warlords, and kings flooded my mind.

The spirits entered me.

I was no longer who I had been. I was the joy of war reborn. I was Sin Tzu.

And all of my many lives shouted a single message: The treasure was not the baubles, but the teachings etched on the walls.

In the endless days of pillaging the tomb, I quickly learned to read the inscriptions on the walls and on the nameplates of the soldiers. I worked in secret, for as I concentrated on the tablets, I entered a deep meditative trance. The visions of Mehta-Sua opened my inner eye. I gained the ability to channel energy into thought, thought into energy, energy into matter. I learned to reverse the normal ebb and flow of thought, pulling realizations in from outside and directing them outward again with killing force. I practiced the art of summoning the energy of the universe, channeling it into grand strategy, and broadcasting it to troops and enemies alike. I began to see the inner workings of the material plane. And I discovered, too, that the solid clay soldiers were no mere statues.

They were an ancient form of automaton. Stone golems that moved with the lithe motions of warriors born.

And should I master the tools of Mehta-Sua well, these soldiers would dance at my bidding. These three hundred deathless men would be my Eternal Elite when I was prepared to reenter the world for real conquest and subjugate the hearts and minds of millions.

The other members of the cult were too enthralled by their rapidly growing wealth to be disturbed by my long absences deep in the tomb. This was to my advantage, for when the voices of the spirits spoke to me, their words were heard by no others. In fact, during my first brief experiences with them, I would respond, as if an ordinary person had spoken. And when the others, who did not share the enlightenment, were nearby and witnessed the spectacle of my speaking to phantom voices, they naturally assumed I was quite mad.

They were fools of weak chakra. I had little hope that they would either understand the new path or follow it.

But there were those who knew that the gods possessed me. My spirits warned me that Dakur suspected I was using the voices as a ruse to gain power in the cult. He would soon try to destroy me. By then, the spirits and I were so powerfully attuned that I knew, without question, that I must kill him first.

But I had to do it in such a way that blame would not come back to me. So, for the first time, I practiced the Yanjin actively against other living beings, and placed suspicion in the hearts of others. It was stupidly simple. I led them to believe that Dakur had taken more than his share of the tomb treasure.

In truth, such a petty theft hardly mattered. Even the lowest member of the cult could live like a prince on his share of the goods. But greed knows no bounds. In fact, I discovered that greed escalates within itself. The more a weak mortal has, the more he will crave. Such is the very basis of capitalism.

I watched with amusement as the Yanjin stalked and infected each of the thugees in turn as they leapt to kill, maim, and torture one another. The final man, so terrified and infested with greed that he could not trust even himself with his huge bounty, finally slit his own throat for fear that he would steal his own treasure away.

That may have been the last time that I laughed.

It was in this way that I learned that the true art of diplomacy is to arrange your enemies so that they will destroy one another, leaving you free of toil and blame. And it was in this way that I was left alone with the voices in the tomb.

I now lived amidst the spirits and the dead—alone to study and to conquer. I played the forbidden game of strategy. I was no longer the son of faceless, dead refugees, but the spiritual descendant of emperors and generals. The void that had existed in my soul had been filled to brimming. I radiated the energy of the Mehta-Sua.

The first step to becoming a great commander is to learn to defer all gratification. Having grown up with the holy men as a sort of ill-gotten adoptee, I had an advantage on this score, for I was always the last to eat and the last to sleep. I had learned techniques for overcoming hunger with the mind, and was able to survive for great periods of time without sleep; now I discovered that the hallucinations that come with deprivation could be turned into a forceful creative tool.

The next lesson was singleness of purpose. That purpose, always, is to achieve victory. There are many different manifestations of victory, but only one determinant: breaking the enemy's will to fight. Often, in long dialogues with the spirits, we discussed will. Will is that place where the spirit meets the flesh. The place where the boundless "I will" overcomes the mortal "I cannot."

I would leave the cave and wander to study the art of reading the minds of other humans. At first I could not help but kill them with my mental intrusions, but soon I learned the art of gentle nudging, the slow exploration of the ego and the psyche. I learned to recognize fears, desires, wants, needs. I learned to pull the levers of human desire to force men to work for my interests.

My discoveries could not help but change me. My skin turned golden from the inner light of Mehta-Sua. My eyes glowed with the white fire of enlightenment. My body's carriage changed to support the deliberate, graceful movements necessary to better deliver the intricate motions of Yanjin Alchemy. The jagged yin-yang sign, the symbol of Mehta-Sua, the martial art of meditation, etched itself deeply into the bones of my brow, echoing the circular saw blade of thought I use to cut through my enemies. My hands became long, tapered weapons of precision and destruction, heavy with death.

So when at last I reentered the world, the Eternal Elite at my back, it is no wonder that some thought me a demon.

My military exploits are legendary. They pass before my eyes in blurs of conquest. My deeds, past and present, in this life and in my hundreds of others, will be studied for centuries to come.

Of course, without the spirit voices to decipher the hidden code of war, any mere human discoveries about my life will be less than useless. But these everlasting secrets will never be divulged by me. Revealing the forbidden knowledge is one way to enrage the spirits. They would torment me to the point of death. That is the pact I made with them. For if they are tied to me, I am equally tied to them.

As they taught me the arts of breaking the will of other men, so they have learned my weaknesses. We are one, but is not every creature sometimes of two minds? When I am doing their will, they fill my body with unnatural power—such a great power that it can be seen by other men. When they sense I am straying from the true path, they shriek at me like banshees, threaten to desert me, remind me of my mortal flaws.

Or flee altogether. I have only suffered the hint of that loss once in my life, when I was very young and foolish, and thought I might like to experience the embrace of human love.

It was not worth the trade. Death is preferable to the endless torment that is desertion by the spirits. My lover, barely able to understand and acknowledge their presence, begged me to forsake them, as if that were even possible. Wringing her small white hands, she claimed that they were spiteful and jealous, and would forever come between me and any meaningful connection to another living human being. I thought to force her into submission, but the spirits guided me away, deeming her unworthy of the effort. They bade me merely to forget.

So I abandoned her to her base humanity. What need have I for mortal softness? I have conquest to warm me.

Only victory brings satisfaction.

And it is true to say that I have had great victories. Never did I lose a battle that was winnable, and when a battle is not winnable, no matter what the outcome, it cannot be called a defeat. It is called a submission to inevitability. Or so my rivals have claimed when I planted my flag in their vitals.

The spirits and I live only for this battle. I am no governor. I have no interest in ruling my conquered territories. Peacetime for me is nothing more than a pause between wars.

And here is where my malaise set in.

After my campaigns and proxy wars in Asia, I began to grow restless. The spirits droned and moaned. Too often, my conquests devolved to the point of slaughter of civilians. While I have no qualms about this when necessary, crushing a third-world country or defeating dictators who pose as generals is not the stuff of glory. I feared that my skills were losing finesse. The spirit voices agreed, taunting me, pushing me further on. My soul was filled with an enervating apathy. I retreated to the hills to meditate upon a suitable course of action.

And so I began my search for an adversary worthy of my attention.

As I meditated, probing the globe, a chance flash in the web of the world caught my interest. It was a foreign-language newspaper, rolling off the press. The pain and fear in every printed page itself wasn't the draw, nor was the article about a masked vigilante—it was the picture that accompanied it. A drawing of a creature half-human, half-bat, looming over the skyline of Gotham City.

All of a sudden, my inner eye filled with a vision. The same drawing, but with myself depicted hovering over this terrible city. The image seemed to flicker. At one moment, it was the Batman—at the next, myself. I knew this creature. I knew his single-mindedness and dedication. I knew his obsession with strategy, his devotion to his cause.

Such men are rare. He deserved to be engaged and defeated.

By me.

I quote my own maxim:

A great conqueror must have a worthy opponent and a worthy prize.

From that moment, my campaign was born. This bizarre creature and I shared a fate. He was worthy. I would conquer the unconquerable. I would defeat the undefeatable.

I studied the Batman. He fascinated me. The bat, like myself, is a creature of darkness, a creature of the caves. Even as I learned my lessons in the caves of Chulan, the Batman must have learned his in the cliff caves of Gotham. No man who had not lived in caves would pick the symbol of the bat. To conquer him, I must find his cave, and to do so, I must learn to hear the soft sounds he makes in the dark though his darkness is not a physical darkness, but of a very different nature.

In my meditations on the Batman, I tried to find the source of this blight. It must have come in childhood, for a creature like him can only exist after years of training. Has he lost his parents? Did he see them die? As he fights crime, I can deduce that his life was scarred in some way by violence. Perhaps it was a tragedy very much like my own. Is the Batman, too, an orphan? A gifted orphan, blessed with intelligence and physical prowess? Unlike myself, he must have had extraordinary resources at his disposal. No one of modest means could have fashioned the equipment, the automobile, the airplane, the boat, that he has at his disposal. But then, why the bat? He must have had a cave near his home. A home near Gotham, as he protects it so fiercely.

Perhaps he hears his own voices.

But I am not a detective and I do not wish to know the Batman's true identity. To best him, I do not need to know his physical house, but the protective structure he has built around his soul. I bear the man-creature no personal grudge. To simply kill him would be artless. I must defeat him first. And therefore, I am determined to threaten what is most important to him.

Gotham City.

For the Batman is the commander of Gotham City. He has no official title or address, but the men who own these things turn to him when peril closes in. It is what the Batman most fiercely protects.

So, I would attack Gotham City. But it could not be an overt military attack. It was my objective to fight him on his terms, his "turf." As the Batman is not a military commander, to visit such an asymmetrical attack on him would not only be ingenuous, but would entirely miss the point of my objective.

Likewise, positioning myself as yet another costumed criminal would put me at a disadvantage and ensure my defeat. Whatever my opinion of the laughing man and the riddling man and the rest of their ilk, there can be no doubt that they are better criminals than I. If the Batman had defeated their petty plans, he would defeat mine should I emulate them.

Like all profound insights, my revelation was obvious when it came. The greatest of war plans are eternal, only the particulars change. What really is the difference between a rock and a rocket as weapons, save for the size of the battlefield and the nature of the target? I would base my conquest of Gotham City on the taking of the Nanchok Dynasty, three thousand years ago, when a great general defeated an entire kingdom by collecting those banished for crime, insanity, or sorcery and using them to conquer all of Nanchok.

Yes. I would build an army of the Batman's natural enemies: the criminal, and the criminally insane. I would bring him not just individual battles, but a finely developed war. Faced with a multifaceted assault, the Batman would show his true colors as a commander, or he would die.

I would take the field. The first step of a military campaign is always a survey. I had to find a way to slip into Gotham unnoticed. Basic Mehta-Sua techniques dictate that criminals are among the easiest people to manipulate, because they often lack the ability to control their impulses and thus are susceptible to suggestion. Curiously, this is true of brilliant criminals as well as stupid ones.

It is also true of American Covert Operations officers. It was a small matter to arrange my capture by U.S. operatives and manipulate them into taking me to Arkham Asylum for study. After all, to the mind of the bureaucrat, there is little difference between a costumed clown and a foreign terrorist.

And so my campaign for Gotham began.

The spirit voices release me. I have seen again my entire earthly existence—and yet mere moments have passed. The clock clangs discordantly; one of the released convicts has scaled the tower and is violently dismantling the chimes. The fires rage. The sirens are softer now; there are fewer blue police lights in the sky. I am winning this battle.

What are the spirits trying to show me? What warning is this, to tell me a history I already know? I am baffled. Am I not fulfilling their desires?

For surely, despite the fact that he has defeated Scarecrow, the Batman knows he is losing this night. He is beginning to discern that there is a much greater hand in this.

Does he suspect me? I would be surprised. He hasn't received one word of information about my proximity. Commissioner Gordon, who was, of course, informed the moment I arrived at Arkham, has spilled not one precious drop of revelation regarding my identity on any of the frequencies I monitor. Curious how soldiers so often conceal critical battle information from their commander. I would imagine that the Commissioner was ordered by governmental agents not to speak of my incarceration at Arkham, but could he truly possess enough pointless honor to obey that command even as it applies to furnishing a lawless vigilante with crucial intelligence?

Men such as Gordon puzzle me. They make up "codes" to live their lives by, willfully blind to the rampant and obvious chaos that engulfs us all.

I do know one thing. At this moment, the Batman is doing the same thing as I. He is in a place from where he feels he can command, a place of high ground. Probably the top of a building, plotting his next move. But he will take the action I want him to take, for I have the initiative.

Gotham City means nothing to me. When I am done, I care not what happens to it. It will perhaps be rebuilt, better than ever, or it will perhaps become an uninhabited ruin. It makes no difference. I have no desire to rule, simply to conquer.

I have written that men should be slow to make decisions and never look back when a decision is made. Destruction follows him who changes his mind. I will not change mine now. Whatever the sprits' objections, I overrule them. I am the victor here, and I will defeat the Batman. He cannot escape me. Our destinies are linked.

Perhaps my one fleshly intimate was right all those

years ago. Perhaps the spirits are merely jealous of my attention towards the Batman. It is true that I have never before taken such an obsessive interest in an individual opponent. But never before has an opponent so purely presented such a true and meaningful challenge. I am drawn to him, yes. But the moment I defeat him in battle, the spirits may once again have my undivided attention.

I reach out and dial the Police Commissioner's number to tell him of the being named Clayface.

The next threat to Gotham has been unleashed.

SIX

Nightwing/Dick Grayson
1:20 A.M.

ightwing. Two enc one," Batman says into the comm link. Two-Face, encounter one. He's referring to a case from nearly nine years ago that ended in a rather unforgettable fight on top of the First Bank of Gotham building in the Diamond District by Robinson Park. It's his way of telling me he wants a meet where no one can hear us.

I answer with a simple "Ten-four," and start moving across town, trying not to think about what the recent Stonegate Prison and Arkham Asylum breakouts must be doing to him. Since midnight, Gotham City's been in total chaos. Not just a riot or a gang war, not just a crime spree Uptown or Downtown, not just a friend being terrorized or a fire or two blazing out of control in residential districts, but all of the above, all at once.

Multiple officer-down calls on the police wire; sounds of gunfire and glass breaking and alarms blaring and stolen cars screeching through the streets; the smell of cordite and burning fuel and the sickly chemical residue of Scarecrow's fear gas carried on the frigid wind. You can't spit without hitting a felon, and the real genius of the organization behind this attack is that it isn't organized. Every criminal for himself, all doing whatever their sick minds can think up. It's chaos, a nightmare. The worst Gotham's seen in a long, long time.

And Gotham City, well, she's maybe the closest thing Batman has to a lover—he spends every night with her, ministers to her tirelessly when she's sick, buys her presents (cop cars rather than Mercedeses, but, hey . . . whatever works). He can't stand it when she's in pain, and I know how he feels.

I can't stand it when he is.

God knows he never shows weakness and hardly anything fazes him but . . . he's been my mentor for my entire professional crime-fighting life, and I know when something gets under his skin. I just know.

I met Batman when I was eight. My life can be neatly divided into "Before Batman" and "After Batman." I even got a name change, kind of. One minute I'm just Dick Grayson, and the next minute I'm Robin, the Boy Wonder. Now I go by Nightwing.

Without Batman, I never would have been able to channel the grief and rage I felt at the loss of my parents. It's hard to even imagine where I'd be now if our paths hadn't crossed. My best guess is jail.

Yeah, I'm an orphan, too. Just like Bruce.

Only my folks weren't rich, not by a long shot. My parents were John and Mary Grayson, and together the three of us were "the Amazing Flying Graysons," the center-ring aerial act for Haley's Circus.

The circus was my world. I loved it with every fiber of my being. I remember Dad once telling me that my mom had been training to be a dental assistant before she met and ran away with him. I wrinkled my nose, and asked her why anyone would ever want to do anything but work for a circus. She laughed, and kissed me on the ear, and said she had no idea.

I do miss them.

Later that same night, a small-time crook named Tony Zucco threatened the livelihood of the circus after Mr. Haley refused to pay him extortion money. Not ten minutes later I saw Zucco exiting the back of the big top. I knew he didn't belong there, and I tried to point him out to Mom, but it was time for our performance, and no matter what, the show must go on.

I was there on the platform, getting ready to fly, when the guy wire that holds up the trapeze came apart like a spiderweb under my father's weight. He'd just caught Mom by the wrists, and he managed not to scream as the tent floor came rushing up to claim him.

Mom did scream. And so did I.

I tried to catch them. And when I couldn't, I tried not to watch. I tried not to hear the thud of their bodies as they hit the sawdust, broken and lifeless. Once on the ground, I tried not to step in the still-warm blood seeping out from the back of my father's skull. I shook my mom, desperate for a flash of recognition from her sightless blue eyes. She didn't recognize me. She was already dead.

She would never recognize me again.

I can still feel my chest constrict when I think about it. I don't think my body could even hold that much grief at that age. So, instead of grief, I felt rage. Kneeling there under the unbearably absent shadow of the missing safety net—we never worked with one, that was our hubris, I guess, our fault—I raised a fist to the tent top and swore revenge.

I'd get Tony Zucco if it was the last thing I ever did.

That night, Jim Gordon drove me to Wayne Manor. Jim was the new Police Commissioner of Gotham City, where we'd been playing when the "accident" occurred. Since I had boldly told him that I'd seen Zucco and could identify him in a lineup, he insisted on taking me to a safe house.

Safe house . . . that's actually pretty funny, now that I think about it. There's no safer house in all of Gotham.

I didn't think it was the least bit funny at the time, though. I didn't want to leave the circus, and I certainly didn't want to leave the circus with a cop. Aside from truant officers, there's nobody scarier to a circus kid than a policeman.

Jim wasn't frightening, though. He had a sort of fatherly look to him and he spoke to me seriously and kindly, which is a sign of someone who understands kids. I remember something he said to me in the circular gravel driveway in front of Wayne Manor. We'd just gotten out of the car and he stopped to put a hand on my shoulder.

"Be brave, son," he said. For a second, I wished I was staying with him. And then he rang the doorbell.

As the giant front door swung open, I found myself looking up into the perfectly composed face of an older gentleman whose eyes were half-closed as he politely greeted the Commissioner in a soft British accent. And then he glanced down at me. I remember that he bent down to my height and smiled very gently. "And you must be Master Richard," he said.

"Dick," I insisted. It's what my dad called me. He nodded seriously.

"Master Dick, then," he said, without a hint of condescension. He straightened up and motioned for us both to enter. "I am Alfred. Do please come in."

If it had been any other day, I would have been knocked out by the size of the place alone. Until that night, I'd slept in a trailer with my parents. Now I found myself entering a living room easily the size of eight trailers, with a fire roaring in a fireplace that was literally as big as a Mack truck. I remember thinking that if worse came to worst, I could probably get up to one of the chandeliers, snag a crystal droplet, and pawn it to live comfortably for the rest of my short life.

I did notice Bruce, though. There's no way I couldn't have. Within moments of my entry into the living room, he appeared and knelt in front of me, placing both hands on my shoulders and steadily watching my face until I finally met his eyes. Even with one knee on the floor like that, he was huge. His hands on my shoulders were massive and warm.

"I lost my parents too, Dick," he said, the very first words he spoke to me. "I won't say I know how you feel, but if you ever want to tell me, I'm relatively certain I would understand."

Alfred ushered me away for dinner and I started to comprehend how far I'd really traveled. We were less than twenty minutes away from the fairgrounds in Newtown, but this was a whole different world.

Over time, Alfred became like a parent to me. He taught me how to play chess, how to cook, how to recite Shakespeare, how to repair cars. He played opera for me and laughed at every single one of my stupid jokes, and sat with me by my bed all night when I couldn't sleep for the nightmares.

And Bruce . . . well, obviously, in many ways he became a father to me. He's so different than my dad was . . . I mean, if you asked John Grayson where babies came from, he'd laugh and say, "Beer bottles." You ask Bruce Wayne and you get a humorless two-hour lecture on reproductive biology. My dad didn't take anything seriously but flying, and Bruce, well . . . the only thing he *doesn't* take seriously is me, and I mean that in a good way. I mean, I can sometimes make him loosen up a little, but it takes serious effort.

I don't mind, though. Part of my job.

In those first few days at the manor, however, as kind as they were, neither Alfred nor Bruce made much of an impression on me. I was obsessed with Tony Zucco. No matter how nice the smart rich guy and his thoughtful butler were, it didn't do a thing to cure me of the notion that the man who murdered my parents had to die.

The only person or thing with enough power to break through that obsession was Batman.

I still remember the first time I saw him.

I had run away from Wayne Manor to go after Zucco. Finding him was harder than I thought. I stole a picture from the PD and fearlessly canvassed the wrong side of town. I had made it all the way out to Burnley when I absolutely and totally lucked into his location. Only my luck quickly topped out when, tiptoeing to a phone booth to call Commissioner Gordon, I stepped on a soda can.

Next thing I knew I was standing outside in the dark by the rushing waters of the Sprang River, with a grown man's hands around my throat, less than two minutes away from being killed by the murderer of my own parents. Zucco had been packing to leave town and was terrifically pleased to have his only material witness show up at his hideout, weaponless and without much of a plan.

And then suddenly I heard Zucco grunt—hit by a Batarang, I later came to realize—and his grip on me slackened. I knew someone else was there with us, but I didn't care. I had Zucco in my sights and I was gonna beat him to death with my eight-year-old fists, come hell or high water. I moved as fast as I could, kicking at his shins and hurtling my fists into his ribs again and again, until I finally hurt him enough to annoy him. Hollering at me, infuriated, he tossed me away, towards a weak railing. A weak railing that overhung the Sprang River.

And that's when I saw Batman.

He was over six feet tall and almost completely concealed by a dark, swirling cape. His mask was like a demon's—terrifying—eyes narrow and glinting white in the dark. Sharp pointy ears rose from his covered head, and only his jaw remained exposed, an afterthought of bristly human flesh that was really no less intimidating. A black bat was emblazoned across the impenetrable armor of his chest, his gloved hands in fists, booted feet planted solidly in the earth.

He was awesome. I knew immediately that he was *real;* the most serious, dangerous, effective, real thing I'd ever seen.

I should have been petrified. But instead a feeling of intense calm came over me. There was no question in my mind that this creature would destroy Tony Zucco. Maybe he'd kill me too, but that was fine. He was my own personal dark angel, come to answer my dearest wish: the avenging of my parents' murders.

A second before I hit the cold water of the river, Batman called my name in a voice so rough and dark that it could not possibly have existed in the daylight. It didn't seem strange to me that he knew who I was. After all, I'd conjured him. I sank under the icy water almost blissfully.

I think I would have drowned peacefully right then except for the image of my mother's face, floating into my soaking consciousness so vividly that it knocked the little bit of air remaining out of my lungs. Where Batman's face had filled me with tranquillity and acceptance, my mother's filled me with grief and negation. I couldn't die. It would break her heart. Suddenly, I needed to live. I began to panic in the water, to flounder and kick and cry out for help.

And then, all at once, there was something solid, something that didn't yield, that grabbed me and hauled me back into the air with savage force. With my back against his chest and his arm around me holding my head up out of the water, Batman felt like hope.

Not that I was appreciative, mind you. Once Batman had me safely back on land I looked around expectantly for Tony Zucco's corpse . . . and realized with a slow, dawning horror that my dark angel had messed up. He'd let Zucco go and saved me instead.

I was furious.

"You let him go!" I shouted, and began pounding the bat on his chest plate with my fists. "Why'd you do it!? Why? WHY!?"

I meant, *why did you let Zucco go?* But I also meant, *why did you bother saving me?*

The fountain of anguish inside of me, held in check until then by dreams of revenge, now threatened to well up and overflow. My mother was gone. And it was my fault, really—didn't Batman understand that?—because I'd seen Zucco leave the tent and I didn't stop the show, I didn't do enough to save her, I didn't save my dad. And now Zucco had escaped. My body was shaking with violence and I hit that bat chest plate over and over again as hard as I could.

Even so, even though I hit Batman with all the force my sopping-wet body could muster, he remained solid and unyielding. When he did finally move, it was to put a large gloved hand against the back of my head, almost tenderly, almost like my dad would have done.

I came undone, falling against his chest plate sobbing. I was sure, somehow, that he understood and could withstand my streaming grief.

And he did. He let me cry for what felt like hours, saying nothing, sturdy and still. And when I finally started to catch my breath in long, jagged gulps, a deafening whirring sound filled the sky. I looked up through tear-stained eyes to see a giant metallic bat hovering above us, clearly at his command. It was, with the one exception of Batman himself, the coolest frickin' thing I had ever seen.

"Where're we going?" I asked him with the casual ease of a lost soul. It didn't occur to me for one minute that he wouldn't take me with him. Wherever he was going, I was going.

"Home," he said gruffly. I remember wondering if we were going to heaven or to hell. Instead, we went to the Batcave, which is a little bit of both.

And then Batman did the weirdest thing I'd ever seen. He pulled his cowl back and transformed into my host, Bruce Wayne.

I don't think it would surprise him now to know that my first thought was a wish that he'd put the mask back on. My relationship has always been more with Batman than with Bruce.

Of course, that's partly because Batman is more real than Bruce. Batman is what happened to the orphaned Bruce Wayne's soul. Batman is the answer and the choice and the holy mission. Bruce Wayne, well . . . he's the disguise that makes it possible to move around in the light of day.

I'm not like that. Hardly anyone else I know is like that. I put on the Nightwing mask so that no one notices it's really Dick Grayson who's kicking their butt. That's the way it usually works among us "capes," but not with Batman. He's the real thing.

And I still don't know what made him take me in. At that moment in time, in the dark of that cave under Wayne

Manor, still soaking wet and lost and clearly too small to be of any actual use to him, I became the only person in the whole world besides Alfred who knew the secret. And let me tell you—not that I don't appreciate the trust fund, and the education, and the endless training he's bestowed upon me over the years—but nothing anyone has ever given me or ever will could be more valuable to me than his confidence that night.

Batman changed the entire trajectory of my life. With the utterance of one simple vow—"I swear that I will fight against crime and corruption and never swerve from the path of justice"—I went from being one of life's many casualties to being the luckiest kid in the world.

Yeah, I became Robin, the Boy Wonder. I became Bruce's ward and Batman's sidekick. I trained beside him, fought beside him, shared all the hazards of the dark as night after night we went out together to stop crime in the streets of Gotham City. Sometimes we'd break up drug rings or stop a burglary in progress. Other times we'd battle against the costumed freaks like Joker and Two-Face who began to line up to get a shot at us.

Together, years later, we even took down Tony Zucco. And by that time, as much as I adored and missed them, I didn't need my parents back. I was completely in love with my new life.

Not that Batman doesn't drive me crazy. Have you ever broken a house rule and waited with trepidation for Dad to show up and dole out the punishment? Well, now imagine that your dad's Batman. And that's just a start.

He's moody, and hyper-disciplined, and unforgiving. And he can push my buttons like no one else on the planet. Sometimes I'm convinced that he's determined to eradicate all of my self-confidence. Sometimes I can't believe how cold and distant he can be, even with his tiny handful of confidants like me. Sometimes he gets me so worked up I catch myself screaming at him like the hotheaded scrapper he sometimes accuses me of being.

And then I remember what a tremendous honor it all is. I realize that he pushes me because if he doesn't, I might die. He's distant because if he's not, he's going to miss something, and then someone somewhere else will die. Everything in his world really is a matter of life and death—and he never forgets that, even if I sometimes do.

There was one fight, less than a year ago now, when I stopped dead in the middle of yelling at him—about not including me in a particular decision-making process, I think, but even I can't always keep track of these things— to laugh.

"What's so funny?" he asked, his voice dark and irritated.

"I can't believe I'm yelling at Batman." I grinned, and was gratified to see his posture soften.

"You've earned the right," he said quietly, turning away. That's pretty good for him, these days. When I was younger and snottier, I could sometimes even make him laugh.

Throughout everything, he's remained the coolest person I've ever met. I'd die for him without hesitation, and I hope he knows that. Of course, he'd be too busy preparing to die to save me to take me up on the offer. That's just the kinda guy he is.

So when he calls me in, like he did tonight, I'm there.

It takes me longer than the normal four minutes to get from my location to his. The city is buzzing like an all-night carnival. There's trouble everywhere you look. I have to stop three times: once to interrupt an in-progress burglary at the Gotham Gem Exchange before tracking down the moron selling guns out of the back of his van to guys still wearing penitentiary jumpsuits; once to deescalate a turf war between the Escabedo Cartel and a handful of Stonegate convicts who seemed to feel they'd been sold out in the last big legal shakedown; and once, with grim pleasure, to stop a two-twenty in progress.

I heard the woman's scream and saw a flash of orange in the alley behind the Suhr complex. I knew I had to get to the meet with Batman, but—unlike the parked-car thefts and petty acts of vandalism I let slide for the time being—there was no way I could pass by this one.

I slid halfway down an ornate drainpipe, and dropped the rest of the way to the sidewalk, landing behind Mike "Hardcore" Connolly. He got the nickname "Hardcore" in Stonegate, a derisive joke about his compulsive need to lie about his supposedly extensive bedpost notching.

I landed with an unmistakable thud. I wanted him to know I was there.

Next I kicked his knee in from behind while simultaneously grabbing the wrist of his right hand. He went down on his knees in front of his would-be victim with a grunt while I twisted his arm painfully behind his back in a straightforward jujitsu lock Batman taught me when I was twelve. Batman said it was good for fast takedowns and he was right. Works every time.

"Wanna kick him?" I said to the woman, who was crying and scared and trying to hold her ripped blouse together. She looked at me, startled, and then back down at Hardcore. And then, to my great satisfaction, she snapped a sweet straight kick right into his chin.

Hardcore let out a torrent of curses and I stepped on the backs of his ankles as he struggled to get up.

"Shut up," I growled at him, sliding my right boot up to place painful pressure on the back of his prone calf. Then I looked back up at the woman and nodded to her.

"I'll hold him as long as you'd like me to, ma'am."

She didn't hesitate. The world tries to rob you of your sense of action, and for those of us who don't have Batman's patience for planning and preparation, sometimes it really does help to kick and scream a little. Besides, it was about time this loser got the notion that women weren't easy prey. I only hope he runs into some of the women *I* know sometime later tonight.

Understandably, the civilian didn't want to get near Mike with her hands, but she kicked him three more times: one snap kick to the throat, a beautiful roundhouse to his left shoulder, and finally a fierce, if unsteady, side kick aimed towards his chest. By the third kick, she wasn't crying anymore, just breathing hard, her small hands balled into fists, her dark hair falling out of her ponytail in wavy wisps. This was one woman who now knew she could fight back.

"Do you live nearby?" I asked quietly. She nodded, cheeks flushed. Hardcore was still on his knees, though now he was moaning more than cursing. "Hold on," I told her. "I'll walk ya."

She wiped the tears off of her face with her palms, wincing when she touched the nasty bruise Hardcore had left on her cheek—lousy creep. I grabbed a discarded plastic six-pack holder off the ground and used it to tie Hardcore to the bottom of the drainpipe, still on his knees. Then I backhanded him, maybe a little harder than I needed to. He went out.

I turned towards the woman as gallantly as I could, trying to show her that I wasn't a threat. I wished I wore a cape so that I could drape it over her. Batman draped a cape over me once, when I was about fourteen and lost with him in the snow of Katmandu, and I have never felt so safe.

But no, I dropped the cape when I dropped the Robin costume. Thought it was too restricting for a former Flying Grayson. Now I wear neck-to-toe Kevlar in black, with a large blue bird pattern over my chest to draw punches towards the armor's apex (another lesson Batman taught me early. You don't think that big bat is there just for show, do you?). Slap a small black mask over my eyes, mess up my hair a little, and presto, change-o, mysterious vigilante.

So I merely gestured to her to go ahead, and then walked beside her for a block and a half until she turned and ran up the steps of a modest brownstone. She unlocked the heavy front door and then turned, with a slight smile, and waved at me.

"Thanks," she squeaked, before stepping into the well-lit entranceway and closing the door behind her.

"Anytime," I told the door. There's nothing like a woman smiling in your direction to tell you you've done good.

But don't let me even *start* thinking about women. It's already taking a full half of my concentration not to check every shadow for a bright yellow bat and a flame of red hair. Batman's city is bleeding from every orifice, and all I can think is, *Whoo-hooo! A bona fide emergency! Maybe Batgirl will come out to help!*

Priorities, Grayson. Priorities.

It was a shift in priorities that made me finally give up being Robin. It was a difficult decision, actually, but I think I did the right thing. After college, I left Gotham to travel, like Bruce did when he was that age. I studied a whole bunch of different martial arts and crime-fighting techniques, and thought about what it would mean to go back to Gotham and put those tights back on.

And I knew it meant that I'd forever live in Batman's

shadow. That I would become predictable to him. I couldn't let that happen. It's my job as a surrogate son to grow out from under that shadow, and my job as a partner to keep him on his toes.

Besides, this way, as Nightwing, I get to come to him on my own terms.

Batman is still waiting on the rooftop of the bank by the time I get to the Diamond District. He's crouching next to one of the hulking stone gargoyles, his heavy cape stirring slightly in the wind. Below him Gotham spreads out in an unceasing scene of pandemonium. I can tell by the way he's watching the street that he's been up and down the building's edge a dozen times already, stopping every crime that passes beneath him.

I watch him for a moment from the top of the building across the street, marveling at his complete stillness. I personally am not, truth be told, all that great at holding still. I mean, I can do it when it needs to be done, but I *hate* it; it feels entirely unnatural to me. But Batman can remain motionless for hours.

Unless he feels eyes on him.

I've been watching him for less than two seconds when his cowled face tilts up towards me, eyes narrow. I smile and offer a friendly two-finger salute. And then I get the hell across the street as fast as my grapnel line will carry me.

"Sorry to keep you waiting." I'm apologizing before my boots even touch down on the rooftop. "Crazy night out there. You okay?"

Batman straightens and turns towards me. His expression is completely impassive, as usual, but I can sense his distress, and his anger—something about the way he holds his jaw, maybe, or possibly by now just a sixth sense I've developed.

What I know for sure is that whoever's behind all of this is going to be very, very sorry when they finally find themselves face to face with Gotham's Dark Knight.

"Are you aware that our enemy may have one of our communicators?"

That's Batman's way of saying hello.

I nod. "Yeah, I'd heard that rumor. Spoke with Robin a little while ago. He said Alfred lost his in a scrap."

That's the other good thing about deciding to be Nightwing. Batman went out and got another Robin. If I'd known it'd be that easy to get more people watching Batman's back, I would have given up the outfit years ago.

Batman looks back over the city. "Continue to use the frequency for everything but deployment orders and acknowledgments."

"You sure? We could just turn them off if they're compromised."

"No. Our opponent is relaxed and comfortable right now, thinks he's got one up on me. Let him keep thinking that."

"So this one's personal?"

"I . . . don't think so. Not a rematch, in any event. I'm not completely sure who we're dealing with yet, but I have a few theories. None of them bode well."

I nod. This doesn't look like your average skell to me, either.

"As chaotic as this seems," Batman continues, "it is organized. Highly organized, actually. The Stonegate and Arkham releases, as well as Scarecrow's attack on Jim, were too well timed to be coincidence. The individual behind this is very aware of my presence in this city, and he wants me at a disadvantage."

Well, that, I think, *just makes him smart.* Woe to the bad guy who takes on Batman head-on.

"I'm beginning to think the breakout at Stonegate is just a distraction—a tactic, rather, to exhaust my resources."

I nod again, listening. I love trying to follow the way his mind works, how he puts things together. I'm still learning from him all the time. It also pleases me that he trusts me enough to use me as a sounding board.

He continues. "This man we're up against, he has a military background of some kind. Not as a soldier, though. This man's a strategist."

Robin once joked that he couldn't understand why anyone would be stupid enough to commit a crime in Gotham, knowing that Batman might come for them. I agree with the sentiment completely, but the truth is that Batman attracts the worst of the bad. They all want to go up against him, to be the one who takes him down. Sometimes it's egomania, and sometimes it's a need for quick street cred, but the crazier they are, the hungrier they seem to be to take their chances with the Bat. Some of them, like Joker, are even so obsessed with Batman that most of their crimes are directed at him the way the rest of us would send a social invitation.

"What about Arkham?" I ask, thinking it through. "Another tactical distraction?"

Batman's quiet for a moment. "No," he says finally. "There's something else going on at Arkham. Something more complex."

He's almost talking to himself, and I'm beginning to wonder if I should make myself scarce when he suddenly turns to me with an energy I haven't felt coming off of him in years. He's confessional, worried. He flashes a gloved palm at me in an unconscious gesture of trust, before balling his whole hand into a fist again.

What am I saying? Nothing he does is unconscious. He's letting me know that he really needs my help.

"Jim . . . isn't being straight with me." It's hard for him to say. He has a tremendous amount of respect for Commissioner Gordon. In their own weird way, they're best friends.

"You think he's still under Scarecrow's influence?"

Batman shakes his head. "I dosed him with anti-fear serum. But he's deliberately holding something back. I don't know why he'd do that unless—"

"Unless he were protecting somebody!" My heart rate accelerates by an easy thirty percent. Where is Jim's daughter, Barbara, she of the red hair and yellow bat on her costume? Maybe the Scarecrow took her, too! Maybe somebody's holding her ransom and Jim's afraid to ask Batman for help. Maybe she—

"Or unless he's prohibited to say anything by law," Batman interjects.

"You don't think maybe Barbara's—?"

"She's fine," he interrupts, with such confidence that I wonder if he hasn't already been by her place to check on her. I feel foolish suddenly, and regain control of my breathing. I'm sure Batman's noticed my little panic attack, but he politely fails to mention it.

Babs would be annoyed with me for it, too. It's not like she's the damsel in distress type. I don't usually worry about her at all, but this night is starting to get under my skin, too.

We both turn our attention back to the city below us. It seems like things are getting worse by the minute. Together we notice a storefront go up in flames to our right and hear gunshots from the left.

"You want me to swing by Arkham and check it out?" I volunteer.

"Did you secure Stonegate?" he asks.

I nod. "Most of the guards are okay. I guess the idea was to get the convicts out on the street as quickly as possible, with no one stopping for grudge matches."

"I have another mission for you. Recon that I think might help me isolate—"

He's interrupted by a hail from his communicator, the same one we both now know the baddie has a bead on. We exchange glances and I step back into the shadows as he opens the channel.

"Batman," comes Commissioner Gordon's voice, "Clayface has taken over the Gotham Chemical Plant."

"Neither Scarecrow nor Clayface could do this alone," Batman tells the Commissioner, leadingly. "There's someone else behind all this . . ."

He lets his sentence trail off, giving Jim plenty of room to maneuver. When he answers, Jim's voice is tight. Batman's right. He *is* hiding something. "You'd better hurry, Batman," is all he says.

I step forward just enough to remind Batman that I'm there. I know it's stupid, but I hate the idea of him feeling alone, or betrayed. I fight off an internal wave of anger aimed in Jim's general direction. *After everything Batman's done for you, you can't even come clean with him now? What the hell are you hiding?*

"Jim . . . is there something you're not telling me?" Batman's voice isn't angry. He knows there's a logical explanation behind Jim's actions, and is patient enough to let it play out.

Still, I can hear the worry in his voice when no answer comes. "Jim . . . ? Jim . . . ?"

He's quiet another moment and then clicks the communicator off and turns back to me. All emotion has been erased from his face and I realize it won't come back until this is over. We're down to brass tacks now, I can feel it. Batman will not quit until this new enemy is behind bars, or at least lying, unconscious and handcuffed, at his feet.

His strategies are incredibly intricate and his skill is inhuman, but the rules Batman works and lives by are simple. They're practically maxims of battle:

Never take, sacrifice, fail to aid, or in any way endanger another human life.

Never give up on a friend, ally, mission, case, or worthy cause.

Never go into battle without careful planning or hesitate to extract yourself from battle if additional planning is needed.

Never tell anyone you love them. They might die.

That last one is an add-on from his eight-year-old self, and one of which I doubt he's consciously aware. But one through three make mighty good sense to me, and I've followed them, along with him, faithfully.

"I want you to locate the recent clinical files of a man named Gareth Baxter," he says. "It won't be easy—he's a federal agent. As soon as you get a bead on him, you'll understand what information I need."

He pauses to gauge my reaction to this cryptic command. I meet his eyes calmly. He'll get no arguments from me tonight. If he doesn't yet want me aware of the contents of Baxter's files, there's a reason. I'll figure it out as I go along.

"Tell Robin to continue patrolling the city in east-to-west sweeps," he continues, satisfied by my lack of protest. "He can go light on the City Hall district—I'll tell Gordon to continue concentrating police forces there."

I start to speak, but Batman is already way ahead of me.

"I know that's a lot of territory for Robin to cover

alone, but I need you on target-specific offensives to secure critical intel while I address specialized, high-level threats like Scarecrow and Clayface."

He pauses again to make sure I'm still fully on board. I've been known to get . . . creative at times. I square my shoulders and hold his gaze, silently promising him that I'll toe the line. If anything in my countenance tells him I'm playing wildcard tonight, he'll simply walk away from me. He knows his troops better than we know ourselves. I'm therefore gratified when he continues.

"Alfred is on humanitarian assistance at Dr. Thompkins' clinic and can be utilized as a drop-point for victims in need of aid or shelter. That's the best force structure we can manage at the moment, but I want you to leave your channel open for reassignment."

I nod. He surprises me by taking the time to place a hand on my shoulder. "The information I'm sending you after is crucial. Keep me informed of your progress. Back up Tim if he needs it, and choose your battles. Our objective is to neutralize from the top down."

"You can count on me, Batman," I say, freaked out for the second time tonight. Freaked out because he used Robin's civilian name, which means he's worried about us, and because he specifically mentioned a victim drop-point, which means he's expecting prolonged multiple casualties.

He squeezes my shoulder and my doubts dissipate; he's got it under control. From this point on, it's just a matter of following his orders and watching for the endgame.

He releases my shoulder, turns, fires his grapnel, and shoots off into the night in one flowing movement. He's off to get Clayface and then make an offensive on whomever it is who's behind all of this, hopefully with the assistance of intel I'll feed him. Batman won't play catch-up forever. I look forward to him turning the tables.

I turn north to head for the Batcave, the best place to start my search, diving off the rooftop of the bank into the cold night air. I cast my line from midway between the sky and the ground and move with great purpose through Gotham City.

Batman's city.

No matter what this mystery opponent might think.

SEVEN

Matt Hagen/Clayface
1:42 a.m.

This is gonna be frigging great.

That's what keeps going through my mind, over and over again, as I stand on the roof of Gotham Chemical all alone and lug this batch of chemicals over towards that batch of chemicals. *This is just frigging* awesome, *baby!*

No question about it, Sin Tzu is my new best friend and hero. It isn't just being out of Arkham Asylum, although that's nice, too. It's the way Sin Tzu worked it so that in the process of helping him, I'm helping myself. I have a part to play in his million-dollar production, and it really is a scene-stealer.

I glance down at the city—as much as I can see from on top of the building, anyway—and marvel at the production value. Oh, Sin Tzu is really pulling all the stops out on this one, baby.

The main plot, as I understand it, is Sin Tzu conquering Gotham City. First he helps the entire population of Stonegate Prison break out, unleashing them onto the streets. This is the first big action sequence, with literally thousands of extras. Most of it's improvised; that's the real genius of Sin Tzu's plan, he just has everybody doing what they do best anyway.

In the case of the convicts, fifteen hundred of them swarm out into Gotham and start creating mayhem. I mean truly, anything goes. They can steal, murder, start fires, set off on complicated revenge missions of their own choosing, or just swagger through the streets makin' trouble and crackin' skulls. Stonegate's hardcore, too—these guys aren't in for petty misdemeanors, they're the real thing, evil to their bones, most of them.

As I look down at them now, I know they weren't miscast. It's only about two hours into Sin Tzu's plan, and the city already looks totally sacked. Even I'd be a little nervous about being down on that street right now.

So then the antagonist—that's the Batman, of course—he goes out to start trying to put a lid on all of this, but there's more in store for him. Much more. Sin Tzu's also let a few of us out of Arkham—his "captains," he calls us—each in charge of a different military campaign. Scarecrow was up first, specifically targeting Commissioner Gordon, which was nothing short of brilliant since Gordon and the Batman are pretty tight. It also means that Scarecrow is working on the other side of town, which is fine by me. I know I ain't nothing nice to look at, but that guy majorly creeps me out.

Anyway, when the Batman catches Scarecrow—and Sin Tzu knew he would, he kept lecturing us about not underestimating the enemy and all of that—well, that's my cue.

My plan is to drench Gotham City in the same chemicals that made me a monster, so that they'll finally be forced to find a cure for me. I figure all I have to do is break into Gotham Chemical, carry a couple hundred vats up on to the roof, mix them up right, and then pour them out over Mortimer Ave, where they'll find their way into the sewer and then eventually leak into the reservoir. No way chemical water processing is gonna neutralize that stuff.

Sin Tzu likes the idea, though I suspect he thinks I'm gonna fail, too—there's all kinds of other strikes lined up for the Batman after me. But this is the one thing Sin Tzu's wrong about.

I'm not gonna fail. I can't afford to.

And I don't think that'll mess up Sin Tzu's plan too much. He can do all the other stuff he has lined up regardless. I wouldn't stop him. I mean, anyone who could help turn me back into a human being again has my vote. No need to even ask twice.

Oh, sure, I can resemble a regular person whenever I want—anyone I want, in fact. I'm a first-rate shape-shifter. I just have to think about it and I can look just like my old self, or like the Batman, or even like you. But just because one of those freaky hairless sphinx cats looks like an overgrown rat doesn't mean it's not really a cat deep down inside. So no matter how much I can look like anybody, deep down, my name is nothing but mud.

If I could be a *real* regular guy again, maybe—

No. There's no use thinking of that. Not yet, at any rate. What happens, happens. Don't count your chickens and all that mumbo-jumbo.

And I should know from mumbo-jumbo. You don't spend a couple years—on and off, of course—in Arkham Asylum for the Criminally Insane without knowing pretty much all there is to know about mumbo-jumbo. You spend some time in the worst place on the face of the entire earth and, oh yeah, you learn a whole lot of stuff. Stuff you had no idea existed. Just not stuff you ever wanted to know. Who knew that minds were capable of thinking like that? Too bad they're not capable of thinking any *other* way, like the normal way, for instance.

Then again, who am I to talk about normal, right? I'm an eight-foot-tall, five-hundred-pound walking pile of grayish brown goop. My head is splattered onto the top of my massive chest like an afterthought, a melting brown snowball with teeth. Right where my waist should be, two short, thick, muddy legs emerge, chunky and dripping. My arms are massive pillars of oozing clay ending in giant, squashy, splattering paws.

One look at me and people run screaming. Women and children you might expect, but strong men have been known to faint at the sight of me. Even some of the inmates at Arkham, although most of them were doing it just to yank my chain.

'Specially that Joker bastard. I hate that guy.

From a respectful distance, of course. It's always been psychological with him so far, but I'm sure he could find a way to physically torture mud if he wanted to. So I try to never make him want to. Of course, you never know with him. Maybe he thinks my attitude's too standoffish and that I need a little help readjusting it. And maybe he's planning to—

There I go again. Have to stay focused on the task at hand. Because this . . . this could change everything. No. Stay positive. This *will* change everything. Just like in the early days, when I was one of ten thousand guys trying to make it in Hollywood: Focus on a goal, and see yourself achieving that goal. If you can dream it, you can be it. Imagine it and make it come true.

Imagine and change. That's me backwards and forwards.

Times like this, you do get to thinking about how it all started. For me, it was an automobile accident. Flipped my '65 Mustang and got pinned while the whole thing went up in flames. Sitting in that driver's seat, upside down, flames licking around me everywhere, listening to the firemen shout outside, well, I thought it was the scariest moment of my life.

Now I only wish that were true.

They rushed me to the Gotham burn clinic and that's when I had my Faustian moment of weakness—yeah, I'll take responsibility for that much. That's the difference between tragedy and pathos, after all. Pathos is when you get railroaded, like a piano falling out of the sky on your head. But tragedy, that's when there is a possibility for things working out all right . . . and you muff it.

So the devil, he appears to me at my hospital bedside in the guise of Roland frigging Daggett. He's a suit, a crook, one of those businessmen who doesn't care who he hurts. And he's got this new "miracle product" he's hawking, RenuYou, a special cream that he said could restore my features within minutes as compared to years of only half-successful and wholly painful plastic surgery. The catch was—and, oh yeah, even then he admitted there was a catch—the drug wasn't FDA approved, and he had reason to believe it was highly addictive. So of course I said, "Oh, you know, thanks, but I think I'll stick to the tried and true."

In my dreams.

In the hospital what I said was, "Hell yeah, where do I sign up?"

RenuYou was everything Daggett said it would be. Within minutes of the first application, I was back to my old handsome self again. It really was amazing. It really was a miracle drug.

And it really was addictive.

As it played out, if I wanted to stay supplied with

RenuYou, I was gonna have to do some "favors" for Mr. Daggett. This included everything from robbing other chemical factories to strong-arming people Daggett felt owed him money or services. I barely even had time for acting anymore, and finally I got fed up enough to refuse him. And *poof* went my supply of RenuYou.

At first it was just the itching. Then my skin started to burn, and sag, and scar. I was hideous, worse than before I started using the stuff. Soon it was all I could think about. I had the shakes, the world was pale and gray and three feet away from me, like I was seeing it through some kinda vacuum, all the time. Finally, I couldn't take it anymore. Out of my mind, totally crazed for the damn cream, I broke into Daggett Industries one night to steal some.

And I got some, all right. Daggett had some goons stationed there, probably other poor schlubs like me who owed him for something or another. But they were poor schlubs with guns, and as punishment for the break-in, they held me down and poured gallons upon gallons of RenuYou right down my throat.

Now we get to the scariest moment of my life.

I imagine Daggett's goons assumed I'd just die. I mean, this stuff was toxic, untested, and not meant for human consumption in the first place. You were just supposed to rub it into your skin. I know *I* sure thought I'd die, and I pretty much wanted to. The pain was excruciating. I was vomiting and feverish and sweating and it felt like every single cell in my body was being held down underwater and drowned, one by one.

Finally I passed out.

When at last I woke up, I was alone. As I struggled to my feet, I felt thick and heavy, sluggish, drugged. My breathing felt wet and labored. I glanced at my hand and figured I must be hallucinating. It was a big brown glob of clay, an oozing mess of mud. I staggered out of the building and back to my car and tried to get in and couldn't. The movements of bending my knees and ducking my head and sliding into the driver's seat—movements that were totally rote, you know, not the kind of thing you even think about—well, I just couldn't make them work, it was like all of my joints were swollen tight and all of my muscles were shredded, jelly.

Finally I made the mistake of glancing into the car's side mirror.

And that's when I realized that I was a monster.

And I guess being a monster does have some advantages. Up on the roof of Gotham Chemical, lugging big barrels of chemical soup, I notice how heavy they are, especially after having carried them all the frigging way up the stairs, but I don't let that stop me. I guess I've gotten used to being able to pick up small cars and stuff—I don't even really think about it now, I just do it—but even by those standards, these huge containers weigh a ton . . . literally.

After an hour, a ton starts to feel like real weight.

I stop to take a break. I'm a little disappointed that I don't have a cigarette; it's been years since I smoked, but back when I was just another struggling actor, I smoked like a chimney, just like all the other hopefuls I knew. I know it's probably a bad idea to light up out here—who knows what kind of flammable stuff is around: the chemicals, the two energy generators behind me, all the construction machinery they keep on the roof for hauling—but it just seems like the right thing to do. Besides, it's been years since I've worked this much, and old habits die hard.

I lean back against one of those huge vats of RenuYou that dominate the roof. I couldn't even guess how many gallons of it they have in this place: Ten thousand? A hundred thousand? Even a million?

I may have played a brain surgeon on a soap opera for a while, but that doesn't mean I am one; not back then, certainly not now. But even I can tell that there is a whole lot of the stuff here. A whole hell of a lot. Enough for Gotham, that's for sure. Sin Tzu was right about that, too.

They've got this crazy suit for me at Arkham Asylum that keeps me from shifting. It's kinda like a full-body girdle, though of course it feels more like a full-body straitjacket. As long as I'm wearing it, I can be outside of my cell sometimes, so I first met Sin Tzu in the cafeteria, where most of the hardcore crazies aren't even allowed to go.

It was weird. He didn't eat. The guards—my nurse, even—acted like he wasn't there. They just looked right through him. Creepy.

And all the more so 'cause of the way he looked. I mean, I can see missing the Ventriloquist when he walks into a room, or not noticing, say, the Clock King. But Sin Tzu? He's gold, for cryin' out loud, and his eyes glow in this sort of pupilless, dead, white way. He's got a big tat right in the middle of his forehead—some Chinese somethin' or another in red and black—and his hands look like something you'd see on a reptile, all claws and nails.

He came and sat next to me as a nurse fed me spoonfuls of sloppy joe. I can't move my arms in the suit, and it was a little embarrassing to be so incapacitated in front of someone else, especially someone as stately and composed-looking as Sin Tzu, but he immediately put me at ease.

"Look how you have them all at your service," he teased, smiling blandly at the nurse.

"Oh yeah, I'm a big hotshot around here," I joked. He

introduced himself and launched straight into this huge
attack plan he had going, which of course included breaking me out of Arkham. I couldn't believe he was saying all
of this right in front of the nurse, and I started to freak.

"What are you, crazy?" I asked, immediately recog-
nizing the stupidity of the question. We were in Arkham,
after all. Turns out, though, he wasn't. Not even a little, to
my mind.

"Don't worry about her," he told me. I glanced over at
the nurse. I thought she was acting weird before, not even
seeing Sin Tzu, but this was wild. She had a sort of glazed
look in her eyes, and was just holding the spoonful of slop
up for me without any hint of fatigue or impatience.

"Can you make her throw that swill across the room?"
I joked.

Sin Tzu smiled, and the nurse lifted the tray and
hurled it at the far wall. From that moment on, I loved the
guy.

After that, we spoke about the big plan almost every
day at lunch, and he offered me all kinds of help, like a
bunch of his own soldiers should I need them. He said I'd
like them, but I'm not entirely sure what he meant by that.
When I asked, he just smiled cryptically.

Anyway, I told him I was okay on my own. I'm practically a one-man army. And that's when he started to really help me crystallize my attack plan against the Batman.

Back up on the roof of Gotham Chemical, I catch
sight of my reflection in one of the open vats and jump a
little. Even now, after all these years—even when I'm in
this place just so I can change it—I sometimes forget what
I look like.

Strange. My fifteen minutes lasted a few years and
had been gone long before the Batman ever entered my
life. By the end I was doing dinner theater for blue-haired

old ladies who gummed their food and bitched right at us, right to us, in the middle of a damn performance because we weren't loud enough. A commercial for hemorrhoid cream seemed like a great gig by then.

But I still think of myself as Matt Hagen, dashing young actor. Average height, good build, nice dark brown hair, dazzling smile. The toast of the town. Every woman wants me and every guy wants to be me. And why not? I've got every woman and all the money and most of the fame any guy could ever dream of. Who wouldn't want to be me?

The vat distorts me. The face staring back at me isn't Matt Hagen, young lion about town, star of *Love and Lust in the Emergency Room*. It isn't even Matt Hagen, star of Acme Doggie Bites, *the treats that'll make you* dog's *best friend*. No, I'm looking at a big clump of mud roughly shaped like a man—a very, very big man—but that no one would ever mistake for the real thing.

Ladies and gentlemen, for your viewing pleasure, the star of tonight's drama, give him a big hand because he could use one, a real one at least, the one, the only, Clay-face! Isn't he great? Well, then, isn't he at least freakishly interesting?

But that is all going to change. One way or the other. Either I'm going to become a real man again . . . or every-one else is going to be joining me.

I can't help it. I laugh out loud. Not in some twisted, mad-scientist sort of way. I laugh because I realize I sound like an evil mirror of Pinocchio. *Really, Gepetto? Everyone else can become a puppet?*

Just for the hell of it, I shift form. First to Pinocchio, then to Gepetto. I do a little dance on the roof, using the gunfire and car alarms from the street as my music.

Right. Once you start acting out old cartoons, it's time to get back to the task at hand. Especially when you look much more like something out of a horror flick than a kids' movie. I shift back to my hideous, gloopy mud form, shake my head to clear my thoughts, little bits of clay splattering all over the roof as I do so, make the little alteration to my oh-so-pliable form that Sin Tzu had suggested, and start moving the chemicals again.

It's even harder now. My big, ugly, slippery paws aren't helping. Part of it is the rest—I know better by now than to wallow in the past; it never helps and it always hurts. It hurts so damn bad, in fact. Part of the difficulty is the modification I just made. And a big chunk of it is the tension.

He is getting closer. I know it.

You pretty much never see the Batman coming. And even if there are three windows and one door and you got two people watching each entrance, he'll find a way to get in without you seeing him. You could be in a locked bank vault and he'd sneak in. A submarine two miles down— he'd sneak in. The moon lander—in like Flynn. Doesn't matter. None of it matters. He'll find a way. He always finds a damn way.

Except for this time. This time it's going to be different. He may have taken me out every time in the past, but I always gave him a better fight than almost any of those other psychos. I'm smart—not as smart as the Riddler or Bane or Two-Face (he was a district attorney, after all, so he better be smart), okay, or maybe Mr. Freeze (he was a big-deal scientist) or Poison Ivy (another scientist), and definitely not the Joker (who the hell knows what he was before, except maybe a demon from hell they kicked out for being too frigging twisted).

But still, I'm smart. Smarter than Killer Croc, sure, but smarter than Maxie Zeus or Scarface, too. And probably some of the others.

And I'm big. And strong.

I'm not as big or strong at this exact moment as I am sometimes . . . but that's on purpose. And I have a plan. A rock-solid plan . . . so to speak. There's no chance it's not going to work.

Sin Tzu assures me it will, and I believe him.

Five seconds with that guy and you know. You just know. Actually, he's kind of like the Batman that way. I've never actually been sure that the Batman's any more human than I am. There's definitely something about that guy that's off. And not just a bit, either. He's way the hell off. Not that Sin Tzu seems like Joe Normal, either.

But whatever. I'm big, strong, smart, and with a perfect plan courtesy of Sin Tzu.

Everything is going to be great. Just frigging great.

I move the final container into place and am about to pour it into one of the few empty vats, trying to recall what Sin Tzu had told me, whether I'm supposed to add two of the big blue barrels and one each of the red and green, or whether it was one blue, one red, and two green. I've long since given up trying to read the names on their sides after the seventh syllable; if I thought Marlowe was confusing and didn't understand a word of Albee, I'm sure not going to be really grasping the names of these chemical compositions. *Hydromethotrexawhoosiewhatever. Right.*

That's when the small beveled window on the rooftop door leading down to the stairway shatters, showering me with millions of razor-sharp diamonds. The deadly little nuggets look like they're dancing as they fall all around me. They don't hurt me, of course, although they might have cut a regular man to ribbons—no safety glass in *this* place. There are times it's an advantage to be an enormous lump of moist dirt.

I spin around, my right arm already snaking out faster

than a Peruvian mudslide and with more force than a bull-dozer. Like a giant mudworm launch. If the Batman had been standing there, I would have either punched a hole right through his chest, or slammed him into one of the vats so hard that his insides would have been jellied.

But he isn't. I don't know if he broke the door window with something else to make me *think* that was how he was coming, or if he is just so damn quick that he's already disappeared before I turn around. Or maybe he came from up the side of the building, and leapt up on top of one of the vats, rather than onto the floor behind me.

Whatever. He isn't there, that's the point.

So I don't turn him to mush. I just rip a tiny hole in the solid steel vat. No RenuYou in that one, fortunately. Just boiling water. Which comes shooting out. And hits me. It *hurts*. Not as much as it would hurt an ordinary guy—it probably woulda killed one of them—but still, it doesn't exactly tickle. Worse, it's starting to melt me.

I reach down and scoop up the parts of my feet that are beginning to dissolve and slap the mess onto my chest, where it—they—solidify again almost immediately. I spin around, knowing the Batman's coming up behind me.

Nothing. No sign of him. I spin around again, knowing that he'll have expected me to turn around, thinking he's trying to get the drop on me, so he'll be coming from the first direction. He's a tricky bastard.

Still nothing. I spin around again, thinking that he'll have already anticipated my first two moves and has simply hesitated but now is coming up from behind me, meaning the original behind-me direction. Or, wait, maybe it's the original behind-me direction behind me, and that's where he's coming from. I turn again and suddenly realize I am going around in circles. I look like a dog chasing its own tail. *If you're going to play that hard, little buddy, you need Acme Doggie Bites*, I find myself thinking wildly. *It's got all the nutrients you need, and it'll give you shiny teeth and a glossy coat!*

I know my brain is starting to go on the fritz and try desperately to get myself under control. *Breathe*, I remind myself. *Breathe from your diaphragm*. Of course, I don't have a diaphragm anymore, which is the whole reason I had jumped at Sin Tzu's plan.

And then the Batman speaks.

"Hagen," he says in that freaky voice of his. I hate it so much. It's like he's whispering through the world's loudest bullhorn. It's soft and deafening at the same time. I wish I had known how to do that back when I was normal. I could have added decades to my career. Then again, no one has ever known quite how to do that with their voice either. No one but him.

And I hate it when he calls me "Hagen." Maybe that's how I can't help but think of myself, but that's me. That's my problem. It's just another example of him looking right through you. He should be like the rest of the world. He should see me as the big, gross, slimy, lumpy monster I am. He should call me "Clayface" like everyone else. Bastard.

I still have no idea where he is.

"Why are you doing this?"

Nope. No good. I can't locate him from his voice—it seems to be coming from everywhere and nowhere. Even with my extra help, all those additional vantage points, I still can't figure out where he is.

Now I get mad. I know as I'm doing it that I shouldn't, that he probably wants me to. I remind myself that I'm a Method actor, and it's all about getting into the role in every way, and that letting my emotions run away with me has no place in this particular drama. But I get mad anyway. He's just . . . maddening.

"You know why I'm doing this!" I yell.

"Tell me anyway."

I realize I'm shaking with anger when I catch sight of myself in one of the vats and see I'm jiggling like a big tub of gelatin.

That helps get me under control, even if it doesn't do a whole lot for my self-esteem.

I take a deep breath. "I was promised that the best scientific minds in the world would fix my condition," I say softly. "It never happened. I tried to rejoin society, but it rejected me. I tried to beat society, but I ended up in Arkham Asylum, courtesy of *you*."

I catch my breath again and force a smile. "So now I have a new plan—if I can't beat 'em, I'll have 'em *join* me. Even as we speak, I'm formulating enough of the chemical composition that created me to turn every man, woman, and child in Gotham to clay. For all I know, even the dogs, cats, and rats'll turn into freaks like me."

I find myself rubbing my hands together. I must be more into the part than I realize. "What do you think?" I ask. "Think they might come up with a cure then?"

"It won't work."

I spin around. "What won't? Yes it will! Why not?"

"Several reasons. First, you've got the formula wrong—your proportions are all off. You're about to create an extremely fragrant solution that might kill all the grass in Gotham, but that's about it."

He's lying, I tell myself.

Only I know he isn't.

Dammit! Why hadn't I taken that part in the remake of *The Island of Doctor Moreau*? Could have come in handy here.

"Besides . . . I'm not going to let you contaminate the water supply with anything."

"Oh yeah?" I sneer. "You don't think so?"

"I know so."

"How can you be so sure? There's already enough RenuYou in this factory below me that I don't *need* to make more!"

"Hagen."

"What?!"

"It won't help."

I pause. *He couldn't know*, I tell myself. *Not that. There's just no way. He couldn't possibly.* If I'd had ears, I woulda put my hands over them and said "la la la la I can't hear you" to drown out his whisper. Because he does know. I know it. I don't know how he knows . . . but he does.

"What won't?" I stammer, bluffing—always a bad move with him.

"The best scientists at Wayne Tech have tried, Hagen. There's no cure."

"There is!" I scream. "You lie! I'm going to be cured! I am! I know it!"

"I'm sorry, Hagen. You're not. There's no miracle cure waiting to happen. You made a mistake looking for a miracle cure once—there *is* no potion that'll give you or anyone else eternal youth—and this is what resulted. Now your body and your mind are the way they are. Cut your losses and learn from your mistakes. Whatever happens next is up to you. You should know that by now."

"No!" I shriek. "I'm going to get back the way I was. I am! I can't stay this way! I can't! Looking like this is bad enough, but to be so . . . I *will* get better."

I fumble for the words. In desperation, I picture a pencil. It was an old trick I learned in acting school. If you forget a line, just imagine a pencil. Think about its shape, its color, its texture. Imagine it in complete detail. Suddenly you remember your line. Of course, that was also where I learned about the Method acting school of . . . uh . . . acting, and here I was getting *too* into the part. And it's not like Sin Tzu gave me a script anyway, just a battle plan. Screw it. I never was any good at improv. Time for the smackdown.

And then the Batman is behind me. I turn slowly. It's for real this time.

Even in my current state, I'm larger than him. Taller, wider, heavier. He is just a man, and not even all that huge a guy either. But his stage presence . . . you could put him next to all the big-time movie stars from Hollywood and nobody would even notice that there was anyone there but the Batman.

"I'm sorry, Hagen," he says again. He pauses, watching me with narrowed eyes. "If Sin Tzu told you you'd be cured, he lied."

"No." I shake my head. "Sin Tzu just gave me the plan. Everything else is just . . . just me."

The Batman nods, more to himself than to me.

Wait a minute.

"How—how did you know Sin Tzu was behind this?"

"The nature of the attack fits his profile. But it wasn't confirmed until just now."

Dammit, what's wrong with me!? Why can't I keep my big mouth shut? Well, never mind. It won't matter that I gave away Sin Tzu's identity anyway. Not if I beat the Batman.

I force myself to grin. If I'm gonna have any chance, I've gotta get back into the supervillain role. *I can beat him. I can beat him. I can beat him.* Pretty soon I'm feeling like myself again. My new self, that is. Clayface. "Okay, hero," I snarl. "Time to end it one way or the other, Batman."

The Batman looks at me in a way I don't like at all. At all at all. Like I'm some bug he's studying. What the hell, I suppose a walking, talking mountain of oily mud *is* pretty interesting. I turn my head slightly, never taking my eyes off of him for a second. My *main* eyes, that is. "Children, to me!" I call.

It's beautiful. Even the Batman is surprised. I can tell. Even the high-and-mighty, smarter-than-everyone-else Batman is taken aback as all my little claybabies come running from their hiding places.

This is what I meant when I told Sin Tzu I didn't need his soldiers. I could make my own.

As the mini-Clayfaces jump onto me, I open up and absorb them back into myself, spinning around to take them in faster. Earlier, when I sent them off, it was a strange, sickening sensation, like that feeling you get when you accidentally peel off a fingernail or something, and your stomach lurches. Bringing them back in, though—it's strangely comforting. I can feel myself growing taller and filling out. With their added bulk, I'm back to my normal size, which isn't normal at all. I'm towering over the Batman, easily six times as big as him. Now this is more like it! I look down at him and leer. "Still look like an easy fight?" I ask.

He doesn't reply; he almost never does. The strong, silent type. Total leading-man material. He wouldn't have been competition for me ten years ago. He would have wiped me, and every other actor, off the face of the earth.

But not now. Now I loom over him and weigh five times what he does.

I'm going to pound him until he looks like my little claybabies.

I lead with my left and he dodges it easily. He ducks to avoid my right uppercut too. But every time I am able to splatter him with a little bit of clay. After a minute there's enough on his arms and chest and legs to start to slow him down a little.

That's when I pull out the heavy artillery. Morphing my hands into giant scythes, I slice at the Batman, over and over again. And yet each time he somehow manages to dodge out of my way, graceful to the end, his cape billowing out behind him.

Without even really thinking about it, acting out of rage and blood lust, I transform my hands into giant hammers, easily three times the Batman's puny size. When I miss him, they pound down onto the rooftop, causing the entire building to shudder.

The Batman looks in danger of losing his balance, so I press forward, this time throwing big, snotty mud balls at him. These he dodges, of course, but I still have a surprise for him. After splattering on the ground into ugly clay smears, my mud balls pull themselves back together, becoming little claybabies, just about the Batman's size. The Batman takes the first one out with a sharp undercut, but minutes after he's spattered it, it slowly reforms, rising up again to fight him.

Won't Sin Tzu be surprised if it's me who takes down the great Batman? Me! That should make up for me accidentally giving away his involvement.

I have four claybabies surrounding the Batman and am coming at him again with one hammer fist and one scythe when I notice something silver glinting in his gloved hand

Crap.

The Batman tosses the Batarang and I get ready to duck, but it doesn't arc towards me. I've fought the Batman enough times to know that he doesn't miss, so I start to turn to look behind me, squinting with my repulsive little beady eyes.

The two huge energy generators. I just catch a glimpse of them in my clay-stained peripheral vision when they short out, blasting me with streams of crackling electricity.

I managed to avoid electroshock therapy all those years in Arkham for *this*?

The current jolts through my muddy clay body like burning spears of acid. My little claybabies melt where they stand, needing my concentration to sustain them. The lights go out in that entire section of Gotham. When at last the generators short out completely, I fall to my knees, dazed.

I smell myself cooking. Not exactly fun, but it actually isn't as awful as you might expect. It smells kind of like a campfire. I can't move. I've been baked solid.

I can still see, though—the Batman has turned on a flashlight. The electricity musta done a number on my already RenuYou-enfeebled mind. *Wow*, I think. *That flashlight's so small, but it sure is bright. Unlike me.*

I fall forward onto the concrete floor and shatter into a million pieces. Two million of my eyes find themselves looking up at the Batman. He's won, but he has an expression of such sadness on what I can see of his face.

You bastard, I think. *Don't you dare feel sorry for me. Just enjoy your body and your brain . . . while you can. Because you never know when it's going to be gone forever. Trust me on that one. And if I have anything to do with it, you are going to be losing them both sooner rather than later.*

"Gloat now, Batman," I mutter. I can just barely move my mouth, but I do the best I can; the sound comes from a million little fragments of clay scattered all over the rooftop. "By dawn, Sin Tzu will have conquered Gotham."

As I say it, I realize it's true. Okay, so it won't be me, that was nothing new. But Sin Tzu, he's large and in charge, and he still has a world of hurt planned for the Batman.

Good.

I just hope I'm back together in time to see him take the Batman all the way down.

The Batman just stares a moment longer and then he's gone. My two million eyes stare up at the stars, which are twinkling into view now that the lights are out for eight city blocks. Then even the stars start to blur and fade and I lose consciousness, just one thought goes through my head.

You've got it coming, Batman. And this is gonna be great. This is gonna be just frigging great.

EIGHT

Commissioner James Gordon
2:07 a.m.

I'm out on the street, on the radio with all of my officers, every one of whom is on beat tonight, trying to contain the chaos.

Bullock and Montoya are on the Hill in a shootout with five Stonegate escapees who managed to get their hands on a stockpile of automatic weapons. Bock just called in from Chinatown where he's single-handedly trying to suppress a looming gang riot between the Luck Hand Triad and Blackmask's gang, who seem to be up from Blüdhaven just for the occasion. I send tactical up to Murphy Ave where reports are coming in about an orange–jumper-wearing convict rigging explosives to the base of the R.H. Kane building. Precinct Four is covering the Bowery while Precinct Two assists the fire department with a public-housing inferno up in Coventry being guarded by a pyromaniac sniper with a rifle. I've got Scarecrow—after that stunt he pulled taking me hostage earlier tonight—in a holding tank downstairs.

And now there's the latest threat, and this one makes all the others look like a party game. A ship is coming into

Gotham Harbor carrying a weapon of mass destruction. I don't know which harbor, which ship, what kind of weapon, or when. Could be biochemical warfare, a dirty bomb . . . could even be nuclear. All I know for sure is that this is no bluff.

The kid on the emergency line doesn't even know who called it in. But I know. And I know that, once again this night, I have to call Batman and lie to him.

The moment I pick up my communicator, the one that gives me a direct line to Batman, I feel my gut clench. Over the years I've come to regard him as a friend. And over the years he's proven to be the best friend I have.

It's strange to come to trust someone whose face you've never seen. And it's strange to be an officer of the law depending on someone who operates outside of it. But I trust Batman with my life, and with the life of the men and women under my command. I trust him with the life of my daughter, Barbara, and with the life of Robin, who is clearly not much more than a child.

And in a funny way, I guess he trusts me as well. With the thing that matters most to him: his city. Because Gotham does belong to Batman. You can't live here and not realize that eventually. He's this city's protector, and also its heart. I expect him to appear with the night now the way most people expect the glow of streetlights and the moon.

On many levels, he's the most moral man I know. Even without the rules and regulations of the police or the military, he works under his own code. I can't go into someone else's home without a warrant, but I can shoot them once I'm in. While he moves freely in and out of private residences, he has vowed to never take a life. I've got a camera on me in the interview room and a fleet of officers who will come to my aid at a moment's notice. He conducts his interrogations in the back of dark alleys, accountable to no one, and works chiefly alone. The exception is one or two young sidekicks who work mostly, as far as I can tell, as moral ballast, keeping him grounded in his humanity and encouraging him to stay in touch with his own compassion and benevolence. We come out of different corners, Batman and I, but when the bell rings, we're both fighting in the same ring and on the same side.

I honestly don't know what I'd do without him.

Which is why I hate this so much.

Gotham City—Batman's city, *my* city—is being pillaged and raped. And Sin Tzu, the international terrorist, is the one behind it all. Only a handful of people know it. In fact, only a handful of people even know he's in Gotham at all.

And I can't tell Batman a thing to help him.

Sin Tzu came to Arkham eight months ago, brought over by a Special Ops team and under a heavy veil of secrecy. Locally, the Mayor knows, the staff at Arkham knows, and I know, and that's it. Mayor Dickinson told me it was a matter of national security, and as a former Green Beret, what am I going to say to that? *I'm sorry, sir, but I don't keep secrets from my daughter, Barbara, and by the way, I think we should tell the Dark Knight Detective?*

No. I said, "I understand, sir," and quietly prayed they'd move the sonofabitch to Metropolis.

They didn't.

And now Sin Tzu has decided to use our eccentricities against us, releasing a flood of psychotic inmates from Arkham Asylum—including Jonathan "Scarecrow" Crane and Matt "Clayface" Hagen, and staging a huge breakout from Stonegate Prison. Not to mention this new threat— this weapon of mass destruction that might conceivably be designed to put an end to all life in Gotham once and for all. I'm not cleared to read most of Sin Tzu's files, but what I have read tells me that this man isn't out to free himself and disappear quietly into the night. He's an exploiter of terror and a wager of wars. He lives for conquest, and he must be after my city—Batman's city, Gotham City. He's going to conquer it, and if everyone in it is dead or alive when it's over concerns him not one whit.

Well, he can't have it. But I don't know how to stop him. And the one man who could figure it out doesn't have the right information. He's relying on me to get it to him, and I can't. Batman, I'm sorry.

I've already asked for his help too many times tonight, without being able to give him the information he needs in return. First, the rescue from Scarecrow. Then, without my asking, Batman deployed Robin and Nightwing to aid my—I'll admit it—completely overwhelmed police force in containing the rioting, violence, theft, and general mayhem triggered by over a thousand Stonegate and Arkham inmates rampaging through the streets.

It was only a few hours later when that bastard Sin Tzu himself called to alert me to Hagen's presence at the Gotham Chemical Plant. Which of course means that he *wanted* me to send Batman there to stop Clayface. Which suggests that it's some kind of trap. But I sent Batman anyway. What am I supposed to do? My people simply don't possess the equipment or experience necessary to capture Hagen, and Batman does. And if I had told him it was a trap and warned him not to go, he would have gone anyway.

Do I sound like I'm rationalizing? Well, maybe. This whole thing is turning into a nightmare.

And now I have to ask again. I steel myself, take a breath.

But, as usual, before I press a single button, my communicator goes off with a pattern of beeps denoting a frequency open only to Batman. I step back into the shadows of the courthouse and open the hail, immediately receiving an image of Batman surveying a grim scene on the rooftop of Gotham Chemical.

I see him probably more often than any other non-mask-wearing civilian in Gotham, and his silhouette still stops my heart. His presence is arresting.

He waits for me to speak. I finally manage the words.

"Batman . . . We just received a tip that a weapon of mass destruction is heading towards Gotham City."

Batman's voice is level. We've known each other and worked together for years. He knows something is wrong. How could he *not* know?

"Where did the tip come from?"

I can't answer.

He repeats the question. "Jim? Where did the tip come from?"

I choke it out. "I can't say."

Batman pauses for the briefest moment. "Meaning you don't know, or you won't tell?"

I hedge. I can't help it. "I just can't say."

My mind is racing with images of death and mayhem. Maybe there's some way to give him just enough of a clue so that he can draw his own conclusions. Clearly he already realizes he's not dealing with one of our recurrent Gotham psychotics. Hell, maybe he already knows, and is just trying to get additional information out of me. Maybe he's trying to give me the chance to clear my conscience.

"I . . . have been sworn to silence," I continue, and then add, quietly, "National security . . ."

"I know, Jim," he says.

". . . You know?"

"I had the suspects narrowed down. Rā's al Ghūl

would be capable of this, but it wouldn't support his objective. The others were just as easily ruled out. Given the military precision of the planning, it could only be one man. Sin Tzu, Warlord of Asia."

There's relief in my voice as I answer. "I can neither confirm nor deny." Once again I thank my lucky stars for his brilliance, and his presence in this city. Maybe he will be able to defeat Sin Tzu after all. He's certainly the only one who could.

Batman continues.

"Sin Tzu was captured by Special Ops thirty-one weeks ago . . ." He's still thinking it through and then his voice is confident and firm: ". . . and brought to Arkham Asylum for observation."

He sighs in frustration, but I know it's not directed towards me. I'm about to apologize again—

—when a new voice breaks into the line, slippery and hypnotic and softened very slightly by a vaguely Asian accent.

"Very good, Batman. You prove to be the worthy opponent I desire."

The image of Batman's masked face flickers and then breaks down into visual static, finally replaced by what must be Sin Tzu's countenance, a frightening mask of mutable gold accented with a red-and-black yin and yang symbol on his forehead.

There's something at once mesmerizing and threatening about him, like a beautifully colored poisonous snake you don't dare take your eyes from for even a moment.

"The battle is fully joined, albeit its outcome is a certainty."

I'm amazed. I have access to this frequency because Batman arranged it—I couldn't find it on my own if my life depended on it (as in fact it sometimes does). As far as

I know, only the smallest handful of Batman's devoted acolytes use this channel. How much does Sin Tzu know? How far has he burrowed under Gotham's skin?

Or did Batman know he was listening? Was this whole conversation a stratagem to draw him out? I'm no dummy, but the game these two are playing is over my head.

"First rule of war, Sin Tzu," Batman answers calmly. "There are no certainties."

I can hear the smile in Sin Tzu's silky voice as he answers Batman's dark rumble. "I am pleased to learn that you have read my tome," he says.

I realize that this must be the first time they've ever spoken. How long has Sin Tzu been anticipating this moment?

I glance back down at the visual feed in time to watch Sin Tzu's eyes narrow as his expression hardens. I realize with a swallow that the gold covering his face is not a mask, it is somehow grafted onto his skin. "When you surrender, the war will stop."

A cop car comes racing down Commerce, siren blaring. Instinctively, I step farther back into the shadows as I continue to eavesdrop on Batman and Sin Tzu's exchange.

"Like it did in Cyanna when you marched the entire population into a 'reeducation' camp?" Batman growls.

"Education is the cure for ignorance," Sin Tzu answers, obviously amused by Batman's anger.

"Or in Unglong when you forced thousands into slavery?" Batman is warning Sin Tzu, both that he's read up on him and also that he doesn't like him one little bit.

Sin Tzu chuckles. "Idle citizens are the fuel of insurrection."

"You were once a great strategist, Sin Tzu," Batman answers, the tenor of his voice changing again. He sounds as if he's just wrestled his personal feelings back into submission. "But now you're just a common thug."

I jump as a pager vibrates on my belt. Glancing down with a frown, I see the letters "DXD" flash back up at me. That can only mean one thing. We're closing in on the location of the latest threat.

I can't keep myself from imagining the repercussions of Sin Tzu's weapon of mass destruction. I hate that term, both the specificity and the vagueness of it. It would be just Gotham's luck to be the first U.S. city to come under nuclear attack. I remember photos I saw from Hiroshima and Nagasaki. More than one hundred thousand citizens gone in a flash, and hundreds of thousands more poisoned by radiation. Babies hideously deformed, children who stopped growing, adults picking glass and shrapnel out of their scalps for years to come. The cancer, the vomiting, the seared skin . . . Though maybe it's a biological weapon? Gotham citizens puking up their guts in the avenues, scratching their own eyes out, dying in their own defecation in tiny apartments and overcrowded subways.

I push the talk button on the handheld communicator hard with my thumb. I feel like I'm stepping between a viper and a demon, but the lives of Gotham's eight million citizens depend on getting this information to Batman.

"Batman," I interrupt, "I don't know which ship, or even which pier, but my military sources suspect activity at the Dixon Docks."

That may not sound like much of a lead, until you remember that Gotham is an island. Being able to cross off the Tricorner Yards, Port Adams, Miller Harbor, and Rogers Yacht Basin from the list is a major accomplishment. Even if it does leave us with over one hundred and twenty-eight individual docking sites to search.

"I'm on it," Batman responds, and I'm flushed once more with a sense of gratitude for his presence in this city.

"I'll disarm your weapon," he says to Sin Tzu, "and when I do, I'm coming for you."

"If only you knew where to find me," taunts Sin Tzu.

Batman's linkup goes dead as he flips off his communicator, and I snap mine off in a hurry, not wanting Sin Tzu to get a trace on my location.

Can Batman really do it? If I had to bet on anyone, I'd put my money on Batman, but even so, he's got less than an hour to search the entire west side of the Gotham waterfront for a single ship carrying an unknown weapon of mass destruction, and then defuse it before it causes anyone harm. Many of the things he's managed in the past remain mysterious to me even now, and I can't manage to wrap my brain around how he'll handle this new threat, either.

It could be anything on that boat—a nuclear device, a biological weapon, a chemical bomb. It could be set to go off at any time or at any one of a thousand prompts, and it could be on any one of a ten-ton capacity worth of crates and containers found aboard any large commercial vessel.

As a man of action, I long to join Batman on the docks—at least to send a bomb squad along with him. But the truth is that he works faster alone, and we would most likely prove a hindrance to him. The best I can do for him now is to continue to orchestrate the efforts of the GCPD, so that there are at least a handful of catastrophes he needn't feel personally responsible for.

Sin Tzu's right, this truly is a war. I sigh and head back to my office to rally the troops. I think longingly of the cigar on my desk, behind the glass case marked "break in case of emergency," wondering if this qualifies.

This city has a lot to recommend it. That's what I'm telling myself, anyway. It's the answer, the recital I go through before I let myself ask the always lingering question: Why the hell do I live here? In the twelve years since I transferred from Chicago, I must have asked myself that question every day of the week, and twice on Sundays. So here's my list, a work in progress:

There's the citizenry. It takes guts to live in Gotham, real backbone, and these are people I'm proud to serve and proud to buy coffee from and proud to share subway rides with in the morning. Robinson Park in the spring is a delight. The curry at Bhagwansingh's will knock your socks off. Gotham Cathedral, no matter how you're feeling about God, is an architectural marvel. Barbecued pork bows on Englehart in Chinatown, the Tuesday afternoon local art fair at Burnley Harbor, an early evening stroll through the Wayne Botanical Gardens in The Scituate, a late evening of cold beer and hot jazz in Burnley, "civic pride" night on WKGC, a filet mignon and three-olive martini at the Blue Heron, a hot-out-of-the-oven freshly glazed MM Good Donut and a piping-hot cup of coffee at five in the morning, Saturday afternoon at the Knights Dome with the home team winning, the half-price Monday Cowboy matinee at the beautiful old Majestic, young couples necking on the Ferris wheel at Amusement Mile— any of these will make you glad to be alive. And then there's the police force, though there, of course, I'm biased. I'm the Commissioner for Gotham's finest, and a finer lot you won't find anywhere.

There's Batman.

And then there's my daughter, Barbara. Babs.

Despite my worry, she's flourished here, taking the city in stride, making it her own. Just last year she graduated from Gotham State University with honors. She's a computer science whiz kid, already overhauling the entire police department filing system, bringing us into the twenty-first century with charm and an almost incomprehensible talent for all things cyber.

And my God, what a beauty. She gets that red hair from her mother. The minute she blossomed from a girl into a young lady, I knew there was a reason I'd decided to be a cop. I cheerfully polished my service revolver as she introduced her high school dates to me, thanking God for her no-nonsense nature and level head.

I'd do anything to protect her. She's the reason I get out of bed in the morning.

I'm just glad that tonight, she's safe and sound at home . . .

NINE

Batgirl/Barbara Gordon
2:15 A.M.

Just think, right now I could be safe and sound at home. But nooOOOoo, instead I'm out in the middle of the biggest brawl Gotham's ever seen, dressed in a form-fitting, face-hiding costume with a bright yellow bat in the middle of my chest.

Just another typical night as a masked crime-fighter in Gotham.

At least my dad doesn't know I'm out here. As Gotham City's Police Commissioner, he's got a pretty good idea of just how dangerous crime-fighting in this city can be, and the closest he'll let me get to it is overhauling the PD's filing system from paper to electronic.

When I think about all the police reports tonight is going to generate, it's enough to make me want to cry. I'll be typing in data entry for months. That is, if there's still a police department by the time this whole ordeal is over.

And if there's still a Gotham.

Something's really wrong in the city tonight. More wrong than usual. Fortunately, I was still home when Dad called around midnight to tell me to stay in.

"What's going on?" I asked, trying to sound sleepy. The truth was, I was already in my basement polishing my Batarangs, getting ready to hit the streets.

"It's not clear yet, but there may have been a breakout at Arkham."

"Who—"

"We don't know yet, but that's not all—Stonegate Prison seems to have been breached as well. Gotham's a madhouse."

"What—"

"I'm going back in. I wondered about whether to call and risk waking you up, but I just want to make sure you've got all your windows locked and the alarm on."

There was a pause as I debated whether or not to risk trying to get in touch with Batman. If things were as bad as Dad said, then he was probably extremely busy, but he also probably needed help.

"Do you? Have the alarm on?" My dad said on the other end of the line, snapping me out of my reverie.

"Yeah, yeah—tucked in all safe and snug."

"Well, keep it that way. And you still have that shotgun I gave you, right? Hm . . . maybe I should send over an officer to—"

I laughed. "You're not going to be able to spare any men. Don't worry about me, Dad. I'll be okay."

"I know you will, honey, I just . . ."

"You worry. I know. It's part of your job as a dad. But I'll be fine."

"All right, Miss Judo Black Belt. I love you!"

"Love you, too, Dad!"

By the time he hung up, I was already in high gear, tearing apart my secret basement crime lab, gathering the equipment I was going to need. Rope, grapnel, a couple of Batarangs, an old communicator I took from the Batcave a few years ago—I doubted it still worked, but just in case—and of course, my Batgirl costume. I'm nothing if not practical; if Gotham was exploding, Batman, Robin and Nightwing, not to mention my dad, were going to need all the help they could get.

Even if they didn't want it.

I've had a little bit of trouble, I guess you could say, breaking into the boys' club. And breaking in wasn't even my intent to begin with. The first time I went out in costume I was actually trying to impersonate Batman.

Okay, I know how that sounds. Five-foot-five, curvy, flaming-red-haired me fooling anyone into thinking I was Batman. But I had it pretty well planned. One of our local costumed crazies, Two-Face, had set up my dad for taking bribes from a local thug named Rupert Thorne. I wanted Batman to make an appearance at the public rally in support of Dad—just a quick fly-by, you know, a show of support—but Batman doesn't really do things on request. So I made my own Batman costume and planned it so I'd be way up high above the rally and mostly in the shadows.

And it totally worked, too. The Gotham populace cheered and thought Batman was communicating his belief in the Commissioner's innocence, and I was all set to get out of there with no one any the wiser when Robin came up out of nowhere behind me and ripped off the back of my cowl as I started to run away. My hair came tumbling out.

By the time I got home, I realized it was a nice alteration to the costume. I shortened the cape to a stylish mid-hip length and added a little color—yellow boots, gloves, and the aforementioned bat—and violà! Batgirl was born.

Hm. When I put it that way, I guess it's really Robin's fault for trying to get me out of my clothes! Oh, not the kid who's Robin now—no, I mean the first Robin, who now goes by Nightwing, also known as Dick Grayson. I think he liked the idea of me joining the Dynamic Duo from the beginning, but Batman wasn't so convinced. He hadn't trained me, didn't have time to train me, didn't want me out on the streets.

I don't think it took Batman long to figure out who I really was, either, and I don't blame him from not wanting to take his best friend's daughter into the line of fire. But by then, even with Batman saying no, I was hooked.

I guess crime-fighting was just in my blood.

I worked with Batman and Robin on and off, always in an unofficial capacity, never fully enlisted. I even went out on dates once or twice—okay, exactly twice—with Dick (who was Robin, but is now Nightwing). I was in on the secrets, part of their world. And then when I started college I found myself crime-fighting less and less—there just weren't enough hours in the day.

But by the time I had graduated from Gotham State University with honors in the field of computer science, Batman was working solo. It turned out that Robin— Dick—had graduated from college, too, and had left Gotham to travel. Batman was alone . . . and more to the point, though he never admitted it, I think he was lonely.

He began to let me work with him in a more official capacity. Eventually, he even let me into the Batcave. Was that like being drafted? We never talked about my new role, but I could tell that he was beginning to trust me.

Now I'm sort of the resident expert on the Bat-computer, and Batman grants me free access to most of his domain. But he'll still send me home when he thinks the risk is too great. He's obviously wholly unwilling to have my blood on his hands.

I find his domineering attitude kind of frustrating sometimes, but Dick assures me that's just the way it goes.

And he should know. He's been with Batman since the beginning, the closest thing the Dark Knight has to a son, the most loyal soldier.

I'm remembering all of this as I climb up my building's fire escape. And then I'm on the rooftop, looking out at the lights of the city. A quick glance is enough to tell me that Dad was right, as usual. The place looks like hell on earth.

Gotham's never exactly been a garden of Eden—not for a couple hundred years, at the very least, and probably not since the Miagini started building huts here back in the fifteen hundreds—but this is *nuts*. Lights are there that shouldn't be—a bonfire in the middle of Robinson Park?—and no lights where they *should* be—all eighty-nine floors of the Levins building are dark. Gunshots are going off like firecrackers and the night is punctuated every few minutes by screams of terror or yells of hate.

In other words, standard Tuesday night Gotham City fare, times bazillion.

I take out the grapnel gun and stare at it. How had it come to this? What was I thinking? I was about to shoot out a line with enough force to send the grapnel a quarter mile—which is to say, enough power to drive it through the chest of a very large man, if one so chose or had poor aim—hoping the grapnel was secured successfully to a gargoyle or outcropping on some adjacent building, and then I'd jump out into space. I'd allow my body to plummet far enough to build up enough momentum to take me across the street and up a few stories higher than my present location, while making sure I didn't reach a sufficient speed that the g-force would cause my arms to be ripped out of their sockets.

Once upon a time, I was a regular girl. I had two loving parents, a happy home, and plenty of friends. Then

Mom died and Dad and I were left to fend for ourselves. He did the best he could, all things considered. I thought I'd turned out fairly well.

So I decide not to jump.

I dive instead.

And as the lights of the city rapidly turn into a blur, and the force of the wind rushing up at me causes my eyes to water, and the street below begins to resemble some sort of urban impressionist painting before I reach the nadir of my line's arc, my body instantly remembers its training, honed by years of practice, and instinctively goes with the centrifugal force so that I am whooshing away from the street below. And as, at the apex of my swing, I push the button that will release the grapnel and hang, weightless, for a fraction of a second before beginning to fall to the rooftop which had previously been across the street and is now just ten feet below me, I can't help but wonder—how had I ever given this up?

Filled with delight at my rediscovery, I quickly make my way to the Levins building; it isn't the tallest building in Gotham, but it's one of them, and it's close. Moreover, its lack of lights would help me with my recon—the dearth of any troublesome glare to contend with would improve visibility considerably, and allow me to get a better feel for the area and decide where I should concentrate first.

I'm not there more than two minutes before I spot someone entering Gotham City Police Headquarters, aka Dad's office. Nothing unusual there—people, mainly cops, flood in and out around the clock, even at this time of night.

Of course, they all use doors.

This guy is going in a window on the top floor.

Ninety seconds later I enter through the same window, which he has so thoughtfully left open. If I have anything to say about it, he's not going to be making the quick escape he's planned for. And I *am* going to have something to say about it.

The room takes up the entire top floor and is filled with computers, filing cabinets, and shelves and shelves of old records that I haven't had time to transfer. The infiltrator is no more than fifteen feet away. It's completely dark and utterly silent; the only sounds audible are a few street noises drifting up from the avenue through the still-open window.

I stand completely still and wait for the break-in artist to move. Finally, he does. I hear a page turn, so quietly that if I'd been breathing I'd have missed it.

Concentrating on not pushing air in front of me as I move, I make my way towards him until I'm within eighteen inches of his back. He doesn't even twitch.

"When'd you develop asthma?" Nightwing asks casually.

I drop and balance myself on one hand, then sweep his feet out from underneath him with my legs. He goes over backwards, but before any part of him can even touch the floor, he turns his fall into a backflip and lands in a crouch behind me. He falls on top of me immediately and pins me to the floor face-first. He outweighs me by at least sixty pounds.

There's nothing I can do. I relax.

As soon as he feels my muscles release, he begins to take some of his weight off of me. Instantly I roll over and turn on my flashlight.

He turns his head to the side and throws up his hands. "What are you, crazy?" he asks. "You *know* I my have night vision activated!"

I laugh. "How did rule number one go again? Hold

on, don't tell me . . . it'll come . . . expect the . . . expect the . . . the something . . ."

"Yeah, yeah." Nightwing laughs. "*Expect the unexpected* isn't supposed to apply to your supposed allies trying to do permanent damage to your retinas."

"Oh, please," I answer. "That was barely enough to blind you for more than, say, ten or fifteen minutes. Your ponytail, on the other hand, has almost certainly scarred me for life."

Nightwing usually wears his hair long and down. For whatever reason, he'd tied it back to read the records.

"You don't like?" he asks, pretending to be wounded. "I think it makes me look *manly*."

I nod. "Mm. It does help in that regard. Add a purse and some high heels and you'll complete the look."

He grins. "I didn't know you noticed me that way. Shall we plan a shopping excursion, make a day of it, Batgirlfriend?"

I shake my head. Nothing seems to faze this guy. I know it isn't true—plenty gets to him, but little that comes from anyone but Batman.

Of course, it's a bit easier to be unflappable when you're the best-looking, smartest, most talented guy in Gotham, heir to the richest man in town, and capable of performing physical feats that would stun a professional acrobat . . . which Dick Grayson had been at age three.

I suddenly realize that my palms are sweaty and my heart is beating faster than it did when I jumped off that building ten minutes earlier. This guy . . .

"So whatcha lookin' for?" I ask finally, trying to keep my voice steady.

Nightwing grins at me again. I hate him. Or at least I try to.

"What'd I find, actually," he answers, staring into my

eyes in that way he has that no one else in the world has. *It'd never work*, I remind myself. *Never, ever, ever, so stop even thinking about it. True, but . . .* I begin to argue, until I realize that he is still staring at me and that I haven't said anything yet. For a moment I am insanely grateful that he is wearing his black facemask. If I'd been able to see the sun-warmed dark blue of his eyes, I think I'd have . . .

I try to remember what he'd said, and then pretend he'd been talking about the files.

"Okay, former Boy Wonder, what'd you find?"

Nightwing gazes at me for what seems like an hour, giving me way too much time to take in the glossy sheen of his black hair and the high cut of his cheekbones, and then suddenly he becomes all business.

"An address. Batman asked me to find files belonging to a shrink who works for the government. He said I'd understand what he wanted as soon as I figured out who my mark was, and he was right. My guy's assigned to an international terrorist named Sin Tzu, so we have to assume that's who's behind the assault tonight. I just found the psychiatrist's home address and a lead on which branch of the CBI he works for, so I figured I'd run by his office and see if I can't dig up Sin Tzu's psych eval. Knowing those guys, it's probably worthless, but you never know."

"Won't the CBI be heavily guarded?" I ask.

"I sure hope so," Nightwing answers, grinning again. He takes his work very seriously, but he also seems to enjoy it more than your average costumed vigilante. I'm with him there. I think it's a blast.

"So these psychiatric files will help Batman profile his enemy. Good. What's he doing now?"

"Clayface has taken over Gotham Chemical, and is threatening to contaminate the whole city with RenuYou. Batman went off to stop him, but here's the thing. About three seconds after Clayface went down, your dad got a tip about a weapon of mass destruction coming into Gotham Harbor."

"A weapon of mass destruction? Like a nuclear device?"

"Maybe. Or maybe a chemical bomb, or some sort of germ warfare—it could be anything. Or nothing for that matter, though Batman doesn't think Sin Tzu would bluff. The ship has probably already docked by now, so the longer it takes Batman to get through Gotham to the docks, the less time he has to find the weapon before it's too late."

"Which docks?" I ask, a note of panic in my voice. Hopefully it was Port Adams, which was a reasonable size, or Miller Harbor. Just not—

"The Dixon Docks," he answers gravely. They cover the entire west side of the South Island. "But we don't know which pier or which ship."

"Shouldn't you be there looking?" I ask, alarmed.

"That was my thought when I heard the news, but Batman's orders were very clear. He says we have to neutralize from the top down, which means finding Sin Tzu himself. And right now, Sin Tzu's psychiatrist is our best lead for that, so that's the mission objective Batman wants me to cover."

"Okay," I say, running the possibilities through in my head; in my mind I was already at the docks, looking for likely hiding places. "But that doesn't mean *I* can't head down there . . . What?" I ask, finally realizing he's looking at me sort of funny.

"Nothing," he says, smiling in a way unlike his previous grins. This one was more . . . thoughtful, tender almost. "I just . . . the way you kind of check out when something really grabs your attention—it's just been a while since I've seen that, that's all." He pauses, then adds, "I guess I've really missed it." He hesitates again, then says, almost shyly, "I guess I really missed you."

I laugh, waiting for the punch line. "Yeah, yeah. Like a case of Lyme disease that keeps coming back, right?"

"Exactly." He laughs too, then shakes his head, his voice softening again, like a caress. "No, dummy, I mean it. You haven't been around much and I really have, you know, missed you."

I smile at him, swallowing. I hadn't forgotten how unexpectedly sweet he could sometimes be, but it is still startling. Of course, he has no idea that his light banter is killing me. So I do the only thing I can do; I give it right back.

"Mm. Which explains why you left Gotham for a year. You don't call, you don't write, and here you are expecting me to just fall into your arms once again."

"Well," he says. "I don't really recall that you ever actually fell into my arms before—except for that one time the Riddler managed to knock you off Parobeck Towers—and I wouldn't say I was exactly *expecting* it . . . but I've thought about it."

He lets his easy smile slowly heat up into a full-wattage grin. "And I've heard worse ideas."

I shake my head at him. For someone so nice and so brilliant, he can sure be obtuse sometimes. Well, two can play at that game. "Uh-huh. Don't we have a few lunatics to stop first?"

He nods good-naturedly, but I think I see a shift in his jaw, and for the first time I wonder if maybe, just maybe, behind all the playful give-and-take, he is serious. I half start to say something, but he's already turned away. *Idiot, idiot, idiot,* I yell to myself, not sure to whom I'm referring.

We head for the window. He steps back and allows me

to go first, gesturing in an exaggeratedly gallant way. I curtsy in response, which draws a surprised laugh from him. As I pass him, his hand lightly brushes my hip. For the first time in my life, I almost swoon, as much from the adrenaline rush I receive whenever we touch as from the knowledge that when a guy controls his every movement the way this one does, a brief, gentle, accidental contact is no accident.

"I'm . . . heading for the docks," I say quietly, over my shoulder. Behind me, Nightwing nods.

"I feel safer already." He smiles. And then I'm on my way towards the docks and he's gone, off to search for our enemy's confidant.

It's impossible not to worry about Dad on my way over. The whole city, really, but for me, that tends to crystallize down to just Dad, who I know is always on the front lines of the action. I have a moment of panic and frustration, worrying over him and everybody else in Gotham and wondering what I can do.

And then I realize that there is no greater service I can perform than working for Batman, under direct orders or not. And that's what I have to concentrate on.

So now I'm perched on a water tower at the edge of the docks, looking at the hundreds of ships, any one of which could take an entire day for one person to search. Which one holds the Big Surprise . . . and what, exactly, *is* the Big Surprise? If I knew that, maybe figuring out which ship was the lucky winner would be easier.

Yeah, and if they just held up a sign saying "Weapon of Mass Destruction Here!" that'd help too, now wouldn't it? Time to stop wishing I had a Magic 8-Ball and get to work.

I slow my heart rate down to fifty beats a minute, and open all my senses. I remember Dick teaching me this back when he was still Robin, and my pulse starts to race again. *Down, girl,* I remind myself. *You've got a job to do.* I begin to get my heart rate back under control, but not before remembering that casual brush and deciding that maybe, just maybe, he felt the same way. Was that really possible?

Okay. Hundreds of enormous ships, three dock night watchmen, eighteen visible crew members from my position. What doesn't belong here? What's missing? What *does* belong here but isn't?

I've already swiped the manifests for each of the ships from the dock's office—one more thing I'd picked up from Nightwing—and have them memorized. None of the Bat-guys had to teach me to do that, I happen to be blessed with an eidetic memory—photographic memory in layman's terms. One glance at something and I've memorized it for life. Now I just have to let my subconscious do the work and hope it filters fast enough.

Less than two percent of all ships coming into this country get inspected—there are simply way too many to do otherwise—so the chances that the normal procedures will nail this one are miniscule. If it's going to happen, it's up to me.

One by one, my brain matches up the memorized manifests to the ships. So far, everything is copacetic. I move farther north up the docks, now running across the warehouse rooftops adjacent to the piers. My heart seems more aware of the passage of time than I would like, and starts to speed up again. I force myself to calm back down and just look without looking. It'll come eventually. I head a bit farther north.

Something about one of the ships feels wrong.

It is quite a ways farther down the dock, at number forty-seven. I make my way towards it, keeping to the shadows—not an easy thing to do when a large percentage of your costume is yellow. What had I been thinking? Of course, Nightwing didn't seem to mind . . .

Knock it off, I say, slapping myself mentally.

By now I'm on one of the freighters opposite the suspicious one. But what about it makes it suspicious? Nothing obvious leaps out at me. Was I wrong? Had I jumped to an erroneous conclusion?

Let's see. There are several crew members on board, walking around slowly. Some of the other ships had none, others had even more than this one. Nothing concrete there.

It is flying a French flag, yet the few words I'd heard the crew members speak were certainly not French. Again, nothing unusual—shipping companies register their ships with whatever country has the best insurance rates and policies at that point in time, regardless of the owners' nationalities or residences. And the nationality of the crew has equally little to do with the nationality of the owner.

The crew, I realize, is speaking Quraci. Okay, that is a little bit odd—without normalized relations with Qurac, there wasn't a whole lot of trade between our two countries. But it also isn't unknown to happen, so in and of itself, nothing conclusive.

Come on, come on. There's gotta be something there. You're just not seeing it. Or more accurately, you already saw it, you just don't know what it is you saw. Now figure it out.

All right. The ship's manifest says it's carrying textiles—rugs and sweaters, mainly—and that's consistent with a Quraci crew, as well as its port of origin, Cairo. So what's making me jumpy?

Two things, I realize suddenly: First of all, now that I'm closer, I notice that there aren't an unusual number of crewmen walking around on deck, but I sure am seeing an unusually large number of them peering out from here and there. Far, far more than is normal for two in the morning.

And the second thing is that the ship is sitting much lower in the water than it should be. The displacement for a ship this size is considerable. Add a full cargo of textiles and it's even larger. This one, however, is riding way too low in the water.

There is something more than textiles in there.

"What are you doing here?"

My blood goes cold. It's as if every muscle in my body instantly cramps. My pulse doubles immediately. My mouth goes dry. I force myself to speak. I can just barely hear the tremble in my voice. Unfortunately, I'm sure *he* does.

"Trying to stop a madman from destroying Gotham. And how are *you?*"

Having thus delivered this devastating *bon mot*, I'm able to glance casually over my shoulder. What I see makes my heart stop for a moment. It's only a moment . . . but it seems like an age.

It doesn't matter that I've seen him hundreds of times. It doesn't matter that I've seen him bleed, that I know he's human. It doesn't matter that I even know his secret identity—not who he is, mind you, but who he sometimes pretends to be during the day—and where he lives and how he became what he is today. No matter how much I try, none of that matters.

Because when you're in his presence you have a hard time thinking anything but, *Oh. Wow. Where did he come from? I sure hope he doesn't hurt me.*

He's not actually that tall—somewhere around six foot three, give or take an inch. And he's not that big, per se—usually around two twenty-five.

Except that he's huge. He's somehow bigger than you

would have thought a human being could get. It's utterly inexplicable. It's like trying to wrap your head around the actual size and scope of the universe, and then trying to imagine that it's still expanding, and then trying to place yourself in relation to something of that magnitude.

Batman knocks out all perspective.

"How many aboard?"

And that's another thing. His voice, it's like broken glass and sand that a heavy boot is crushing against concrete. It's usually soft, but it always carries exactly as far as he wants it to. And it's as clear as crystal and as sharp as a scalpel. It's not a fun thing to hear coming from behind you.

"I've counted twelve so far." *Hey*, I think, *he trusts my intelligence report. Cool.*

"Have you determined what's inside?"

"Not yet," I admit. "But I noticed the water displacement and—"

"And it didn't match up with the cargo listed on the manifest."

Unbelievable. "Lucky guess," I say. And then, more sulkily than I mean to, "How did *you* figure out which one it was?"

He cocks his head slightly to one side, and then shakes it.

"I just got here. I'm following your lead on this one."

"Oh." I nod. What I was thinking was, *You mean I found the ship with the weapon of mass destruction!? All by myself? And if not for my being here, you'd still be looking for it? Really for real? How cool is that?*

"Thank you for your help, Miss Gordon," he says. "You've saved me a great deal of time. Now go home."

I finally turn all the way around. "Now, wait—there

are at *least* a dozen guys on there, and maybe three times that number. You're going to need me to—"

He's gone.

Which at least gives me a chance to catch my breath. Batman is a good guy, a hero, the best chance we've got of surviving the night. And yet he's utterly terrifying, like everything dark and unpredictable about the city personified and set loose and arbitrarily on your side.

A moment later I notice that two of the crew members up top are no longer present.

The final crewman is still walking around slowly. And then he isn't.

A shadow moves across his body, as though a cloud were crossing the full moon, and he simply goes limp. But he doesn't hit the deck. He starts to collapse, as though all the bones have instantly vanished from his body, and he falls backwards, as if a gale-force wind has blown the sack of skin which had seconds earlier been a massive sailor into a dark corner where it wouldn't be noticed for hours.

I wait. A minute later, all but one of the few lights on board have been extinguished. Finally, after three minutes I hear a shriek coming from the lighted room near the top.

I know how the screamer feels. I'd been there, only I'd known that Batman wouldn't hurt me. I'd known that, in fact, he wouldn't hesitate to give his life to save me—yet every time he snuck up on me in the dark, I felt like screaming. And the people on that ship had no such luck. Batman had no problem at all about hurting the people guarding Sin Tzu's weapon of mass destruction.

There is the sound of shattering glass, running feet, and gunshots. More screams. A snapping sound. A few grunts, as air is expelled from lungs that will gasp uselessly for an eternal fifteen seconds before they begin to work again. Two more gunshots. Someone begging for mercy in Quraci. A soft thud. And then silence.

I realize I am shaking. I'd witnessed this kind of scene before. But there are some things you just never get used to.

When I see a dark shape glide across the deck and toss something large and orange over the side, I understand why I'd heard the scream so close by—among his other attributes, Batman's practical. He wanted to get as many near the top as possible so he wouldn't have far to move them. Why he is tossing them overboard is still a mystery, however, so I decide to do a little detective work.

As I learned in my one college journalism class, nothing beats going right to the source. I make my way across to the freighter, stepping over the unconscious bodies, and see him tossing another crew member off the side—he'd thoughtfully put a life jacket on each of them first. "What are you doing? Why not just keep them on board?"

"Because I don't want them waking up in the Batcave."

My mouth falls open and I take a step back. "You . . . you don't . . . you . . . *what?*"

He tosses another pair over. "I don't know what's on this ship and I can't risk it going off here before I find out—the entire city could be contaminated for decades for all I know. In the cave the city will be shielded by a hundred feet of sheer rock. The risk is minimal."

"Except to yourself!" I nearly shout.

For the first time, Batman stops and looks me in the eyes. "Yes?" he asks, clearly implying, *And what's your point? Would you prefer I risk others?*

I turn away, gritting my teeth. Of course that wasn't what I meant. I know as well as anyone the risks we take, especially him. I grab one of the unconscious sailors, slipping a life jacket on him—not easy to do with two hundred and fifty unconscious pounds—drag him up and over to the railing, then tip him over. He hits with a satisfying splash and immediately begins to sputter and then curse in Quraci. My Quraci's a bit rusty, but I more than get the gist.

Batman and I each dump several more overboard—I lose count but I'm sure there were at least nineteen—and then he disappears. I have just noticed when he reappears behind me, like an afterthought.

"Thank you for finding the ship," he says darkly, staring at me hard. There is no mistaking that what he means is, *Go home right now.* Still, I appreciate his effort to couch it in more gracious terms.

"Nightwing deployed me," I offer, wondering if that will make any difference to him.

"Get clear." He nods. And then he is gone again.

"Good luck," I whisper.

A minute later the deck begins to hum. Shortly after that, the ship begins to move. I run to the edge and jump as far as I can. I just make the dock.

I stand there, catching my breath, watching the freighter slowly get smaller. One word keeps going through my head: *incredible*; I'm not entirely sure to what or to whom it refers. I gradually become aware of the sounds of wet clothing rustling, accompanied by the spitting of water; the sailors are gradually making their way up onto the dock.

As the first crewman stands up, I step out of the shadows. His eyes get very large, his face gets very red, and he says something extremely uncharitable in Quraci about my family history and my extracurricular activities. He pulls a very large knife out of his pocket and runs towards me. He must have seven inches and a hundred and fifty pounds on me.

It isn't even close.

As he tries to impale me on his dagger, I step back, placing my weight on my right foot. I grab his right wrist with my right hand, place my left hand on his right elbow, and push up, over, and then down towards the ground. The guy has no sense of balance. He goes down like a sack of wet, crushed bricks. As he does, a very clear snap can be heard.

I've never experienced it, but I understand that having a broken elbow is extremely painful.

It must be, because he can't even scream. He just lies on the ground, his mouth open, his eyes practically falling out of his head, breathing slowly but very, very hard.

I don't have time to admire my work, though, because two more are coming towards me and I can hear others on their way. One down, at least eighteen to go. I'd be going home, just like Batman had oh-so-politely requested. But not for a while, it seemed.

No one in Batman's army would ever surrender the field.

TEN

Sin Tzu
3:15 A.M.

Clayface has been defeated. The weapon of mass destruction will soon be in the Batman's hands, if it is not already. In mere moments, he will convey it to his secret lair. It is the only location he can take the weapon to disarm it, given that Gotham is in chaos.

He must know that I have carefully crafted the dilemma that binds him. The Batman has proven to be a scholar of my work. He knows the best defense is always a devastating attack on your enemy's stronghold. Attack it openly, if you know its location, to draw your opponent to defend it. Or, if it is secret, attack it by stealth, the better to take him unawares.

In his heart he must now know that, had destruction of the city been my goal, I would simply have unleashed my lethal weapon openly. So, clearly, this ship of deadly crates is a trap. A trap he must take back with him to his hidden fortress, the Batcave.

I have already assaulted the Batman's city. But I have not yet violated his home, his secret nest. Now he is forced to open his most private, most vulnerable place to me. He has no choice. He must either ignore the weapon of mass destruction or ignore the battle on the streets.

And he loves his city. He is mired in compassion for its citizenry. So he cannot take the chance that this weapon is a ruse. He cannot follow his heart and yet he does not believe his mind. He is torn between the yin and the yang. This is the most artful and exquisite dilemma in which one commander can place another.

But even within that art, there is a greater art still.

The Batman and I have spoken, at last. We have seen each other's faces. He begins to understand the scope of our conflict. And he knows that he dances to my tune.

It goes well.

I reflect on what was said: his verbal sparring, his obvious knowledge of my writings. I think about his voice, dark and jagged. Was it that conversation that made me hunger for more direct contact? Or was this always our fate?

For, after our conversation and as he made his way from the defeated monster's arena atop Gotham Chemical to the docks, I allowed myself a moment's indulgence. I dipped gently into Mehta-Sua and sent my inner eye roving through the streets, seeking out one of the warriors I had planted in Gotham's byways. I had planned a small diversion for the Batman on his way to the mysterious weapon of mass destruction. One of my Eternal Elite guards, planted along his likeliest route. Certainly my warrior could face the Batman on its own. But I longed to see the Batman in action myself.

I spied the Dark Knight from the corners of my consciousness. As expected, he had chosen his path through the most problematic streets, the ones not covered by his costumed warriors. Compassion again, his incessant need to care for and protect this city.

When I found him, he was effortlessly dispatching some of the denizens of Stonegate Prison. I settled in behind the eyes of my guard to watch.

His fighting style is truly remarkable. He possesses both speed and power, and eliminates anticipation of his blows by never using the same move twice. Each opponent was neutralized in a unique manner. He effortlessly switched strategies from intimidation to stealth and back again. Never had I seen such a creature.

My appetite for battle was honed. I abandoned my earlier plans of creating a slight delay for the Batman, and resolved to truly test his skill against my best guards, one of the Eternal Elite, face to face.

The sensation of pain broke suddenly through my mental armor: a hot, tight cramp in my left temple. The spirits screeched. They told me that I was foolish, arrogant, brash. I shouted them down: It is quite possible that before this night ends, I will face the Batman myself. It would be ludicrous to ignore that opportunity to gain an upper hand! And should my Elite kill him, then the matter will be solved, his unworthiness proved. I had kept away from the field long enough this night. I had earned this one match.

The spirits clamored for my attention, filling my mind with curses and mumbles in a thousand voices, but I ignored them. I am Sin Tzu. This night is mine.

I activated my Eternal Elite. A moment before, he had appeared to be a life-sized clay statue on the streets of Chinatown. Once initiated, he revealed himself for what he truly was: a master of the ancient arts of killing.

The Batman spun and saw him instantly. Never before had I witnessed such an eye for the battlefield. He's instinctive, hyper-alert. He leapt into action. Even as he flew through the air in a move that was both evasive and offensive, a move with no name I know, he was assessing the skills of my warrior. He saw the dagger, useful as both a ranged and close weapon. He saw the sword. He was fully in the moment.

He landed on top of a scowling stone foo dog that guarded a nearby Chinese restaurant. He seemed to balance uneasily. Before I could consider, I telepathed to the guard to throw the dagger. It whizzed through the air, directly towards the bat on my enemy's chest. I saw a flash of teeth. A laugh or a grimace? My answer came as the Batman deftly swiped the dagger from the air and then calmly inspected it.

I realized that his off-balanced appearance was, in fact, a ruse which effectively disarmed my guard of both a close-kill and ranged weapon. And although I cursed my gullibility, I could not help but feel a thrill of anticipation. This battle will indeed be an even match.

The Batman regarded the dagger first as a weapon and then as an artifact.

"Pre-dynastic . . ." he said, to himself as much as to my automaton. "Flawless craftsmanship. This ought to be in a museum, not a street fight." He jumped from the foo dog to a flagpole, from the flagpole to a balcony, from the balcony to statuary, and then from building to building, from light to darkness, circling behind my fighter, causing him to reposition himself in the center of the street.

I realized that he was testing both for speed and range of motion. He had seized the facing initiative so that my guard had to react to whatever he did. He fought in the street the way one might command a battle. His strategy and tactics were flawless.

The Batman feinted, close enough to watch how my guard handled a sword—close enough that the automaton was forced to swing at him, far enough that he couldn't hit.

The Batman had not yet used an offensive attack. All know that the Batman does not use firearms or explosives, which would have ended the fight in an instant. But why didn't he use one of his curved Batarangs? I saw him size up in a glance the studded leather armor that my guard wore. No, a Batarang would not penetrate its thickness. The Batman probed for weakness. Quickly, I reviewed. I could think of nothing extraordinary, save for the vulnerability all armor possesses by necessity . . . the eye slits, the breathing holes, the joints . . . the thickness that could slow my warriors down.

And then I knew that that was precisely what the Batman would exploit.

Finally, the Batman made his first attack. Gas. He dropped a pellet. I forced the guard to collapse. He resisted; a true warrior does not give up the fight. For a moment, I was surprised—my Eternal Elite, questioning my command? But it passed swiftly. The guard dropped to the ground.

The Batman approached him warily. I waited for the precise moment to strike.

And then I had to laugh. The Batman had anticipated this. He jumped out of the way as the sword moved in an arcing blow.

By then I knew that my intended ruse of falling was a mistake. The Batman had immediately detected my deceit. He had traded the risk of a stunning sword blow for the advantage he would gain if my guard ever hit the ground.

As my guard attempted to get up in his bulky armor, the Batman was quick. He slid his hand under the guard's helmet and around to the back of his neck. He squeezed. But the response was not what he expected. For the warriors of my Eternal Elite are not living things and cannot be stunned.

The Batman recoiled and looked at his hand, covered in dust. I saw his face shift as he realized that the guard was dead—thousands of years dead. But yet living.

He acted instantly. His hand swung in a mighty blow, dislodging the soldier's mask. My guard fell again to the ground. I was taken aback. How did the Batman discover my Eternal Elite's weakness so quickly? I rushed to disengage myself from the shattering clay figure. For few men know this, but all living things die in degrees. Even at the moment of death, some senses live on, polluting the Mehta-Sua for minutes, even hours. The energy of dying is exhilarating, brilliant, overwhelming. I did not want its oily weight distracting my mind.

I retrieved my consciousness just in time. I could only imagine how my guard saw the world as the Batman pulled off its clay mask, and the look of surprise and revulsion on the Batman's face when the soldier crumbled to dust the moment its face was exposed to the air of the night.

The Batman instantly turned and disappeared into the shadows. He did not linger. There is a city to save, still. He resumed his advance towards the docks.

And now my guard is dead. Truly, irretrievably dead. Only a handful more remain with me in the shipment I have allocated to Gotham for this battle.

The spirit voices stab at me with accusing tones. One of the most loyal of their Eternal Elite is gone.

I fight down their cries. I will replenish our army from the vanquished, I tell them. Even the Batman himself might serve as one of my soldiers after his utter and abject defeat. For I have written:

You can not trust a man until you have crushed his soul and then given it back to him.

The spirits growl and hiss and howl. I am too caught up in this challenge, they cry, too caught up in him. I am not heeding their wisdom. I have made the mistake of allowing myself to be distracted from the fight to focus on one figure only. That I myself have selected the Batman as my specific opponent means nothing to the spirits. They care only for conquest on its most impersonal scale.

I argue back. I defend myself with our own words:

If you enter a battle knowing neither your thoughts nor your enemies' thoughts, you have no chance of winning.

I have gained information and I have lost nothing.

But still they clamor. To quiet them, I close my eyes and summon images of hatred and greed; vague, impersonal. I control the masses of Stonegate Prison through general telepathy. With a single Mehta-Sua-fueled mental flick, I exhort my berserker masses to remember the moment of their capture and imprisonment. I send them images of treasure to be plundered.

I care not what happens to them. Many times, I send them to their deaths, if death helps accomplish their objective.

Oh great spirits, you think me weak, my plans foolish? You think I cannot spare a moment to plumb the weaknesses of my enemy counterpart in this war? You are wrong, and you distract me from my greater purpose. Perhaps the student has finally outstripped the masters. See my strategy in action!

I show them one criminal among my thousands, a hulking, sweaty mass of a man with four-day stubble on his iron jaw. Even now, he rushes a police barricade with a bottle full of gasoline. Fear drips from the police officer, who is contaminated with compassion; he does not want to kill the man. As the criminal draws close, the policeman hesitates, his finger on the trigger. At the last possible moment he fires his weapon. There is a loud detonation. Lead rips through the chest of the attacker, but still he comes.

He lets go of the bottle. As with many crises, this creates a moment of temporal distortion, a long-drawn-out instant as the bottle tumbles through the air. All eyes watch. The criminal falls backward, instinctively clutching a hand to his bleeding wound. The policeman dives, eyes dilated with fear. There is an exquisite sound of shattering glass as the bottle strikes a police car. There is the WHUMPH! of gasoline igniting. The squad car is instantly consumed by flames.

The police retreat. The vicious fire spreads. I withdraw from the scene, secure in the knowledge that I have shown the spirits enough. It is clear what will happen next. The flames will eat their way through to the gas tank of the police car and force it to explode, sending fire and metal soaring in all directions. Many of the attackers will be killed. Police will be wounded. The conflagration will spread to buildings nearby. Eventually the heat of the twisted metal will ignite the many rounds of live ammunition in the police car. Stray bullets will fly, spreading chaos. Other abandoned police cars nearby will flame and the pattern will repeat. The fires in the buildings will spread. When the firemen reach the scene, some of their own will be hit by exploding bullets.

In the end, it will be necessary for all of the Stonegate criminals to die. One cannot command troops for long when he does not fully trust them. They are useful, but expendable. Ultimately of low karma and unworthy.

The spirits seem appeased. They do not distrust the

plan. It is only my obsession with the Batman as a rival that makes them uneasy. I wish I understood why.

Behind me, I feel the two ninja guards on the balcony shift.

My guards. I have written:

Soldiers only fight for a small set of motives: love of their commander, fear of their commander, hatred of the enemy, hope for treasure, or love of battle itself. The more of these motives that are present, the harder the troops will fight. The commanding general must fuel all of these when possible. The great commander knows why his forces fight for him.

My Eternal Elite fight for me out of necessity, for I am the Sin Tzu, the incarnation of the great commanders they have followed for thousands of years. I use them sparingly, because they are finite. I was granted three hundred of them in the tomb. Some dozens of them have been spent through the years in my earlier battles. I shipped a mere handful here with me, to Gotham. And now one of this precious number is gone, due to my lust to engage the Batman.

Then so be it. When Gotham is conquered, I will write a new maxim of battle:

All troops, no matter how loyal or specialized, are expendable in the face of battle.

Perhaps the spirits become oversentimental.

The guards behind me are humans, ninja. They fight for me out of reverence, awed by my powers and by what I have allowed the Eternal Guard to teach them. I can sense their slow, polluted minds. Behind me, one is unquestioning. But the other entertains doubt in his sad excuse for a brain, that pathetic muddy wad denser even than the clay bricks within my stone Eternal Elite.

He does not approve of my choice of tactics. He does not like the way I use the Batman's strange modern communicator to steer the battle. Like the spirits, he does not trust the way I turned from the battle to focus on my foe.

This distrust cannot be tolerated. I have written:

Far more dangerous than any enemy is an ally who stands in the way of victory. The worst of those is he who doubts his commander, for he will sow the seeds of insurrection.

It does not matter that he has fighting skills beyond the ken of most mortal men. Nor does it matter that he sacrificed any chance at a normal life to join my ranks. The spirits, from whom I receive my power, may question. My foot soldiers may not.

Still facing the theater of my war, my back to both ninja guards, I summon the Yanjin with a motion in my mind that is echoed by my body: a slow, graceful coming together of the hands, collecting the power, and then throwing it outward in a sudden, deathly release.

It radiates from my entire being, hitting the targeted ninja like a shock wave. His eyes grow huge, and his mouth opens in a terrified, questioning *O*. His face and body begin to compact, as if all his flesh is being squeezed together by some invisible exterior force. Blood seeps from his bulging eyes, his ears. His body starts to vibrate on an increasingly frantic frequency, forcing his posture to go rigid as his tongue rolls out from his mouth, flaccid and dry.

The ninja beside him steps quickly away, an instinctive

move tinged as much with revulsion as fear. The Yanjin will not touch him unless I direct it towards his unique energy signature, but in his frantic ignorance he considers throwing himself off the tower to spare himself his associate's fate. I bask in his terror. One component of all reverence is fear. For must not all creatures both love and tremble before their gods?

Vibrating at ever increasing frequencies, the targeted guard finally ceases movement altogether, seeming to hang in midair, as if suspended by his own excruciating pain.

As I again begin to chant and summon the Yanjin, the doubting one doubts no longer. He knows that his fate is sealed. His eyes roll towards me as if begging for forgiveness, but the fool should know better than to expect mercy from Sin Tzu. I do not harbor the Batman's weakness for compassion. I will not be made to entertain limitations such as mercy or doubt.

The entire world twists and distorts as I suck in not only the light and electricity around me, but also the sound and microwaves which constantly flow through the air. I summon them, process them, and then I unleash them, full force, onto my guard.

With one final scream of spiritual agony only I can hear, he crumbles to dust before us, leaving a small pile of sandy ash. I watch as it sifts gently from the bat-carved floor of the balcony. It powders me, the boots of my loyal guard, and those of the second guard who comes instantly to replace the traitor. By now, these guards have washed all thoughts of him from their minds. They think only of the battles ahead.

From my vantage post at Arkham, I survey the grounds. My eyes burn. The sky is filled with fire and smoke. All of the smells have merged into one smell, a scent so thick it is better called the taste of battle. My ears are filled with cacophony. Sirens wail in all directions. The continuous sounds of shattering glass and gunshots merge with the static of captured police scanners, AM, FM, and satellite radios, televisions playing simultaneously in the homes of frightened civilians across the city. Everywhere, there is confusion. Police call out for backup that will never come. They have no idea what to attack, or where. Citizens can neither fight nor flee.

It is the music of victory.

The spirit voices congratulate me. The swift reprimand has soothed their concerns. Once again, we are of one mind, one body. I have triumphed. United, we turn our attention back to the war on Gotham.

The union of Sin Tzu and the voices of the Mehta-Sua cannot be defeated by any earthly means. The Batman is doomed.

The one device I would like to listen to is silent: the communicator the Batman uses with the others. They are now aware that I share their frequencies, and that I will be listening. Perhaps they knew this earlier, but the Batman now knows that I know, so there is no tactical advantage left in their use. Neither he, nor Gordon, nor the others under the Batman's command will say anything they do not intend for me to hear.

Perhaps the spirits were correct. Was it wise to speak and thus let him know that I was listening to him? Would it have been more judicious to remain silent? Perhaps, one day, I will look back and see that the moment I confronted the Batman after Clayface had fallen was the moment when I turned the battle against myself: the one single, solitary act in which I gave in to my vanity and taunted my opponent.

No. The highest art of generalship is to place one's opponent in the position from which any path he takes will lead to his destruction. My communication was necessary, a part of the overall battle plan. I have achieved my goals here as I have in the past. My skill is uncompromised. My strategy flawless.

The Batman is out of the battle. Even now, he ferries the boxes holding the mysterious weapon of mass destruction to his hidden lair. I will not make the mistake of underestimating him now. No matter what the spirits claim, to know the Batman is to find the tools of his defeat.

On the Gotham pier, the Batman once again made the compassionate choice—to sacrifice himself, if necessary, for Gotham.

And, once again, it will be his downfall.

I close my eyes in meditation. This time, the spirits leap to aid my contemplation. I ignore the sounds around me. I ignore the tastes and smells. I imagine myself in the stygian darkness. I reach out to channel the Batman's thoughts. What is he thinking? Does he suspect the nature of the latest trap I have set for him?

I do not tap the Mehta-Sua to enter and twist his mind. That pleasure I leave for later. For now, I have no need. I know what he is thinking.

He is thinking about me.

I imagine his thoughts, and having finally heard his voice, I am able to have the sense of hearing them aloud: "From Sin Tzu, I must expect deceit, strategies within strategies, tricks within tricks—deceit wrapped in other deceits. The question is: How do I defend against him?"

Perhaps he carries with him a gadget that could disarm a chemical weapon. He is a man of devices and tools, because he lacks extraordinary, superhuman powers. But my weapon of mass destruction is of such a scale that I doubt any mere handheld tool will match the challenge.

Whatever the Batman's secret hideout, he must have a

splendid array of equipment. I know that he has these electronic crutches, because he could not function without them. Somewhere there must be a gymnasium. I suspect there are quintains of amazing complexity, for one cannot keep up such mental focus and physical strength without constant training. Though I am sure his nightly prowls keep him in top physical form, I feel equally sure that he punishes himself with a formal exercise regime. He is a man of iron discipline.

Perhaps he keeps trophies—those things to remember his successes, or, more likely, those things that goad him with his defeats. Intriguing bits of torture to remind him that he is, after all, mortal and fallible. Does he keep something that harkens back to the source of his rage? Is there a shrine?

Or does he keep his den sparse and bare, an altar of technological marvels? I know of the Batmobile, the Batplane and the Batboat. Where I have my spirits and the aid of the Mehta-Sua, he must rely on the earthly network of supercomputer, telecommunications, and surveillance equipment. We each are attached to our net of control.

Is it likely that one mere man can command all of these resources? I know of his costumed captains out on the field. They are effective, true. I counted on their efforts to free the Batman from the raging war in Gotham and isolate him within his cave. But I do not feel the presence of a cohesive team. I do not think the Batman has brothers and sisters. I do not think he has a wife. I do not sense a lover. I suspect his life is as celibate as mine. It is unlikely that he has close relationships at all. Allies, yes, but kept at a distance. He would not possess anything that would distract him from his mission. I am certain that the Batman has no human links.

In that way, the Batman and I are curiously alike.

Perhaps that is what draws me to this polluted Western town, with its meaningless loops of commercial, political, and criminal activity. Of all the generals I have faced, only the Batman seems to feel no love for life. The very things he protects in Gotham—hope, innocence, weakness—he does not value in himself. He has sacrificed them on the altar of Gotham.

Like me, he serves a demanding god. But while I serve War, what does the Batman serve?

No matter. Such speculation is futile. The spirits prickle at the edges of my mind and I obey. I must move quickly now. Should the Batman survive, I must prepare for our inevitable clash. I almost feel joy at the thought. The Master of Fear and the Malleable One have fallen. One more remains.

Bane.

Should he survive this challenge, I can then expect the delight of luring the Batman, oh so battered, oh so broken, to my door. To, as has happened so often this night, the place he least expects. To my fortress. To Arkham.

I patiently await my chance to deliver the final blow.

ELEVEN

Ramon Domingo, Thug
4:07 A.M.

Madre de Dios.

The moment I set eyes on the Batman, I know—I did not sign up for this.

No. I must tell the truth.

In truth, at the time I offered my services for hire, I not only did not know what I was signing up for, I did not care. This was my chance to get away from this stinking hellhole—Peña Duro, the armpit of the earth. An island named for an imaginary saint, and famous for two things: the world's most crooked politicians, and the most dangerous jail on the planet. A jail where the worst of the worst got sent by every other country to fight it out for the spot of top dog.

This was my home.

But not for long.

I was going to the Promised Land. Gotham.

Oh, *sí, sí,* we had all heard the tales, even down here, of Gotham's dark and dangerous and mysterious bogeyman, the Batman. And perhaps some of the children here believed it. But not many. I certainly did not. Only those willing to fight, and even kill, to get—maybe—one meal a day survive to see their fifth birthday in this place. And so, by the time I got my adult hairs, I had killed well over a hundred people, some twice or even three times my age, just to survive. A man who dressed up like a bat held no terror for me.

There were those, of course, who claimed he didn't dress like a bat, that he *was* a bat, a demon from hell. I laughed at this. No, no, I assured them, there is only one hell. It is Peña Duro.

A hell I, Ramon Domingo, was determined to escape.

So when I got word that someone was looking for a few of Peña Duro's toughest men to do some dirty work, I was the first one in line. Well, at least I was after I killed the two men in front of me and the others very graciously decided to allow me to move ahead. Perhaps they would have moved even without this gentle persuasion, based on my reputation alone, but one does not take chances in Peña Duro.

I was a little disappointed, actually. Killing as much as I have, you learn to appreciate the art. And killing only two men, you hardly have time to really get into the mood, to truly enjoy the soft *slish* as your knife slides smoothly into a belly, with no resistance. For if there's resistance, you know you've hit bone, and what kind of idiot makes a mistake like that? Unless you feel the gentle twist of the blade nicking the spine, in which case it means you've gone all the way through. Then it's okay.

Either way, as you pull the blade back out, you keep staring into the guy's eyes. Because it's when you pull the weapon out—no matter how quickly or how slowly—that you see his look of shock turn to confusion, and then to understanding and horror. And to know that you're the one that put it there . . . ah, that just starts your day off right.

Even when looking in his eyes, of course, you have to be aware of the sounds from down below, or you could end up with his blood on your pants and shoes—or worse. And that's no good; that red, sticky *sangre* never comes out.

So I was understandably confident when I saw the weakness of my competition. The word was that only the toughest of the tough would be accepted. And from the looks of my fellow applicants, the man in charge was going to be sorely disappointed by his options.

Except for me, of course.

And from there, it wouldn't be long before I would be the man in charge myself. I, as I had already shown, would kill to make it happen.

Then I met my employer.

I felt his footsteps, approaching from behind me, and heard the whisperings and gasps, the altered breathing of the men around me, long before I saw him. There was an acrid smell and I knew that more than one man had soiled himself. I did not turn around to look; I had no need to. I knew then who this man in charge must be. He was a legend. There could be no other on the island who would turn hardened killers into frightened infants.

Bane.

Yes, I am not ashamed to admit that even I felt fear then. Bane's intelligence, his ruthlessness, his very size were legendary. He had killed twice as many men as I by the time he was half my age. There were some who claimed he was actually one of triplets, but he had killed the others while still in the womb. The truth about him may never be known, except for one thing: He was the top dog on Peña Duro.

For now.

I knew it was unlikely I would ever be able to best him, but I was determined to do so or die trying. For if one cannot be the best, one is worthless. And I was not going to live my life worthless.

My life would mean something. I swore it would.

Bane had reached the front of the line. He was close enough for me to see the black Mexican wrestler mask covering his face and the tubes that ran from the back of his skull to a slim supply canister worn on his left wrist. The substance pumping into his body was called "venom," and there was no doubt what it did. His body mass was incalculable—he was like a walking steroid commercial, solid and huge.

Bane spoke in a dark, intelligent voice. "I require twelve men to do an impossible job which will almost certainly result in their deaths. Any who do manage to survive will live forever, with all the riches they could ever imagine."

Immortality? Riches? All I desired was the chance to leave Peña Duro behind. This job was starting to feel like a calling. Destiny.

Bane continued, his low rumble of a voice snapping me out of my reverie. "Who amongst you is worthy of this honor? We will find out now. You may begin."

Out of the nearly two hundred men in line, only perhaps thirty knew immediately what it was that Bane sought. The others were like sheep, looking around, awaiting further directions. Perhaps some were dazed with hunger because they hadn't eaten in days, and had joined the crowd in hopes of a handout. Others were simply hungry for a kill. And some were clearly now realizing they were far out of their depth. They were all about to discover their mistakes.

They were easy prey. Fifty fell lifeless before half a minute had passed.

Another fifty ran immediately.

Fifty more tried to escape but failed.

That left four dozen of us still standing. We circled each other warily, always mindful of those around us, sensing who might still be dispatched easily and who was true competition. A few gauged badly, and fell. The battle became even trickier now, as the ground was slick with blood. Lifeless bodies lay everywhere, and were easy to stumble over if you weren't careful.

I was careful. Many others were not—and died for it.

By now, I had extinguished the light of over twenty-five men, but only ten could truly be counted as competition. Many of the others were taken in the first minute, before they had any idea what was upon them.

There were now no more than twenty-five men left alive. And these men . . . these men meant business. They knew what they had to do and they had no qualms about doing so. In fact, they looked forward to it. I would come out triumphant, of course, that was a given, but it might be difficult. That was fine. It would make my eventual victory all the sweeter.

But it was not to be. As I lunged forward to slash the ligaments at the back of one man's knees, I felt a hand grab the hair on the back of my head and lift me off my feet.

I attempted to spin around, knowing it would likely rip half of my hairs out, and indeed, the pain which shot through my scalp told me I would have a bald spot for no short while. I swung out backhanded with my knife, waiting to feel the gratifying sensation of the blade slicing across my opponent's neck. I might even be able to cut through half of it, leaving a semi-decapitated corpse as my calling card. There would be no doubt then who was the alpha male here.

And indeed there was none.

My arm somehow swung against a brick wall. A sledgehammer slammed down on my wrist, causing me to drop my knife for the first time ever in my entire life. Faster than my eyes could see, or perhaps it was simply that my brain could not comprehend what was happening to me, I felt an enormous hand grab my ankle—no, both my ankles—and then in one sickening swoop I was hanging upside down, helpless. And I realized that, impossible as it seemed, all this had been done by one man.

Bane.

It was his arm, and not a wall, I had slammed against. It was his fist and not a sledgehammer which had almost broken my wrist. And the man was now holding me upside down as though I were a mere puppy of a boy. He was holding me straight out, in fact, with only one of his hands. Not both. One.

I was completely helpless.

Clearly, Bane sensed that I understood the situation, for he let me go. I managed to keep my head from slamming against the pavement and rolled away as quickly as I could to avoid the coming blow.

But I need not have bothered. He was not even looking at me. Relaxed, he was observing the fight, not with much interest, but as if, since there was nothing else to do, he might as well.

I stood up warily, unsure of myself. For the first time ever, the fight had not gone as I expected. What was I to do? Should I rejoin the fight? Stay here? Kill Bane? What was the right answer?

Perhaps this was the turning point of my entire life.

I had always been so sure that I would know when

that moment had arrived, the moment that would change everything. And yet here I was with no idea which way to go, like *una poca niña* with a grimy coin at a candy store, unsure which treat is the sweetest.

It took only a moment. I was a man of action. No one, not even Bane, would keep me from taking my rightful place as champion among the gladiators. I would rejoin the fight. It was going to be difficult to win now that I had no weapon, but I would cross that bridge when I got to it—I would simply kill whatever man had the largest knife and take it from him. I would keep my eye on Bane this time, however. And when I was finished with the others, then I would come back. And perhaps I would kill him, too, for the tremendous indignity he had done to me.

My mind thus made up, I felt my power returning. The blood lust was upon me again. I had spilled much blood this morning, but there were more veins yet to be opened.

"Stop."

I froze instantly. Bane had not moved a muscle and he was still not looking at me, but I knew it was I to whom he had spoken.

But no further word seemed to be forthcoming from him. Puzzled, I stood there once again, attempting to figure out the best course of action. But I could not fathom what was expected of me here. This was a situation like none other I had ever encountered before. In the past, whenever I had been unsure, I had simply killed someone and that usually cleared everything right up. But apparently I was not allowed to do so now. It made no sense.

I trembled, both from the urge to go and take a few more lives, to prove myself the greatest man here—although even I was beginning to admit to myself that Bane did not just frighten me, and was not simply much larger than me, but was clearly the better man—and also from the simple act of standing still. I never stood still. That was for the dead. If I was alive, I was moving.

That was how I stayed alive all these years. Moving, like a shark.

Bane laughed as though he read my very thoughts. "Conserve your strength, Ramonito. There is no need for you to prove anything else at this point. You will be joining me for the trip up to Gotham. And it seems as though you need some practice in being still."

I did not know how he knew my name and I did not like his tone as he continued, "Don't worry—you'll get more practice than you could ever have dreamed."

Still speaking to me, he reached out and plucked another man from the fight, much as he had done with me. I did not know his name, but recognized him as the man I had deemed the greatest threat, the one I had intended to go after last.

The battle of the others ended soon enough. Bane picked out another four men, grabbing them unceremoniously from the fight and pulling them silently to the side. They looked as uncomfortable and uncertain as I.

The six he picked, including me, were the best fighters, no question. Apparently unimpressed with the others, he let them fight it out until there were just half a dozen left standing amongst the carnage, covered in blood, wearied but ready to go as long as it took. If Bane was pleased, he showed no sign. "Put your weapons away," he simply said. "It's time to go."

And shortly after that we boarded the ship.

It was an enormous tanker, far larger than any of us had ever seen before—such ships did not usually come to Peña Duro. We had no oil, no automobile factories, nothing of use to anyone but our prison. And they only brought people *to* the prison, never away.

There was a crew of perhaps twenty-five men on board the tanker. They were much larger, thicker, and beefier than most of us Peña Durons—clearly they, unlike ourselves, ate every day. Later I was to learn to my astonishment that they almost always ate not once, but three times a day. I had heard of such people, but thought they were simply another fiction. Like Gotham's Batman.

These crew members were large, yes, some even fat. Yet even these *gordo* ones had a toughness underneath, a steel inside, that was obvious. I knew I could take any of them. But it would not be easy.

And it was not allowed. Our first day on board, Bane had warned us not to kill anyone while on the ship. Not the crew, and not among ourselves. "You will have plenty of opportunities for slaughter later," he assured us. "Do not waste any of my ammunition . . . or you will dearly regret it for the rest of your short lives."

Most of us took his words to heart, difficult as it was to live in peace for the first time.

But one fool among us must have felt he was above such rules. Or perhaps he did not understand the full implication of Bane's words. For he began taunting the others, stepping on feet, pushing, even slaps to the back of the head. It did not take long before tempers ran high, and things would have almost certainly exploded into death. We all knew that once the first blood was spilled, the entire ship would turn into a boat of charnel.

Bane clearly knew it as well. He waited until the fool had finally pushed someone too far—a gentle cupping of another's buttocks did the trick—and knives were drawn. Then out of nowhere he appeared, stepping in between the two men, turning their bloody knives effortlessly. One quick fist to the fool's forehead and he dropped to the deck as one dead.

We soon discovered he was not so, however. Although the fool soon made it quite clear he wished he were. He went on wishing for death for a very, very long time. Bane stripped the fool naked and shaved off all the hair on his body, then bound him with rope. He coated the fool's body with oil and cut one of his toes, just a tiny bit . . . but it was enough. Then he dangled him over the side of the ship, until he was no more than a few inches above the water.

We were going fast enough that the force of the wind and the water stung the fool, or so we gathered from his screams when he awakened. The salt got into his tiny little cut as well and burned. And the oil which coated his body increased the already strong power of the sun here at the equator. Before long the fool began to bake alive.

And then came the sharks.

Bane had been careful to make only a small incision, so the fool would not bleed out too quickly. Bane was very careful indeed. The cut was large enough that even the small drips attracted many, many sharks. After the first time a shark took a bite, gaining the prize of a large toe, Bane raised the fool up a tiny bit. A few more nibbles, and another shark took off half his foot. Bane raised the fool. More small bites and all that was left of that foot was a heel.

It went on for hours.

At one point Bane brought him up far enough to put a tourniquet around the fool's thighs, to ensure the game would not end quite yet. And for the rest of the day Bane gently raised and lowered the fool, ever so precisely, so the sharks would be able to reach him, but not too much of him.

Bane made each and every one of us stay there the entire day, watching. We were all ready to pass out from the heat and lack of food or water, but we would look at the fool screaming there and know better than to complain or faint.

It was amazing how long the fool lasted.

When it was finally all over, Bane left the remains of the body to hang just out of reach of the sharks. Over the next two weeks it was picked apart by birds, until finally there was not enough left for the ropes to hold onto and it fell into the sea.

Bane did not have to tell us the point of this lesson. It was a test, of course. No one had made eye contact with me before—my reputation at Peña Duro made sure of that—and even the fool had been wise enough to avoid me like the plague. But now none so much as looked at, much less came within two feet of, another person for the remainder of the journey.

But at least we had enough food. In fact, we had too much. After a few days, I cut back to one meal a day—one very large meal—so I wouldn't feel so sluggish.

I drank as much *agua* as I could, however, because it was nice to be able to drink water without spending the rest of the day having it pour right back out of you, even if the water's taste—or I should say lack of taste—took some getting used to. Clean water was something else I had previously dismissed as a myth. This adventure was becoming quite the education.

I think Bane noticed my change in diet, but he only smiled slightly. Perhaps he appreciated having at least one lion around who was tough and smart. Like him.

And it seemed that Bane was expecting to be reunited with another smart man, someone he spoke of like a partner. Bane called this man "Sin Tzu," and by his tone it was clear that he had great respect for him. Apparently our mission was part of a much greater plan, set into motion by Sin Tzu. I wondered what kind of man it was who could earn such respect from Bane.

One morning, Bane called us together in the belly of the great ship and informed us that we were within a day of Gotham. I was pleased. Bane still had not fully explained the plan to us—a fact which did not seem to bother my fellow travelers, but had begun to prey on my mind. Bane had mentioned an "old foe," and again, this made me curious. As strange as it was to hear Bane speak of this Sin Tzu man as a sort of friend, it was stranger still to hear him speak of an undefeated enemy.

I knew I could handle anything that came my way, but it was always better to know a little bit ahead of time, to prepare yourself. It was the difference between walking out alive and walking out alive with a wound. I did not mind pain, but if it could be avoided, that was a good thing.

"We now enter the next phase of our mission," Bane said. "Tomorrow we will be in Gotham. The day after that we will destroy it. Whoever survives will have his pick of the spoils."

He told us a little more of Sin Tzu. By the time we got to Gotham, a great battle would already be raging. In addition to aiding Bane in releasing all of us from Peña Duro, Sin Tzu had apparently emptied Gotham City's Stonegate Prison and some of Arkham Asylum, sending criminals and maniacs out into the streets. The mayhem they induced would be the backdrop for our attack, which was to be launched directly at the general opposing Sin Tzu. I supposed this must be the same enemy of whom Bane spoke so darkly.

The mouths of many of my fellow travelers fell open

like babies looking for the teat. Had they dismissed Bane's earlier promises of wealth so easily? I myself simply nodded. Yes. This felt right. My destiny of greatness would be fulfilled. It was as I had always known. I was prepared to do whatever it took. The audacity of the plan held no surprises for me. There can be no greatness without ambition, without willpower. I had all and so I would have all.

Bane gestured to the enormous crate behind him. I had already noticed that, unlike the dozens of identical crates around it, this one was open.

"This," Bane announced, "is to be your home for the next forty-eight hours." He paused. "When the crate is next opened, you will kill the creature before you. I have no need to tell you what that creature is. You will know at the appointed time."

There was not a man aboard that ship who would have dared to question Bane . . . but there was not a man aboard who was happy about this information either. Few of us had ever lived in anything even close to a house for any length of time, and we did not care for enclosed spaces. Just being in the ship's hold was a trial for most of us.

To be packed into that crate like . . . something other than men . . . it was a thought unthinkable.

Yet it was to be so. We went forward. And, amazingly, Bane came with us. He led the way, so he was at the very back of the crate, where he could keep an eye on all. Flesh pressed against flesh. I was the last in line, and thus the first in front. I could see the man to my side, but none behind me. Never before had I been in such a vulnerable position. Always had I watched my back. This thought gave me considerable pause.

The lid came down and we were all smashed together in darkness. And then the torment began.

I cannot begin to describe to you the feeling of being in that crate. The feeling of knowing you were almost certainly going to die without ever getting out. Knowing that, if you did get out, you would die without a doubt, because Bane would kill you for coming out too soon—or this mysterious creature would kill you for coming out on time.

My life has not been a pleasant one, but those two days still stood out amidst all the other routine horrors I had faced. The only thing to do was imagine what nightmares awaited me, should I even live to see them.

To keep my mind occupied, I began to create for myself a small hole where I might get at least a tiny bit of fresh air and perhaps even gain a small bit of sight. Where the seams met at the corners, there was the tiniest crack where the wood was not flush.

I had carried a bottle of water with me everywhere I went on the ship so as to always be flooding my body with this new, delightful, never-ending supply of clean water. I conserved it now—the more I took in, the more would come out, and the air around me was foul enough after only a few hours. I had no wish to add to the already almost unbearable stench.

So I would wet my finger and slide it along the crack between the two boards on the front of the crate. Then I would attempt to wiggle my fingernail between the boards and create a gap. Wet, wiggle. Wet, wiggle. For two days I did this, stopping only when sleep overtook me for up to three minutes at a time. There was no room to sit down, of course, so jammed together were we, so your body was constantly fighting itself: too exhausted to stay awake, too uncomfortable to sleep.

Not all of the men had a task like mine to keep them sane. After the first endless twenty-four hours, a few of them began sobbing quietly or talking to people who were not there. Some began begging Bane to let us out. A week before these had been some of the hardest murderers on the planet, and now they sobbed like frightened children.

Bane spoke once, softly. "Silence," was the only word he said. But it was enough. No one, not even those losing their minds, raised their voices above a whisper again.

After two days my nails were but ragged shards and my fingertips bloodied . . . but I had succeeded. There was a gap no more than a quarter of an inch wide and a half an inch tall in the wooden shell—but it was mine. I briefly reflected upon the fact that it was the first thing I had ever created with my own hands—other than gaping chest wounds—but dismissed the thought quickly. It had no bearing on my current situation and was not useful, so it was to be done away with. Greatness was in my future. Those who perform manual labors are not great, unless the labor is the taking of another's life. Peña Duro, the island of suffering, had taught me that.

The endless vibration of the boat which we had felt for the last forty-eight hours had ceased. So clearly the engines had been switched off, and I knew we had docked. Still we waited. What choice did we have?

And then, after what seemed weeks but must have been more like four hours, I heard a bump. It was simply an ordinary bump, yet it made my heart skip a beat. Something about it just seemed out of place, wrong.

Then I heard something crack, and I knew I had been right before about the bump. Something was going on.

A shadow flitted past the crate—I had thought all was dark in the ship's hold, yet this shadow was somehow darker than black. I held my breath, but it was too late. The shadow was gone by the time I stopped breathing. I tried to figure out if I was losing my mind too, or if I could possibly have seen something which was darker than total darkness. Something that moved so quickly, so lightly. Almost like . . . a bat.

And then we heard the screams.

I had heard screams, oh so many screams in my life. Most I myself caused, but others I remembered from my earliest days on Peña Duro. Screams of pain, of terror, of hunger, of dismay. These were some of my earliest and most powerful memories.

But never had I heard screams such as these.

There was pain involved, *sí*. But that was not the half of it. These were the screams of men who had looked into the maw of hell and seen *El Diablo* himself staring back at them. These were the screams of men who knew that there were things in the dark—things that had never been there in the light.

Bane would terrify any human being. One look at Bane and you knew he would cause you pain such as you could never comprehend. And he would enjoy it.

But I knew, because he was wedged in here, in the crate, with me, that these screams were caused by something much more terrible than Bane.

The screams moved around the ship a bit and then there were running feet. Then a few more cracks . . . another bump or two . . . a gunshot . . . and then . . . nothing but silence.

The engines rumbled to life again and we began to move.

Was this all part of Bane's plan? Had something gone terribly wrong? I had to know, yet there was no way to find out. I had to get out of this crate, yet even I was afraid of what awaited me on the other side. But the need to move was becoming so great, I believed I would have faced *El Diablo* himself if that was the price to be paid. And then there was my everlasting desire, against which my need to stretch my agonized limbs was nothing: to prove my greatness. For, surely, what could be further proof of a man's greatness than if he killed the devil himself?

For it had to have been a demon I saw through the crack in the crate. Dark like the shadow of shadows, swift like a bat, rending screams from grown men that surpassed what even Bane in all his terrifying glory could ever hope to cause.

We did not sail long. Although time no longer held ordinary meaning for us in that crate, I don't believe we could have gone more than an hour at most. And then the engines were cut and all was still.

There was a tremendous sound of machinery and soon we found ourselves jolted and tossed as our entire crate was picked up, dangled in the air, and dropped gently to solid ground. The crate must have weighed nearly ten thousand pounds. I would not have thought it possible to move it so smoothly, yet it happened. The moment the crate touched land, my eye was at the crack.

But it did not help. I was not sure what I was looking at.

We seemed to be in an enormous cave. I could hear the cries of bats, real bats, and then . . . then something worse.

I heard a whisper of movement around us, saw through the hole I had created a light shining across our crate. Something held the light. Something that moved with a smooth, powerful grace.

I thought I had been in awe of Bane before. Bane could see none of this. He was pinned against the back of the crate. Yet he somehow sensed it was the right time and place.

"Now!" he roared and pushed forward with such force that from ten feet away he broke open the front of the crate.

Pity the men who stood in his way—for, to be more accurate, Bane had, in fact, pushed the men in front of him so hard that the force of their bodies is what burst the crate open. Men, swearing and cursing, came flooding out, and light and air came flooding in.

Bane surged towards the front, pushing the others ahead of him. They all staggered into this unknown space, weakened by lack of food, water, and sleep, exhausted from standing for two days. Yet Bane had chosen well. Faced with the unknown, they immediately realized that, once again, they must fight and succeed or they would die. A dozen knives came out, a dozen hardened killers ready to slaughter any who dared stand before them.

And yet I am not amongst them. I who could have taken any of them down and who, just moments ago, would have leapt at the chance.

I am still inside the crate.

For by then I had seen.

The Batman.

And I knew I would never move again.

I had believed him a myth. I had thought myself tough. I had thought Bane the most dangerous man in the world. I knew better now.

The Batman cannot be human. No human being can move like that. He glides as though he were a being made of oil. Each movement flows into the next as though there are no bones in his body, like he is a snake in human form. Which makes sense. Of course he is a serpent.

He is *El Diablo* himself.

He moves from person to person, and each time the man falls, some straight down, some twisting, some tossed as though they were no more than a leaf blown by the wind. He never stops moving, but his costume is so dark and his cape always flows in such a way that you can never see exactly what he does to make these men fall so swiftly. The soft crack of a bone or a skull hitting the rock floor and the screams of men are the only sounds. And of the screams there are fewer and fewer—only the men he has not yet touched are able to scream, and there are no longer many of those left.

And then there is only one.

Bane and the Batman stand facing each other. Bane smiles. "I believe you have at last found that which you sought."

The Batman nods slowly. "Sin Tzu's weapon of mass destruction . . . is you."

Bane laughs. "Perceptive as always, Batman. I shall miss you."

The Batman says nothing. He does not move. I thought I had been forced to be still for two days. I realize now that I know nothing of stillness.

After what seems an eternity—two heartbeats—four breaths—the merest moment—Bane attacks.

Never have I seen such ferocity, such brutality, such pure strength. It is clear that Bane is far, far stronger, but it does not matter. Bane may have been one of the most intelligent people in the world, but he is no match for the Batman.

No movement of the Batman's is wasted. Each of his punches may not have been able to crush a steel door . . . but it would certainly be able to dent it. And his punches are never mistimed, never misplaced. Each and every one of them is exactly where he wants it to be.

Bane gets in a few blows. But they seem to make no impact. If the Batman feels pain, he never shows it. He never hesitates, never doubts, never slows. Bane increases his dosage of venom, growing visibly larger and stronger within a matter of seconds, the force of his attacks loosening stalactites from the chamber ceiling. They plunge down with deadly speed, but the Batman never blinks. Bane strikes and the Batman is not there. A stalactite crashes to the ground, and the Batman is not there. The terrain is his.

I watch in awe as the Batman works Bane's body like a surgeon, breaking a rib here, bruising a kidney there, bloodying first one eye and then the other until Bane is bleeding inside and out.

Bane stands there, swaying uncertainly. The Batman steps back and allows him to crash onto the floor. He kneels down and touches two fingers to the side of Bane's neck, then stands up.

The Batman picks up a small device from the floor. His expression is utterly without emotion, and only the barest rise and fall of his chest give away his recent exertion.

I hear a voice come out of the device he holds. It is an eerie, oily voice that makes my teeth ache.

"Batman," it says, "you have not disappointed me. Would you like to know our next battleground?"

"I already do. And I'm coming for you." The Batman's voice is no better. It is like a whisper heated over red-hot coals, humid and strangling.

"Ah," the oily voice purrs. "But you have no idea where I am. I could be anywhere in Gotham."

"You're hiding in the last place I would expect and yet the best fortress in Gotham—Arkham Asylum."

Even I, in my makeshift hiding spot, can tell that the silence that follows—in the instant before the Batman closes the device with a snap—is one of stunned shock.

And then the Batman walks over to me.

He stands in front of my crate for a moment, then reaches out and rips away the last remaining plank. I stand there like a fool. I cannot move.

I, Ramon Domingo Sanchez Barreto Garcia-Lopez, killer of hundreds, soon to be ruler of the world, or so I had so recently thought, cannot move. Cannot breathe. Can do nothing but dimly feel the tears leaking from my eyes and sliding down my face, a sensation I have never before experienced. I cannot even blink. I have no choice but to stare at the Batman's terrible visage and await my death, knowing now, at the last, that my immortal soul will see him for all eternity as I burn in the depths of hell and he stands over me, making the worst more terrible yet.

And he . . . he knows.

"Learn from this," is all he says. Then he moves too quickly to see.

And I know no more.

Until I awaken here. The movement and sounds tell me before I have even opened my eyes that I am on a boat at sea once more.

I sit up and look around. Pain shoots through my head as I have never known . . . as does joy, something else I have no previous knowledge of. For I, who was damned to everlasting hellfire, am not dead.

It is the same ship I had been on before. All around me lie the bodies of those the Batman had vanquished. I can now see that they, too, are alive, if still unconscious. Even Bane is breathing, although he is also bound from head to foot.

I gaze up at the stars and thank my maker for bestowing his grace on one so unworthy. I know not the reason, but mine is not to question why. Mine is simply, as the Batman had said, to learn.

And learn I would. All my previous desires were forgotten. I have a new one now, one which erases all previous thoughts and needs and wishes.

Madre de Dios, pray for us sinners, now and at the hour of our death—which I hope will not be for many, many decades yet. For I have so, so much work to do, and I am, after all, only twenty-four years old. *Por favor, Padre*, grant me time to make up for my wicked ways.

A great rushing fills my ears, like the beating of a thousand dove wings. Water rises up over the hull and drenches me from head to foot. A new baptism here under the stars of heaven! The ship tosses violently, echoing my joy.

"The Rip!" cries one of the men behind me.

"It's a prison, look!"

The night sky cracks open then, leaking the light of heaven, letting it pour down on me to illuminate my moment of earthly ecstasy.

"Searchlights, get down!"

"*Maria!* That's Stonegate!"

The voice of God then thunders across the water. "Stay where you are," he says. "We have you surrounded. You will drown if you attempt to escape."

Ah, *Padre*, yes! You and your angels surround me! Never again will I drown in sin! From the darkness I have seen the light and I will strive evermore to serve You rather than the dark master whose servant I witnessed tonight.

I shall become a priest, the greatest, most humble priest who ever lived. I shall save more souls, do more good deeds, feed more hungry, clothe more naked, and give more shelter than any priest before me ever has. I shall start in Stonegate Prison, for it is there I am now surely bound. I shall serve my time there with a glad heart, and then I shall move out to cure the entire world.

With your help, Blessed Mother, and in the name of the Father and the Son and the Holy Ghost.

Amen.

TWELVE

Gareth Baxter, U.S. Federal Agent
4:30 A.M.

Soldiers line the verdant fields, as far as the eye can see. There must be hundreds of them, thousands, tens of thousands. They stand in perfect formation, shoulder to shoulder, their uniforms gleaming cream and gold under the hot attention of the sun, their heavy black boots planted firmly in the grass. They hold their chins high and their eyes low as I probe the first assembled row with my eyes.

"Captain!" I bark at the young man to my left. His lucid brown eyes snap up to meet mine as I inspect his broad jaw and clear skin. Salty sweat glimmers on his throat as he nervously licks his lips. He's a model of health and vigor, seeming to grow an inch taller as he stiffens under my inspection.

"Sir, yes, sir!"

"Where's the Tenth Regiment?" I demand.

"Guarding our rear access, sir!"

"Excellent." I shade my eyes from the sun and squint across the battlefield to where our enemies have begun to mass, disordered and drab, a scurrilous bunch of heathens, hard men who must be tamed. Behind me, I hear the approach of hooves.

I turn to see our General riding towards us, powerful and erect on a magnificent steed of purest white. He carries a mighty rod of power which glistens in the beating sun. If the uniforms of our soldiers gleam, he is truly resplendent, his golden skin lustrous in the brilliant daylight, his dark hair like a swathe of midnight to frame his face. His eyes meet mine and, ever so slightly, he smiles.

"Commander," he says quietly. His accent is soft and exotic, his voice at once as smooth as an Asian breeze and rough as the desert sands. Delicious.

I pull myself up to my full height and salute him.

"Sir."

His stallion paws at the dirt, kicking up tufts of grass. From astride the mighty beast, the general's keen eyes rove over our troops before he turns his attention once more to me. I see him slowly take in my cropped brown hair and olive eyes, his glance stroking up and down all six feet of me, the lean musculature and clean-shaven, all-American good looks. Finally he returns the sharp jerk of my salute, thereby allowing me to relax.

"This battle will soon come to a head."

"We'll take 'em, sir. This one will go down in history."

"Good work, Commander."

"I simply followed your orders, sir."

He pauses, cocking his head slightly as he looks at me so that the black-and-red yin-yang symbol stained onto his forehead seems for a moment to pulse, swirl, and then right itself. He reaches down from his stallion and thrusts the rod into my hand as he dismounts. "I know it couldn't have been easy to gather everyone on such short notice."

My chest rises slightly as I inhale, taking the gleaming

staff from him. "When I told them who summoned them, sir, they all came at once."

The general smiles again, his eyes locking onto mine. A frosty, sharp breeze blasts across the combat zone. I frown, turning towards the wind.

And wake up in my bed with a shiver. The room is dark, lit only by the streetlights outside my window, a jumble of blues and blacks, and cold. Too cold. Out of the corner of my eye I catch a fluttering movement—the drapes. I'm sure I didn't fall asleep with the window open. I work covert field operations for the federal government. My hands are always free when I walk, my pistol is always loaded, and I never fall asleep without closing all the windows. Never.

"Don't get up," says an even voice less than two feet away from the side of my bed. I sit up abruptly, instinctively pulling the sheets to my throat with my left hand, as if a few millimeters of Italian silk could protect me, while my right hand goes for my gun. "And do *not* pull a weapon."

The Batman. It has to be. We were briefed on this over and over again—no one gets tasked to Gotham without seeing the file. It's ninety-three pages of testimonials—ninety-three pages of fluff. We've got nothing, not a damned thing that'd stick. That's how dangerous this guy is.

I relax my grip on the .40 caliber H&K USP Law Enforcement Model twelve-shooter under my left pillow and turn towards his voice. Forty-six of the fifty-two testimonies I read mentioned the Batman's complete intolerance of guns.

But he had better understand who he's dealing with here. I may have started out as a civilian—a board-certified, licensed psychiatrist, actually, with a pre-med from Yale, an M.D. from Johns Hopkins, and a residency at S.T.A.R. Labs Psychiatric—but now I'm an FBI PSP IRS. Not a special agent, exactly, but rather part of the Federal Professional Support Personnel concentrating on tasks related to the Intelligence Research Specialist. I started my career with the Feds as a Supervisory Special Agent assigned to the National Center for the Analysis of Violent Crime and worked my way up from major case management advice; threat assessment; and strategy recommendations for investigation, interviewing, and prosecution to case-specific research concerning how individual offenders committed their crimes and how they avoided detection, identification, apprehension, and conviction. I've received every promotion for which I've been eligible and the agent in charge of my background investigation said I had one of the cleanest records he'd ever seen.

That's a matter of pride with me. I'm a straight shooter.

"Batman," I say calmly, just to let him know that I understand who he is. He snickers slightly under his breath.

"No, not this time. But if you don't cooperate—well, next time, just maybe."

"If you're not the Batman, then who are you?"

My eyes begin to adjust more completely to the dark and I can just make out the lines of his figure crouching on my seven-drawer dresser. He doesn't wear a cape, as I was told the Batman does, but his eyes are covered by a small mask that mostly serves to call attention to the bare skin of his face as it contrasts against his dark hair and the rest of his entirely covered body. Gloves. Boots. He's a young man, early twenties, and even in the dark I can make out the long, lean muscles rippling under his skintight costume as he moves. I watch him for ten seconds without blinking and realize that he's in almost constant motion.

"Call me Nightwing," he says, his tone almost conversational. "And hand over the Sin Tzu files."

Nightwing? I shake my head. I don't remember anything about a Nightwing from the files, but he must be one of the Batman's soldiers. We've long suspected that the Batman has a support team operating under the acronym R.O.B.I.N. (Reserve Officers of the Batman's Intelligence Network), most of them alarmingly young (kidnapped children, possibly, or runaways). I've also heard of an operative called the Dark Knight, but never Nightwing.

Nonetheless, Nightwing moves around my room restlessly, lifting objects to peer under them and unobtrusively sliding open drawers. He stops by the shelving unit to peer at my collection of porcelain figurines. I reach for the pack of cigarettes on my nightstand as I watch him, trying not to let his obvious impatience unnerve me and hoping he's not enough of a philistine to break anything.

He picks up one of the figurines in his gloved hand, peering at it with obvious revulsion.

"That's 'Willow Tree Boy,' " I inform him. He immediately sets it back in place.

"Are these some kind of collectibles?" he asks incredulously.

"You don't know about these?" I lean forward, engaged, letting the covers fall to expose my naked chest. At least this young man can leave better informed than when he came in. It would be a shame to be so magnificent-looking and not be capable of civilized conversation.

"They were started by an artist named Goebel more than sixty years ago—some of those are originals, by the way. The figurines are all based on drawings done by a Bavarian artist, and they became popular shortly after World War II when soldiers returning home from Germany brought them back as gifts. Notice they're all wearing some sort of Bavarian garb. And they're all children. Aren't they cute?"

He lifts another off the shelf, one of my favorites, and stares at me blankly.

"That's Max and Morris," I say, smiling.

"What the hell is wrong with you?" he asks with a frown.

"Don't you have a grandmother?" I ask dryly.

"What's this worth?" he counters speculatively, dangling the two porcelain boys a bit too precariously above the floor. I try to calculate how much cushioning the gray long-pile rug will afford them.

"Put them back," I say as authoritatively as I can manage.

"I need Sin Tzu's files."

"I don't know what you're talking about," I tell him. I have just brought a cigarette to my lips to light when he leaps onto my nightstand, squatting just inches from my bed. A gloved hand shoots out of the darkness and flicks away my unlit smoke. I feel certain for a moment that he's going to kill me, and then realize with a swallow that he's unarmed.

Do you have any idea how dangerous someone has to be to break into your bedroom in the middle of the night and threaten you unarmed?

As if to justify my fears, his leg snaps out behind me, kicking my H&K out from under the pillow. We both listen to it skid across the hardwood floor towards the closet before he speaks again. He still holds Max and Moritz hostage in his other gloved fist.

"I'm talking about the psychiatric analysis you've done on your current case-study subject, Sin Tzu. You remember Sin Tzu, right? The international assassin and despot, not to mention highly dangerous coordinator of tonight's Arkham Asylum and Stonegate Prison break-outs, Scarecrow's little fear gas escapade at the courthouse, Clayface's assault on Gotham Chemical, and the threat of a weapon of mass destruction homing in on Gotham?"

His voice takes on a harder, edgy quality as he leans in closer, his white teeth flashing in the sleepy blue of the bedroom. "I want his files. *Now*."

I feel the threat in his voice prickle at the back of my skull before shimmying all the way down my spine to pool in my groin. A glance towards the bedroom door on my part puts him between it and me in a heartbeat. I try a different tack, sitting up straighter and lending an edge of authority to my voice.

"Those files are classified."

This earns me a short, derisive laugh. "Come on, now," he says, suddenly at the foot of my bed, rolling Max and Moritz between long, nimble, gloved fingers. I can hear the smile in his voice. "Do I look like I care?"

"About the authority of the United States government? Maybe not, but you should."

Now he sighs with frustration, moving towards my curtains, which he yanks apart roughly. I wince. It took me fourteen months to find just the right shade of yellow linen to match the dominant shade in the Kandinsky print above the bed. Actually, it's more of a citron. I become distracted for a moment remembering his leg kicking the gun out from under my pillow.

"Do you have any idea what's going on out there, Gareth?" he asks. He's not laughing anymore. If anything, his tone has become achingly earnest. I'm tempted to lower my estimate of his age. "I wasn't kidding when I said your boy emptied out Stonegate. That's one thousand four hundred and eighty-nine former inmates running free through the streets of Gotham tonight. Now, some of them aren't dangerous to the general population, but most of them are. I can think of fourteen serial killers, twenty-nine mass murderers, sixteen repeat-offender pedophiles, forty-three rapists, and sixty-two armed burglars in their midst off the top of my head. Those are guys I know by name. Some of the ones I don't know are even worse." He pauses to let this sink in and then continues. Behind him, out the window, I can see two separate fires raging out of control on the east side of the city, adding an unnatural glow to the room. Sirens wail in the distance as if to underscore his speech. "These are the kind of guys who take nice little boys like Max and Murray here—"

"Morris—"

"—Max and Morris here, play with them for a few hours, and then leave them floating, sans eyeballs, in the Finger River by dawn. I'm sure you've seen some of their files. Kevin 'Shorty' Robinson, Ronnie Dubray, Kurt Lewis 'the Sheldon Park Pedophile' . . ."

He was right, I had read the cases, even helped with the nationwide manhunt for Dubray. But that was all small potatoes compared to the case I carried now.

"The city is under siege," Nightwing continues. "It's a war zone."

He watches me for a moment in the dark and when I don't say anything, he goes on.

"On top of that, Sin Tzu blasted a few inmates—presumably including himself—out of Arkham. You've worked at Arkham Asylum, right? It's a very special place, reserved for the deeply, incurably, criminally insane. The ones we know about for sure are Scarecrow and Clayface. They may sound like harmless loonies you could dress up like for Halloween, but they're far from it."

I still say nothing, so he begins to pace from the window back to the foot of my bed, tossing Max and Morris back and forth between his two gloved hands restlessly. Lucky little boys.

"Scarecrow is a pure sociopath—he has absolutely no awareness that torture and massacre are wrong and compulsively engages in both. He once incited a riot at Gotham State University where he used to teach, encouraging thirty-two college sophomores to tear each other to pieces during a drug-induced panic. To this day, he doesn't understand why he's being punished for that. As for Clayface—"

"I've read the files. That doesn't mean I can hand over Sin Tzu's."

Nightwing comes closer, gently pleading with me, his face briefly illuminated by the streetlamp outside. I watch his lips as they move and swallow hard. "We need to find him, Dr. Baxter. We need to get inside his head and figure out what he's trying to do so we can stop him."

Now it's my turn to laugh. It's not Nightwing's fault. Psychological profiling is a completely legitimate crime-fighting tool and probably the first thing I'd suggest if he were looking for one of the mass murderers or serial killers he mentioned previously. But Sin Tzu? I've been studying the man in person for over a year now and am hardly any closer to understanding his genius than when I started. Sin Tzu has a mind like a blazing sun.

"It's simply not possible," I tell him. "Me giving you the files, or you using them to understand Sin Tzu."

"Why are you protecting him?" Nightwing's voice is hot again, tense.

Once more my training sends a visceral warning through my body—he's volatile, dangerous. I wish I'd taken Central up on their offer of a bodyguard.

As Nightwing resumes his search for the files, now with a renewed energy, my bedroom suddenly feels too small, as if it can't quite contain him. "Believe me, if I think there's something you could do to resolve this crisis tonight that you don't end up doing, I won't hesitate to bring you in."

"Nightwing, I don't know where Sin Tzu is. Honestly. And I don't know the reasoning behind what he's doing tonight. But I do know that he *has* a reason, and a comprehensive plan. It'll probably be beyond our ability to fully comprehend, but . . . but try to understand."

I sit even more forward on the bed, warming to my topic. "We're in the position here to watch this unfold right before our eyes. It's an astonishing opportunity. This is the greatest criminal mind in the history of humankind. Watching him execute an offensive, it's—"

I catch my breath and reach again for the pack of cigarettes and lighter on my nightstand. "It's an honor," I conclude. I'm almost smiling just thinking about it. I'll write a book when it's all over, help share Sin Tzu's brilliance with the world: *The Gotham Offensive: Lessons in Strategic Genius*, or maybe *Intimate Sin: Confessions of a Mastermind*.

"There's no honor in standing by while people get hurt," Nightwing tells me, jaw clenched in frustration. He tosses Max and Morris at me in disgust, and they bounce harmlessly onto the bed. I snatch them up and place them tenderly on the nightstand before extracting another cigarette from the pack. I put the pack down next to Max and Morris and twirl the cigarette between the fingers of one hand while tapping the lighter against my knee with the other. How can I explain Sin Tzu to this young masked man who tracks through the night, deeply believing himself to be a hero?

It's not that I don't understand where he's coming from. When I was first assigned to Sin Tzu, I was shocked by a lot of the things he'd done: the bloody coup in Qurac, for example; the massacre in Chulan. I read his dossier with predictable righteous indignation. I even looked forward to my sessions with him, thinking—and I can laugh about this now—that I'd break him down, bring him back in touch with his *feelings*, help him self-actualize himself as a complete, autonomous, integrated human being. I had no idea what he really was, couldn't see the bigger picture. Sin Tzu operates in a place outside mere morality—he's *beyond* human autonomy, he's reintegrating himself with global energies we don't even have proper names for yet. He's someone we can't categorize in conventional terms. Completely outside the box.

I got the case based on the success I'd had working with Iraqi military personnel during Desert Storm. By the age of thirty-three, I had a reputation as the psychoanalytic go-to guy for military enemies of state. The profiling I'd read on Sin Tzu up to that point was a frantic mess of anxiety and speculation. I looked forward to earning his trust and getting the real man on record.

He was very patient with me in our sessions. He must have known I would never be capable of understanding even half of the knowledge he held, but he was tolerant of my questions, even sent me away with homework assignments, reading lists. When I tried to get personal with him he was direct, but never emotional. What I at first took to be flat affect was really an almost mystical ability to direct his internal energies.

I mean, yes, there was pain in his history, memories that in a more typical patient I might have worked with and tried to bring to a sense of closure. A colleague of mine asked me once about PTSD—post-traumatic stress disorder—but what the hell does that mean anywhere outside of this country? Sin Tzu grew up in a land at war and he lost his parents early. He doesn't have an exact age, but I assume he was around eight.

That's a huge psychological hurdle, no question. Even in the best of circumstances, by which I mean an absence of exterior societal adversity such as war, children orphaned at that age are almost always additionally burdened with developmental, social, and behavioral problems.

Developmentally, an eight-year-old is old enough to understand that he's been abandoned but not old enough to make sense of it. The role parents play in the emergent psychology of their children, especially in a capitalist, pro-individual culture like ours where everyone is supposed to *belong* to someone, well, I can't exaggerate its import. It's imperative to the psychological well-being of the child. Infants, who clearly have no conscious understanding of what's going on, have been known to pine and die for the loss of parents, even while in the care of others.

A child of eight losing one or both parents is likely to be consumed with feelings of abandonment and distress, and no logical explanation of what happened to Mommy and Daddy is gonna cut it on an emotional level. If the death of the parents was violent, that child may also feel the need to be incredibly on guard at all times, lest the danger that took away Mom and Dad circle back for him.

Add to that the desire to get even and the illogical but deeply held belief that there might have been something he could have done to prevent his parents' deaths, and you have a very distressed young human. Hell hath no fury like an orphan forsaken.

These were some of the issues I thought I'd be addressing with Sin Tzu. It occurred to me, too, that I knew nothing about death culture in his native country. As a society organized around the collective rather than the individual, it was possible that the death of one or two people would not be considered so terrible, that orphans in that war-ravaged part of the world might find themselves more fluidly absorbed by their communities than the ones in ours. I thought Sin Tzu might hail from the kind of place where the death of his parents would leave him very focused and with his own solid place in his societal structure, but without the possibility of getting his personal emotional needs met in any meaningful way.

And in fact, all of that is probably true, in terms of where Sin Tzu is from. It just isn't true in terms of Sin Tzu.

Amazingly, he's made healthy translations of any grief he may have held into creative brilliance for military strategizing.

I light my cigarette and regard the last space in which Nightwing stood, even though by the time I'm looking at it, he isn't there anymore.

"I don't like watching people get hurt," I tell him after I take a long drag. The hot smoke filling my lungs seems to displace cold clouds of anxiety that had been threatening to cut off my breath, and I return the lighter to the nightstand, grateful for my failure to quit. "But you have to have faith in Sin Tzu. He won't let this chaos continue unchecked. It's serving some purpose for him, and when that purpose is achieved, he'll end it."

Nightwing appears in my peripheral vision, a small stack of my personal files in his hand, regarding me warily, his head cocked. I think he's just changed his mind about me, is maybe beginning to see the truth of what I say.

"And do you have any idea what purpose that might be?"

"I'm afraid I don't." I smile as I ash the cigarette into

a small glass ashtray also on the nightstand. "It'll blow our minds when we find out, though, I'll tell you that much."

Nightwing touches something on the side of his mask and the material covering his eyes begins to glow a whitish green. He then starts sorting swiftly through the small stack of files which I realize he must have found in my briefcase. He's reading them in the dark and then discarding them, one by one, onto the floor. "What if we don't live that long?" he asks casually, without bothering to look up.

"If Sin Tzu considers us expendable, then so be it. I would rather die as the pawn of a genius than as the savior of an idiot."

Now Nightwing does look up, letting out a low whistle as he turns the glowing eyes of his mask back on me. "Sin Tzu must do a lot of work with mind-altering chemicals and brainwashing techniques, huh?"

"He can control weak minds, yes." I take another drag off my cigarette. "Why?"

He turns his attention back to the files. "Just a hunch."

I smile, catching his drift. He's like a clever little boy, mischievously bantering about insults. I wish I had more time to play with him. "You know," I muse, "it's really fortunate that I was assigned to Sin Tzu. I can fully appreciate his creativity, whereas another psychiatrist might misinterpret his genius as, you know . . ."

"Sociopathic aggression?"

"Sin Tzu is not aggressive. His choices aren't emotional. He's motivated by challenge and . . . and intellectual symmetry."

Nightwing has finished going through the manila folders from my briefcase and dumps the last one on the floor unceremoniously. I watch his gaze rake across my room as he tries to decide what to take apart next. I have to find some way to distract him.

"What about you?" I ask none-too-subtly. "How does one get to be a soldier in Batman's army?"

He chuckles softly under his breath and then beelines to the Kandinsky, hopping up on the bedstand again to gently pry the framed print from the wall and peer behind it. His movements are supple and acrobatic.

"Why? You looking for a new line of work?" he asks.

I start to take another drag off my cigarette, only to have it kicked out of my mouth. I wait for some sensation of pain to blossom across my jaw, but none comes. Nightwing bounds back off of the nightstand and grinds the cigarette out under his boot into the rug. The moment he leaves, I am going to have to treat that with stain remover and pray it's not too late. I wonder if I still have the receipt.

"It's gonna take me a week to get the smell of smoke out of this," he grumbles, sniffing at the arm of his costume with a frown.

"I'm sorry," I say, unable to repress a smile. I consider offering him the use of my shower and then decide against it. So far he hasn't felt the need to assault me. "I hope you don't have a hot date after the insurrection."

My quip earns me a brief flash of one of the most stunning grins I have ever seen. I am suddenly consumed with the desire to get up close to him and rip off his mask. But that, I remind myself, would almost certainly get me killed.

I'm imagining his gloved hands on either side of my head, preparing to snap my neck, when he jumps up onto the bed suddenly, crouching over me like Fuseli's *Nightmare*.

"Baxter, I really need those files."

"They're not here," I lie.

"Yeah," he says, moving back towards the closet. "I'd maybe believe that if I hadn't already been to your office." He begins pulling clothes from their hangers and emptying out shoeboxes, his energy unceasing.

"What would you do with them even if I turned them over to you? Are you schooled in psychiatric intake assessments?"

"I'm just the messenger boy," he answers, emptying out a hatbox full of figurine receipts. He lifts one up and peers at it with a snort. "You paid seven hundred dollars for 'Little Maestro'?"

"Limited edition," I answer flatly, suddenly intent on finding a way under his skin.

Messenger boy, huh? For the Batman, of course. Sin Tzu must know he'd face the Batman's resistance in any attempt to take over Gotham City . . . in fact, that must be his plan.

"I suppose he means to defeat the Batman," I muse aloud. Thinking of Sin Tzu soothes me, but something about my statement makes Nightwing, for the first time since he's been in my room, go still.

"That's not gonna happen," he says, his back to me. I hear the steel in his tone and admire the Batman for being able to instill such loyalty in his soldiers. For the third time in the six minutes he's been in my room, danger radiates off Nightwing in waves.

"I understand your devotion, Nightwing, but you'd better prepare yourself. Sin Tzu has never suffered a defeat."

Nightwing has turned his attention back to ransacking my closet, so I continue, mostly because the already fading nicotine buzz, the sound of my own voice, and especially my thoughts of Sin Tzu are the only things keeping me calm. "If he lets you live, you'll come to marvel at the clean efficiency of his thinking. Your worries about what's happening tonight will seem completely insignificant to you once you grasp the full scope of Sin Tzu's campaign. Wait until you stand before him in person. He's utterly magnificent; enthralling, captivating . . . "

From the closet, his back still to me, Nightwing drops his head with a slight groan. And then with breathtaking alacrity, he executes a perfect backflip that lands him once again by the side of the bed. Frowning at me with something that looks a lot like disgust, he thrusts his gloved hand in between my mattress and the box spring and thus produces the Sin Tzu report.

"Why is everything always in the last place you look?" he says quietly, shaking his head at me.

"I'm warning you again, that information is classified."

"Duly noted," Nightwing answers, flipping through it to verify that it's what he's been looking for. My brow creases in concern as he leaps up onto the windowsill, preparing to exit the way he came in.

"Wait—"

He turns to frown at me over his shoulder, impatient as ever.

"It—it's folly to go after Sin Tzu. If you get in his way he'll . . . "

"He'll *what?*" Nightwing asks menacingly.

"You care about the Batman, don't you?" I ask, softening my voice. Nightwing's eyes narrow. "Tell him to surrender, before it's too late."

"It's already too late," replies Nightwing. "For Sin Tzu."

I think about this for a second and then I nod, softly. Sin Tzu would not have bothered engaging a lesser opponent. I'm happy for him that he has found something to do worthy of his skill and intellect.

"This will sound strange, Nightwing, but if you need someone to talk to, when this is all over . . ."

Nightwing laughs bitterly.

"Prepare yourself, Doctor," is all he says. I glance down at Max and Morris on the bedstand and manage a whimsical smile.

"Prepare myself for what?" I ask, not without affection. I hope Sin Tzu doesn't kill him. I'd like to see if I could break him myself, maybe present him to Sin Tzu once his attitude has been properly adjusted. When I glance back up at the window, however, he's gone.

I remain sitting up in bed, the covers hooked on my hips. There's no way Sin Tzu could have underestimated his opponent, is there? The Batman's soldiers aren't sullied, amateur ruffians, even if they can't appreciate a nice porcelain figurine collection. They're clean, strong, loyal troops with dazzling smiles and the confidence of nightmares. I mean, if Nightwing is that formidable, I can only imagine what the Batman must be like . . .

Where is Sin Tzu? Is he truly prepared for what's coming? I wish I could stand beside him in this final battle, document his strikes and his inevitable triumph. I think about getting dressed and going out into the night to find him myself, but I'm not sure even I could risk the chaos he's unleashed.

For a long while, I simply feel the cold air against my face, and listen to the sirens.

THIRTEEN

Sin Tzu
4:53 A.M.

I have written:

*To have complete victory, the commander must
defeat both the enemy forces and their commander.
To defeat the forces without the commander invites
the commander to rise again. To defeat the
commander and not his forces leaves way for another
to rise and take his place.*

Throughout the night, I have watched the battles
rage. The enemy forces are on the brink of collapse. To
deal the death blow, I need only defeat the Batman, for
their will to fight will crumble with him. Soon comes the
moment when I shall cease to be commander and become
warrior.

The Dark Knight has vanquished Scarecrow, Clayface, and now Bane. The spiritual power of Mehta-Sua
has attuned me so closely to the Batman that this last battle came to me as clearly as if I had fought in it myself. I
felt the crushing blow to Bane; I heard the rush of breath

into his powerful lungs and the beating of his heart . . . I tasted the blood on his teeth . . . I smelled the sour, acrid smell of Bane's fear and the Batman's triumph. Most of all I saw the Bat filling my vision, growing darker and darker until all light was gone.

I have not seen such darkness since the Yanjin first overtook me.

After defeating Bane, the Batman stood victorious for a moment, catching his breath. He was not savoring his conquest—no. I know that he never reflects to gloat, merely turns his thoughts to what lies ahead. Curiously enough, I felt myself doing the same thing.

But unlike the Batman, I felt the thrill of victory. For I have finally found an opponent worthy of my skills. The haunting hollowness of my previous conquests is gone. As I watched his demonic visage, I felt a tingle run through my body that I had not felt in years. I revel in the reaction. My failed captain Scarecrow would recognize it for the galvanizing force it is.

Fear.

For, at last, and for the first time in this mortal life, I am evenly matched.

What was the Batman thinking? Did he anticipate our meeting as eagerly as I? I rejected any attempt to read his mind. Any insight at this stage would be a useless illusion, pointless. And with the battle joined, I knew that I should probably refrain from communicating with him again. The potential existed for him to learn more from me than I from him.

But the desire proved overwhelming. And besides, I am far too cunning to be manipulated so easily.

Mere moments after the battle, I hailed the Batman, and taunted him with the secret of my location, which I was sure he did not know.

But he did. "I'm coming for you," he snarled.

For a moment I was stunned, off balance. The Yanjin swelled like a held breath. The voices hissed. Their disapproval formed a barrier around my thoughts, but again I held firm. This was my battle. I would triumph. I clawed my way through the thick complexities of the Mehta-Sua to once again seize the initiative back into conscious thought.

Perhaps he was bluffing. My voice returned to me. "Ah, but you have no idea where I am," I told him.

He came right back. "You're hiding in the last place I would expect and yet the best fortress in Gotham City—Arkham Asylum."

My turn to bluff, to hide my astonished awe. "I commend you again."

"You can either stand or run," he said. "Your call."

I felt myself swell. "Sin Tzu runs from no man."

His face was hard. It was as if he were staring directly at me, directly into my soul. As I had been staring so long into his. He shut off the communicator, and the line went dead.

Let him come. I am ready.

The technological trinket in my hand is worthless now. I have lost contact with my opponent. But it matters not. Even without Mehta-Sua, I have other ways to track his location, other modern technical tools. Now I set them into action. I mean to know: Where is the Batman's command center, his lair?

But the readings I receive are outlandish. Obviously, the Batman has set up numerous jamming devices in his Batcave in anticipation of being followed. I do not know where he is or where his cave is. He has vanished into the darkness. He could emerge from it at any time. He could come from any direction.

I am intrigued. The feelings of doubt and anticipation add spice to the conflict.

I wonder if I should expend more energy tracking him, or simply prepare for his inevitable arrival. But the spirit voices within me are silent. Perhaps they have not come to a harmonious answer, and so to preserve harmony they say nothing. Perhaps they are testing my knowledge. Or perhaps they agree that this battle I have claimed is indeed to be mine alone.

I care not. I am ready to defeat the Dark Knight without their assistance. And then together the spirits of war and I will rejoice.

Leaving my post on the roof, I march down into the bowels of Arkham Asylum and return to that place where I have chosen to battle the Batman. It is the most defensible location in Arkham; a foul place where the psychic signature of terror still vibrates in the walls from long ago. Torture in the name of science, perhaps, or misguided compassion, or a little of each. The energy here is violent and unsettled, echoing still with tragedy and deceit. It lingers like a wound scarred over, visible but no longer announcing a specific hurt. I find it particularly apt that this energy will flavor my final conflict with the Batman. Physically, too, it possesses all of the elements of an arena destined for a titanic struggle—a large open space with no windows and only one door leading to the outside. Its many other doors lead to unused cells. There, I shall place my Eternal Elite and my private corps of human ninjas in case of the need for unexpected retreat.

I sink to the cool cement floor, center myself, and descend into the familiar deep womb of meditation. In my mind, I return to the beloved caves of my youth, following sheer walls of limestone back past half-buried pools of obsidian water, deep into the skyless cavern of the tomb. There I sit at the carved plaques, shrines to my bodiless teachers, the assembled pantheon of the past Sin Tzu, regulating my breath.

Amid the soft, endless circle, the rise and fall, the in and out, eternal rhythm, I go back to the beginning and retrace my battle plan.

It has worked flawlessly thus far, and grows sweeter still. I can now feel the bat inside me, his claws tightening around my soul. The nature of the battle has changed. When I began this campaign, it was to find a challenge worthy of my skills. In this task I have succeeded. My goal then was to defeat the Batman. Now I yearn to destroy him. It is a subtle difference, but one that I acknowledge with relish.

Without opening my eyes or releasing my other senses, I know that one of my Eternal Elite approaches, carrying word from the world of Arkham that I have left behind. I smile in anticipation, for my guard knows that I am not to be disturbed unless the Batman has been discovered.

The Dark Knight is near.

In my mind, I leave the cave. I open my eyes. As I reemerge into the physical world, I feel the Yanjin inside of me slosh and swill like ocean water forced into an eddy. Its power pulses within me like the great heart of the cosmos. Subjugating it to my will, I close my eyes again and focus it, drawing it into a long tsunami, ready to break. I will no longer use it gently, for telepathy or detection. I will save every drop of it for combat. With it I will drown my foe.

I open my eyes again and turn to see the stone face of my guard. He too yearns for this combat. Anticipation radiates through his iron discipline. He is pointing to the video feed, routed to my inner lair from the security cameras that ring the asylum.

Commissioner Gordon is on the security video screen. He stands before Arkham, surrounded by men in black with large weapons. Police cars flank him in rows, their lights suppressed. He does not appear aware of the blacker-than-black, flitting shadow approaching him, and it is certainly undetected by his men.

I, however, do not take my eyes from it.

One of Gordon's men is speaking. "We can storm it . . ." he begins.

Gordon shakes his head, a tight frown beneath his mustache. "Arkham is impregnable. It was built not only to keep supervillains in, but also to keep their henchmen at bay."

The shadow speaks. "Just make sure nobody gets out."

Gordon and his men spin around. The men have the Batman at gunpoint, for just a second. One of them almost fires. His finger stops at the trigger. The Commissioner is already motioning for them to lower their weapons.

"I'm going in. Don't follow me," the Batman says tersely, and then vanishes into the darkness of Arkham.

Gordon stands alone. For all his soldiers and arms, he rests his hopes on one man . . .

If indeed the Batman is only a man.

The Yanjin rises inside of me and I ache to release it. How satisfying it will be to feel it surge from my body, to watch the mighty Batman be blasted into ash!

I turn my attention back to Gordon on the surveillance. He is troubled. He picks up his communicator. He knows that I can listen in, but he seems not to care. His conscience is troubled.

"Batman, there are some things I should tell you about Sin Tzu . . ."

The Batman does not appear on the communication monitor, but I hear his voice. "Yes?"

Gordon cannot help himself. He hesitates. "He has mastered something they refer to as Yin Yang Alchemy, also know as Yanjin . . ."

"I know," the Batman responds. "Nightwing has his psychiatric evaluation files."

Gordon continues. How touching, I think, that he is able to get this off his chest before his friend is lost to him forever. "Well, I don't know how much his psychiatrist really understood. Yanjin is an ancient mental art. Its practitioners are able to turn mental energy into physical energy to heighten their own abilities and dominate the minds of others . . . That must be how he controlled Scarecrow and Clayface."

And Bane, and the prisoners at Stonegate. It extends much farther than you suspect, little man.

There is something close to mirth in the Batman's voice. "Not much of a trick, since he commanded them to fight me, which is what they wanted to do anyway."

Gordon continues, "He takes his instructions from spiritual 'advisors' he hears in his head . . ."

"So does every schizophrenic in Arkham," replies Batman.

"Just . . . be careful, Batman, he might try to use the Yanjin on you."

"It only works on the weak and the impressionable," the Batman states flatly. "I am neither." And then he turns his communicator off.

I scoff at his lack of comprehension. Does he think this is some paltry parlor trick? Entire countries have gone down on their knees before me! How like the hubris in all heroes to mock what he does not understand. Perhaps I will kill him slowly enough to allow him the opportunity for enlightenment seconds before his physical and spiritual death. Or perhaps I shall simply wipe him out, denying his essence even the small pleasure of entering the universe to be fuel for my future conquest.

For the game is very simple now. Even without the Yanjin surging within me, I know what the Batman is seeing as he enters the tunnel to my lair. For I have arranged it as neatly as any campaign.

It is dark. It is absolutely silent. The Batman peers down the length of the corridor where Gotham's most deranged criminals are housed. He moves as one expecting to be attacked at any moment. The shadows and light of the cell doors and the walls put him in mind of a surreal chessboard. A suitable meditation before this final, deadly game.

I let his tension build.

He looks in the first cell, finds the plant woman, Poison Ivy, standing there in a characteristic pose, frozen. My supposedly imaginary Yanjin has lost none of its power, keeping her in eternal stillness. The sweet but morbid smell of her gardenias touches his nose. Is there a touch of the scent of roses? For I feel that the scent of roses reminds him of something terrible; his formative event, the postulated murder I suspected so long ago. The energy I hold allows me to feel the subtle shift in his emotions. He is haunted, weak.

I speak to him through the asylum intercom.

"Impressive trophy collection, is it not?"

The Batman takes a fighting stance, awaiting attack. None comes. He considers my question. More precisely, he considers his answer.

"Tonight I'll add one more," he says.

A good answer. He remains on the offensive. I laugh. I feel like a racehorse held behind the starting gate. *Come closer, Batman, closer.*

It occurs to me that I have not laughed since I watched that last thugee destroy himself in a fit of greed and fear. That was when I first felt the strength of what I could do. In all the months of hearing the inane cackle of the laughing man they call the Joker, perhaps some of his energy permeated through my cells. I am enjoying this. The urge to fight only strengthens.

The Batman walks slowly, cautiously, past the next several cells. He finds the laughing man and the harlequin girl. They, too, are frozen, still held by the power of Yanjin. He flinches. I can almost feel the goosebumps crawl up his flesh. He knows not whether they are alive or dead. I know that he has never seen anything like this before, and it has its calculated effect. He knows precisely how difficult these costumed obsessives are to best.

In this case, the enemy of his enemy is not his friend. By defeating them, I have just proven myself to be an even more dangerous foe.

The Batman is not sure how to react. I have skillfully regained the initiative.

"What happened to them?" he asks. His voice sounds strangely naive and yet also matter-of-fact. Yes, very American.

"Control the mind . . . and the body soon follows," I say.

The Batman passes the empty cells of my captains. "Why did you choose the ones you did? Why did you pick Scarecrow, Clayface, and Bane?"

A good parry. His question surprises me. It shouldn't, because, after all, he is a detective. In moments of doubt, all men rush to those things they know. They flee to the familiar.

I consider telling him my reasons. I am bursting to share them with one who would understand them, but I steel myself. To know and to keep silent is power. Many battles have been stolen from the jaws of victory by aimless banter. Besides, there are greater mysteries facing him. He should be worrying about the Yanjin: where it comes from, how he might stop it, and how much it will hurt when its full force is unleashed upon him. But I allow him the courtesy of a reply.

"Let us just say that they were less . . . unpredictable than the others."

"Good answer, but it isn't true. You had other, more complex reasons, didn't you? You never intended for them to defeat me. They were a series of diversions, intended to control me while you took the city."

"Indeed. And they worked. You took your eyes from the battlefield . . . A fatal error for a commander."

"Correct. Just as you are doing now."

Fool. It is true that I no longer watch the city, and I suppose his captains could be regaining control of Gotham as we speak. It would be easy enough to maintain a visual on the battlefield and confront my enemy directly at the same time if I relied on the same sort of faulty tools and technologies he uses. It is true, too, that the Batman has maneuvered himself to now block my path back to command. But I need spare no thought for what happens outside. I have mustered all my energies for the duel that is rapidly approaching. The Batman would be wise to do so as well.

He will understand soon enough.

I consider unleashing my guards to destroy him, but

that would be predictable, what he wants. And I will not give him what he wants.

The Batman steps towards my cell, which is still shrouded in darkness. But it is empty. "You did not expect to find me in there, did you?" I taunt over the intercom.

"I expect only the unexpected."

The Batman turns to see a boarded-up doorway on the far wall. I watch as he investigates it. He knows that the boards have been recently hammered in. He knows that he will find me behind them. In a motion that is as surprising as it is deft and accurate, he kicks them down. It is perhaps the most artful display of force I have ever seen without the use of mental channeling.

He stands before me. Proud, indomitable, dark . . . Larger and more graceful than I had anticipated. The moment has arrived. I am struck with a sense of destiny. "Thus it ends as all battles should end . . . two great commanders facing each other on an empty battlefield."

His response is terse. "Let's finish it."

Oh yes, Batman. Indeed we will.

I smile as I unleash my human attackers, my black-clad ninja warriors trained in the martial arts of Chulan. Fourteen of them immediately surround the Batman, who takes out two with a swift fling of a sharp, gleaming Batarang before the circle has even closed. He tries to keep his initiative with a high-speed side kick aimed at the head of one of the remaining twelve ninja, but the ninja blocks, crossing nine-inch metallic claws over his face defensively like two multipronged sai.

Four ninja flip over the shoulders of their teammates, flying into striking range as they all unleash their sai claws simultaneously. The Batman drops low, executing a flawless sweeping hook kick that takes down three of the four. The fourth has time to see it coming and leaps straight up in the air as the Batman's leg passes beneath him. With a movement as fluid as silk, the Batman follows through on the arc and then seems to disappear under his billowing cape. He reappears suddenly, standing precisely behind the fourth ninja the moment his soft tabi boots touch the cement floor. With a gesture too fast for my eyes to follow, the Batman renders this ninja unconscious, hurling his inert body at four more who approach.

The three knocked over by the sweep kick halt in the act of rising to somersault out of the Batman's way, each making a rolling retreat in a different direction as the Batman slides towards them. There's a blur of movement, and then the Batman's boot is crushing the throat of one of the tumbling ninja as his gloved hands knock two hooded heads together.

After that, only two of the fourteen manage to get close enough to him to strike; one tearing the very edge of his cape with his claws while another breaks into an offensive ring of six. His kamikaze attack is meant to deliberately exchange his consciousness for the chance to rake the claws of his right hand across the Batman's briefly exposed left arm. For his sacrifice, he manages to tear the Batman's armor and draw a slight trickle of blood. His shriek of pain as the Batman retaliates, however, makes it clear that, mere seconds after completing the move, the ninja has paid the price for his cunning.

The rest take less than a minute. The Batman dispatches them swiftly, concentrating fully but not yet breathing hard. But a moment is all I need. I chant to summon my chi. I feel the swiftness of the power filling me, the effortless connection of my consciousness to its depth.

It takes a second or two, at most. I expect the Batman to attack, but he does not. He must know that I am at my most dangerous defensively when I chant. He watches me, watches as I absorb the light, as electricity jumps from my sockets and I turn the Mehta-Sua inward, becoming a black hole.

My power grows.

The end is near. The end for the Batman.

He is fascinated. He studies me like a scientific experiment. "The gold skin . . . the symbol . . . I understand it now. You're a human dynamo. You suck in energy . . . harness it and then dispense it tenfold. Were you less mired in megalomania and capable of compassion, you could be a great light in this world."

From the great distance of my power, I respond. "I *absorb* the light."

"Fine," he says. "I am a creature of the darkness."

I focus all of my energy and then fire on him. The room flashes intense white with a soundless roar of pure power and then goes pitch-dark. There is nothing. Silence.

Have I destroyed my enemy with the first blow?

Different emotions, unfamiliar, course through me. Disappointment. Relief. A slight sadness. I have not known these since my days before the cave. I had hoped for a greater finale. But then I resign myself and accept the more recognizable glow of victory, an emotion that does not tarnish, no matter how familiar it becomes.

I listen for the humming approval of the spirit voices and hear nothing. I have destroyed the most fascinating, most worthy opponent I have ever faced for them, and still they scorn me? I am thinking of how best to rouse them when, from the darkness, comes a sudden flash—a jolt of pain—and then blackness once again.

I feel myself hurtling through the air.

The electrical light from above flickers, and I turn to see the Batman's controlled spin as he follows through on his uppercut. Then, in a graceful move more like that of a dancer than a fighter, he comes back to his center of balance and turns to face me.

Rage courses through my blood as I stumble across the room like rubbish in the wind and crash, shoulder first, into a stone wall. He has dared to touch me? I, Sin Tzu? I force down my fury. Surely I had expected no less.

I shrug off the pain as he steps towards me. Again, I summon the Yanjin.

Words flow through my mouth like churning water as the Yanjin courses through me. "For me, the battle is already won. Your armies are defeated. But no matter what happens, my armies fight on," I taunt, circling.

The Batman smiles cryptically. "Wasn't it you who wrote that if the head is cut off, the body soon dies?"

"Do not mock me with my own words!" I hiss.

He sees it coming. Yanjin, once summoned, cannot be stemmed, merely dispersed. I shoot another bolt of pure, enraged energy at him. This time, I use the whip pattern, designing it to strike not where the Batman is standing, but where he will jump. The whip bolt snaps to the side of the Batman, just missing him as he doubles back on his evade. With building fury, I watch it snake into one of the cells where my Eternal Elite wait. A member of my guard bursts into flames.

A negative energy emerges from the flaming corpse. Now the spirit voices of the Yanjin rise around me, shrieking, battering, displeased. Dissonance fills my head. The voice that is mine and not mine is fragmented. I struggle to suppress it and yet cannot help but hear individual voices breaking from the flow of chants—kings long dead and conquerors of ancient history, vanquishers of the ages, all screaming different instructions. Opposite instructions. Some call for me to attack. Some order me to retreat and regroup. Some insist that the enemy must be probed further.

For the first time, I feel a separation from my spirit voices. We no longer act as one; their cacophony fills my head. I force them to order, I still their shrieking cries. This single miscalculation has not lost us the battle! Only one deliberate hit will destroy our enemy, a single hit I am certain to achieve if I could but concentrate!

I do my best to ignore the discord in my head, focusing on the struggle at hand. I do not have time for the foolish arguing of long-dead kings. I must focus on the duel before me. On my mysteriously powerful rival.

But as I focus, his image presents me with only negative information—information of what is not:

The Batman is not hit.

The Batman is not standing where he was when I fired the bolt of energy.

The Batman is nowhere to be seen.

The Batman has slipped within the darkness.

The Batman is the darkness itself.

I summon the Yanjin Flame in order to find him. The energy builds, spins, flares, and illuminates . . . nothing.

I turn around, directly into a striking fist. Again, I tumble through the darkness.

On my back on the ground, I draw the Yanjin from the very walls, from the earth beneath the floor, from a sky I cannot see. Its power grows weaker. If I had begun with the force of one hundred, I now have the force of perhaps sixty. But it is enough. The great tide of Yanjin within me still swells for battle.

I take a great risk, and target three blasts: one to where the Batman is, one to where the Batman leapt after my first attack, and one to where the Batman might leap should he evade in the opposite direction. Three bolts of pure Yanjin lightning streak away from my glowing palms.

The energy of these bolts, once released, turns the room pure black. The light is swallowed. All energy is sucked from the room. For a moment there is only silence, vacuum. The voices that are mine and not mine whisper to each other, still discordant.

Then, I hear him. His breathing is irregular—suppressing a moan of pain. I hear his footsteps. He is staggering. My spirits soar. The voices hum with speculation.

In the darkness a lock turns. Wounded, he is trying to retreat, to escape!

I fire a bolt at where I know the door to the cell to be.

As my reward, I hear another grunt of pain, and then the sound of halting breaths fill the darkness. There, my spirits, do you see? My enemy is badly injured. His powers dissipate, leaking out with his strength.

This battle will be a war of attrition. Who will regain their strength first?

My powers rise, gathering in the expanding emptiness within my soul. For I have written:

In an unknown environment, blind aggression will lead to success three times for each time it leads to failure.

Spurred on by this very real gap in my enemy's defenses, I endeavor to summon the Yanjin once more. To my great frustration, the energy flickers, feebly. I must wait for it to build. But it is not my only weapon; my body, too, is a tool of destruction. Targeting the Batman's breaths, I spin around, kicking, chopping, and punching in the darkness.

I connect only with empty, dead air. The Batman,

even wounded, is swift. The challenge is not yet won. But I am confident. I will smite my enemy with the next volley of attacks.

Slowly, as if seeping sheepishly in through the walls, light slinks back into the chamber.

I behold the Batman crouching against the dank stone floor. He is breathing heavily. His cape is charred, and I can see red, burned flesh on his chest and upper arm.

With an intoxicating rush of adrenaline, I prepare to finish him. I can offer him no quarter . . . no terms for surrender. This man who moves amid the darkness the way I channel the forces of light, this commander who calls upon warm, living soldiers the way I summon cold, dead ones—he must be destroyed!

Movement catches my eye from another corner of the room and I turn to see my five remaining Eternal Elite, standing in their cells, watching. My heart leaps. I will force them to defend me while I conserve the last of my Yanjin and build yet more energy, enough to make my final blow a truly punishing strike that will obliterate the Batman once and for all! I order them to seize the Batman with silent mental commands in the voice that is mine and not mine.

But . . . they do not respond.

For the first time since the caves, I feel the emptiness.

They do not hear me.

I am alone,

It is an old feeling from childhood—from the time before the cave, when I was alone and merely tolerated by the cult, unloved, without nurturing. Abandoned. I refuse to acknowledge it. It is an aftereffect of the energy I have spent. My powers are merely ebbing from me at a greater rate than I have calculated. The battle is not yet lost.

For the Batman's powers are waning as well. He crawls, like a broken, damaged creature, into the darkness. I can still track him by the sound of his ragged breath. I volley. But he is still strong. His returning blows cripple me further. Much as I would like to crush him with my body alone, I know what tactics dictate. I must end this or face defeat.

I summon the Yanjin, gathering its weakening force within me. I speak aloud. "Bring the intruder to me."

But still the Eternal Elite do not respond. They stare back at me blankly with faces as immobile as . . . stone.

"The Bat is defeated! Claim our victory! Make him bow down to me in surrender!" I shout.

A voice startles me, shooting out from the darkness with calm precision. His voice. The Batman's voice. "You have risked control of your own army for vanity, Sin Tzu," he says. His voice is low and grim and unfaltering.

"MOVE!" I shout again to the lifeless stone guards.

"Perhaps your spirit guides feel you have lost focus in this battle."

I ignore him, trying silent mental commands on my Eternal Elite once again. But still there is nothing; no movement, no response. I feel the voices stir petulantly within the recesses of my mind. Now there is no longer cacophony. They sulk, they refuse to speak. This is betrayal! *Has the Yanjin forsaken me?* This is neither the time nor the place for such pettiness! The enemy is in my sights, just waiting to be finished off! How dare the Yanjin toy with me now? I reach into the depth of my being and summon the last of my power with a mighty roar. Trembling with rage, I target all five of the silent stone golems. To defy their general is death. I will finish this myself!

Yanjin lightning flashes around me in a pentagram form. Each shot strikes one of the guards and ricochets off to strike the next and then the next. My guards are blasted apart in a dust storm of destruction. The room thunders with my rage and then their anguish.

And then there is a thunder more deafening than any I have ever heard before. I fall to my knees and press my hands against my ears as the spirit voices rage, screaming and howling and screeching in a thousand discordant tongues inside my head. The noise is like a physical force, abusive, brutalizing.

But then, all at once, it is dark and painfully silent.

I am covered in ash. And despair.

I cough. From the moment I entered the cave at Chulan I have radiated with power. But now . . . now I am depleted of all Yanjin. Mehta-Sua is closed to me. The voices have deserted my head. The spirits of the ancient Sin Tzu have returned to the tomb to protect themselves. I am empty.

As the light sneaks back into the room, I see the Batman's face.

He grabs me roughly and lifts me off the ground. I notice that the heavily muscled arm that grips me is still smoldering from my lightning, though nothing on his countenance betrays his pain. He holds me face to face. I try to summon my strength, but it is like trying to grasp water in my fist; the Yanjin leaks from me wetly, without force. I feel the spirits leaving me, a mass desertion, an exodus. My weakness enrages me. Somehow the Batman is doing this! The demon has driven the spirits from me!

Indeed, the abandoning spirits whisper of enmity. They hiss about obsession. In a panic I reach out for them and feel their cold condemnation as they continue their desertion. Why? WHY?

I search my energy for impurities and am shocked by the sudden density of my own internal space. The spirits are not just leaving of their own accord, they are being crowded out, forced from my soul by a rising tide of sentiment. Fury, envy, hate, revenge, fear, awe, covetousness, suspicion . . . When did my soul begin to fill with such contaminants? These are . . . these are human weaknesses! Is this what the spirits tried to warn me of when they filled my mind with memories of my past earlier this evening? Did they sense that I had begun to take the extraordinary powers they have bequeathed upon me for granted? Or even that, at some level, I wished to desert them myself, reaching out to this dark mirror nemesis with the attention and will they felt rightfully theirs?

For the first time in my life, I plead. I regale the spirits with my need: Let me defeat the Batman, and I will once again prove to be your loyal servant! I have always done what you bid, always thought of nothing but . . .

. . . war.

I have abandoned the war for a petty rivalry.

And so the spirits of war desert me.

The Batman speaks, his harsh and forceful voice stabbing at me. "You made the worst mistake a General can make," he says darkly. "You misjudged your enemy. My motives were nothing like yours."

My heart constricts, and then expands.

Compassion.

I thought it was a weakness. I was wrong. It is his strength.

Language finally comes to me. It is my own. Weak and hollow—echoing of false bravado, although I mean every word. "Savor sweet victory now, for there will be another day."

As I slip into unconsciousness, he speaks again. "Don't count on it."

I fall further and further into oblivion. Back into the

dream of the terrible things that happened once in this room . . . a man, a woman, a fight, blood. Then, the spirits take me to a worse place yet.

I see a young boy. It is night. He is with two adults, his parents. The world is in perfect balance. A loving family. They talk about a movie they have seen that night. They laugh.

A man emerges from the darkness. I feel a chill. The man demands money. The father's internal energy shifts, he comes to a place of resistance. He moves to stop the attacker. A gun goes off . . . twice. The mother falls, a broken strand of pearls raining down beside her. The father falls, first to his knees, and then all the way forward. The boy stands utterly still, a look of shocked incredulity stamped across his face.

The man with the gun could kill the boy, but something stops him. Maybe it is a darkness that comes before his eyes. Maybe it is the Yanjin—or the reverse of the Yanjin—that blinds him. Maybe he doesn't see the boy. Maybe his hand will not squeeze the trigger. Maybe spirit voices scream in his ears and make him run.

Something happens. Something that is hidden in the darkness behind a cowl.

He flees, leaving the boy alone. The boy stands wordlessly over the corpses of his parents, peering upwards into the night and into the endless darkness.

I am a stranger to human sensitivity. The spirits taunt me with my own emotions, still insubstantial and hazy to me. These are a secret ammunition, a source of power I do not comprehend. They are also a liability, waiting in the dark of the mind to be tripped over or fallen into like quicksand.

The Batman can read them, in himself and in others.

My fuming heart betrayed me to him in a tongue I do not know.

The thick tangle of voices in my head falls silent.

Darkness claims me.

FOURTEEN

Batman/Bruce Wayne
6:00 A.M.

I taste blood in my mouth and smell the smoldering of my own flesh, but can once again retire for the night with all my teeth intact. As my heart rate decreases and my blood begins to flow less rapidly, I can feel the muscular aches and bruises begin to set in. Rest and a hot shower will cure these injuries. I wish it were as simple to cure the wounds done to spirit and psyche.

The only way to win a war is to avoid it. By definition, war entails conflict—in this case the struggle over a city that was neither the attacker's nor the defender's to win or lose. Gotham belongs to her citizens, and tonight her citizens were brutalized, bullied, manipulated, and marked as fodder. They were put at risk to satisfy one man's pride, and for this, too, some lost their lives.

I find this completely unacceptable.

Sin Tzu has been taken back into custody, Stonegate and Arkham are once again functional, all but six of the one thousand four hundred and eighty-nine convicts let out of Stonegate earlier this evening have been accounted for, Bane is imprisoned, and Scarecrow and Clayface will make their morning group therapy sessions at the asylum. Gotham is, for the moment, safe, and yet I feel neither victorious nor relieved.

The senselessness of Sin Tzu's attack cloaks me in a cold fury that I have not had time to indulge until now.

As I watch from this rooftop, Gotham begins to wake, moving numbly about her business in the first pale light of morning. Those who survived the night carry on. If they feel outraged or grief-stricken over the attack, they keep it mostly to themselves, confessing their distress only in the impulsive offerings of camaraderie they silently exchange with one another as they brave the streets. A man purchasing coffee from a cart on Vern Avenue meets the eyes of the vendor for a moment as he drops fifty cents into the tip jar. *Alive.* Two women waiting for the bus by the Giella Gardens exchange brief smiles. *We're still alive.* The driver of a black Subaru waves a silver Jetta through the intersection ahead of him. *Go ahead, buddy. At least we're both alive.*

Sin Tzu's ego—my ego—means nothing to these people. Just as these people mean nothing to Sin Tzu. They have jobs to get to, stores to open, children to send off to school. Most of them will be entirely forgotten by history, while Sin Tzu's name lives on in infamy. They have no idea how they managed to survive the night, and they have no idea how important they really are. I don't fight just to protect them. I fight to earn the right to live among them. The 8,168,564 citizens of Gotham City are my neighbors, my inspiration, and my responsibility.

My existence is spent battling for the safety of this city. I don't honestly know if it's possible to live in complete safety, complete peace. But I do know that I'll do everything within my power to bring us as close to that point as I can, even if I have to use violence to do it.

I abhor violence. It is a language of tyrants and thugs, and one I have therefore become fluent in. But it is never my first choice when initiating discourse.

The drag of the wind blowing in from the harbor behind me alters as it confronts new mass. Nightwing must have just appeared on the adjacent roof. The slightest scent of strawberry hair conditioner follows. That would be Miss Gordon. And so Robin will be in attendance as well—Nightwing would not have come to check on me without ascertaining Tim's safety first.

A young man, a young woman, and a child—in the daylight and in normal clothing they would look like an attractive, youthful family. And indeed, they each have every opportunity to live a rich, extraordinary life. Each of them has a razor-sharp intellect, an embarrassment of health, and a safe home. Why, then, are they standing in the icy wind on top of the Von Gruenwald Tower at six in the morning wearing masks and fighting to stay awake?

Because they've been up all night with me, risking their lives repeatedly, loyal soldiers who owe no more allegiance to me than to anyone else in this city. They would tell you that they enjoy the work. For that matter, I would tell you that I prefer to work alone. Some truth in both statements, but also inaccuracies.

On their part, they're omitting tales of physical agony, extreme psychological stress, and the psychic scarring sustained by so regularly seeing so much of humanity at its worst.

On my part, I'm failing to acknowledge the degree to which they anchor me.

And after fighting so close to Sin Tzu tonight, it is not a concept I intend to refute.

Anchoring. I've heard police talk about the difficulties they have dealing with "civilian" life after a long beat.

Spend enough time with criminals, and everyone begins to look suspicious. One comes to understand that most people act from predictable, even selfish, motives. We may all choose to believe that we behave morally, but the very basis of our current social structure encourages competition, vanity, and circumstantial ethics. You can make the choice to be moral, but it's rarely the path of least resistance.

The kids on the roof behind me are three shining examples of the exception that proves the rule. They do not struggle to behave with integrity. It comes naturally to them. Each one of them has supplied me with intel, recon, even assistance in physical combat.

Their true value to me, however, is as envoys of hope. They keep me connected to the physical world, and to the living future. Who would Sin Tzu have been had he had similar connections?

"Sun's coming up," Nightwing says behind me.

This does not require a response.

"You think they'll be able to keep Sin Tzu in Arkham this time?" Robin asks.

"Technically, he never left Arkham," Miss Gordon . . . Batgirl . . . adds.

The edge of the sky is touched with red and I feel a strong impulse to get indoors, back into the dark. Over time, I have learned to honor such impulses, but for now I wait.

"Sin Tzu will be reviewing his failures in this battle for quite some time to come," I tell them, without turning to face them. I am battle-weary and bloodied and find the idea of eye contact with other human beings exhausting. Or maybe I just don't want them to see me injured. Dick, in particular, has a tendency to worry himself over my every scrape and mood change. "He's too egomaniacal not to try another offensive, but he'll need time to re-group."

"For a start, I think he could use a new shrink," Nightwing quips. I am about to smile when I remember the twenty-three Gothamites in critical condition as a result of tonight's turmoil.

"Does anyone know the condition of Mrs. Langley?" I ask.

"The cranial trauma?" says Nightwing. "Alfred said she was still in ICU at Mercy."

"And Mr. Mayfield's still in the burn ward," says Robin, anticipating my next question. "But he was listed as stable as of four A.M."

"I'll run checks on the rest of them," Batgirl adds softly. "Twenty-three total?"

I nod and finally turn to face the three of them, ready to evaluate their condition. All are standing tall and breathing evenly—a small miracle, and precisely what I expected.

Robin looks a bit dazed from exhaustion, his thirteen-year-old body intent on resting and continuing its work of growth. He cannot suppress a slight yawn. Standing between Nightwing and me on this rooftop, he looks relaxed, open, and trusting, his defenses lowered. And yet tonight he fought alone for hours, without pause and without complaint. He exhibited initiative, bravery, and also a great degree of loyalty. The mission I gave him earlier concerning Alfred was the kind of task he might sometimes consider "bogus," or "too far off the action." Tonight he accepted it without argument and saw it through without incident. I would tell him how pleased I am with his performance if I could afford to allow him any slack.

I cannot. His life depends on his continuing to strive to impress me.

As for Alfred, I should have known where we'd find him. He can no more sit still on a night like this than I can. Service defines his life, and his nature. In some strange way his skills as an estate manager, medic, social critic, and perpetual rationalist come together to supply me with everything I need to persevere. I am grateful for his safety and acknowledge to myself once again that I absolutely could not do what I do without him. He is one of a very small handful of people on the planet who can continuously surprise me.

I turn my attention to Nightwing, one of the others, who now stands grinning in the warming dawn. His smile is so familiar that it almost teases a response from me, though when I look at him these days I am filled with equal parts of pride and bewilderment. How can it be possible that this independent, self-governing young man standing nearly as tall as me is Dick, the pint-sized acrobat, the little monkey wrench in the gears? Alfred assures me that this reaction is a very normal fatherly response, but how many fathers look at their grown sons and think, *How on earth did you stay by me all those years and yet survive? Thank God you're still here, thank God you're still alive . . .*

The odds really were against it. Dick knows of my concern and dismisses it as an unexamined reaction to my parents' deaths. But while there was no reason to expect any harm to come to them, there have always been plenty of reasons to fear for Dick's safety. I fought with three of them tonight.

Scarecrow proved as sociopathic as ever, completely unconcerned with the consequences of his actions. However, he also revealed a hint of suicidal ideation, an affect I have not observed in him before. Was he just playing with his own fear of mortality, or is his pathological disregard for mortality progressing to include himself? He seems to be reinventing himself as some sort of avatar of death. His targeting of Jim concerns me as well. I'll have to keep closer tabs on him.

Clayface behaved more predictably. He must have been quite easy for Sin Tzu to manipulate. I still have scientists at Wayne Medical working to find a cure for hydromethotrexamede poisoning—the main ingredient in RenuYou—but so far we have had absolutely no luck. The best Hagen can do for himself now is try to accept his condition as much as possible. People survive with worse.

And Bane. Sin Tzu was not wrong in his assessment of Bane's prowess; he continues to be a dangerous, formidable enemy. I can attribute many of tonight's larger bruises to him and do not feel confident of a long internment for him at Stonegate. His intelligence and strength make him extremely difficult to keep behind bars. Like Sin Tzu himself, I know Bane will be back for a rematch.

The steadily increasing sunlight catches in Miss Gordon's hair, creating a conflagration of beauty. I can only imagine how proud of her Jim must be. If she insists on being out on these streets, I will have to do more work with her. She's a natural athlete and exceedingly sharp—but I cannot vouch for her safety unless I've trained her myself. I have no right to endanger her by accepting her onto my team.

Nor do I have the right to tell her she cannot defend the city she loves.

"I—I should really be getting home," she says, becoming self-conscious in the growing light, or perhaps under my gaze. I note her proximity to Nightwing, who has angled his body in such a way as to subtly impede her departure. For a moment I wish I could free them, send them off into the sunlight to play.

But it is not within my power, for I never constrained them. For whatever reason, they choose to bind themselves to me unbidden.

"I'll walk you," Nightwing tells Batgirl, but she smiles and shakes her head.

"That'd be real hard to explain to Dad."

"Why? Who's your dad?" Robin asks, and Nightwing and Batgirl laugh.

I dive off the roof, the sound of their laughter following me down eight stories. By the time I discharge the grapnel line, the cacophony of city traffic is rising up to meet me.

And then all I can hear is the wind.

Earlier this evening, I laid two roses on the ground where my mother and father were murdered over twenty-five years ago. I also left fresh flowers at their grave. In my early teens, I vowed to them that I would avenge their deaths.

It turned out to be a more difficult promise to keep than I imagined.

My parents were casualties of random urban violence, a robbery gone awry. How is that avenged? It's not as simple as catching the man who shot them, who was merely a symptom of an epidemic of poverty and crime. As far as he was concerned, they could have been any couple in the whole city; as far as they were concerned, he could have been any criminal. The crime was impersonal and arbitrary, and its effect on me was so deeply personal and searing that it is almost impossible to conceive of suitable retaliation. It wouldn't be enough to incarcerate every criminal in the city. Until every couple venturing out in the evening to stroll the streets of Gotham can do so with a reasonable assumption of safety, my parents' deaths mean nothing.

I have a lot of work to do.

My thoughts turn to Sin Tzu as I move northwest across the city rooftops. Two contrasting images of him fight for dominance as I try to appraise this new enemy. Both are more emotional evaluations than I would like.

The first is the image of Sin Tzu the warlord. I can directly connect him to the deaths of seven thousand four hundred and twenty-eight people over the course of his public career, and that does not include murders he may have been involved with before his first official strike in China. The energy he wields is powerful and dangerous, as is his mind, devoid as it is of empathy and social aspiration. War is a compulsion for him, not a means to an end. He's the most treacherous kind of sociopath: disconnected from morality and even his own humanity, incapable of seeing others as anything but military fodder. This is the Sin Tzu whose face first appeared in my communicator monitor; bold, bloody, ruthless, and megalomaniacal; a figure nearly impossible not to hate.

The second, competing image is of Sin Tzu the orphan. He doesn't have a different name for himself in this state, as I do, and the mask he wears is permanent, but I understand the division in his nature all too well. Like me, he turned to discipline to forge an identity for himself that would allow him to move through a world that had seemed to abandon him. Like me, he gave up much of what it means to be fully human in order to be something more effective and less vulnerable than that. Like me, once upon his chosen path, he never hesitated, never looked back. Like me, his mission began to consume him, became much farther-reaching than he had initially dreamed.

But unlike me, the beings that finally did come into his life were unsympathetic, lifeless things, incapable of forming the bonds of family. Unlike me, the things he fought for—the "art" of war, the approval of the dead, the mastery of destruction—were transient and insubstantial. And unlike me, the things he put his trust in could not be looked in the eye, the powers that he drew from depended on more than his own strength and will. This is the Sin Tzu I saw in the final moments of our fight: broken, terrified, lost, and unendurably alone; a figure nearly impossible not to pity.

I understand him well enough to be sure that he will rise again, and that when he does, his wrath will be terrible. I will be waiting for him, and this he knows, too.

Jim is clutching a Styrofoam cup of Colombian coffee and exiting Arkham when I arrive. He has clearly not been home to change clothes or shave. His dedication to the safety of this city unquestionably equals my own.

I have heard the hypothesis that my presence in Gotham attracts as many criminals as it deters. This was certainly true in the case of Sin Tzu, who targeted this city specifically as a means of engaging me. I cannot comment on this phenomenon except to say that it is certainly not true of Jim. Everything he does in this city improves it. He is completely effective and irreproachable, whether acting as a citizen, policeman, or father. My respect for him is boundless.

I deliberately let my shadow pass over him as I head up to the roof, and in short order he dismisses himself from the four officers and two security guards in attendance and joins me above the crowd and away from prying eyes.

"They're mopping up now," he informs me, taking a

sip from his coffee. His slight wince of displeasure tells me it's cold.

"Sin Tzu was not mistaken about the importance of leadership. When the commander is defeated, the army surrenders soon after."

I think about Sin Tzu, once again isolated within a cell in the asylum beneath our feet. It is perhaps disingenuous to dismiss the man as a mere megalomaniac. Like Scarecrow, Sin Tzu is a sociopath, unable to appreciate the difference between wrong and right, but he is also a scientist of sorts, obsessed with the equation of war.

There are some minds I would rather not understand, but all too often the only way to defeat an enemy is to be more aware of his motives and methods than he is himself. The rage and hunger of a genocide survivor boil just under Sin Tzu's detached exterior. He's obsessed with war because war has been a consistent and merciless nemesis for him, costing him everything—his family, his future, and finally, his humanity.

Interesting that the key to his undoing tonight should prove to be his inability to fathom compassion. Did he make a promise to his absent parents to punish them for their perceived abandonment? Or was he determined to survive at all costs just to spite them?

At its most basic level, my self-appointed mission to eradicate crime in this city is a defense against feeling personally cornered and robbed by it. By the same token, Sin Tzu's maniacal warmongering is an expression of his unconscious desire to tame and rule those forces which threaten him. My fear drives me to protect, and so I am regarded as a hero. Sin Tzu's fear drives him to attack, and so he is deemed a criminal.

"I should have told you that Sin Tzu had been transferred to Arkham," Jim says tightly, grinding his back teeth as he eyes his own shoes. "But I was sworn to secrecy."

"I understand," I answer. "We all have to honor our vows."

To the living.

And to the dead.

About the Authors

Devin Kalile Grayson is the award-winning creator of *Batman: Gotham Knights* and current writer of *Nightwing* for DC Comics. She lives in Oakland, California, and says the commute to Gotham City is a breeze.

Screenwriter, game designer, and novelist Flint Dille's works include the *Agent 13* series with David Marconi, the *Sangard Interactive Gamebook* series with E. Gary Gygax, and the *Night of Sin Tzu* video game script. Flint lives in Los Angeles, California, with his wife, Terri, and two children, Zane and Gwynna.

Acknowledgments

DEVIN KALILE GRAYSON would like to thank the following:

Scott Peterson, for helping me out of a jam with such humor and grace, and for introducing me to Batman in the first place; Michael Wright, for leaving the porch light on in Blüdhaven for me; Mark Waid, for being available online at two in the morning for grammar and punctuation lessons; Denny O'Neil, for the inspiration in life as well as writing; Matt Brady and Dwight Williams, for the wonderfully informative *Daily Planet Guide to Gotham City* from which several of the statistics in this book were taken; editor Dana Kurtin, for the support, help, and cheerleading; all the creators of *Batman: The Animated Series*, for this wonderful continuity we've had so much fun playing in; my co-writer Flint Dille, for writing such a cool video game that WB wanted to make it into a novel and for his great work on the Sin Tzu chapters; Dad, Linda, Mom, and Frank, for understanding why they couldn't see me for over a month; and along those same lines, Arnold Feener, Dave Segale,

Kaye Jarrett, and Dave Kinel, for letting me off the hook, game-running-wise, six weeks in a row.

FLINT:
Thanks to Buzz Dixon for the (literally) kick-ass help on the in-game fight voiceovers, and for reading over the game script to catch any embarrassing errors. Thanks to Frank Miller, who took the time to talk to the game's producer, Benoit, designer Mario, and me about Batman over a few beers and lunch; as well as Jim Lee, who brought Sin Tzu to life. Oh yeah, and Paul Dini, who's spent countless hours talking to me about Batman over the years; and John Warden, who taught me more than I'll ever know about Strategy.

VISIT WARNER ASPECT ONLINE!

THE WARNER ASPECT HOMEPAGE
You'll find us at: www.twbookmark.com then by clicking on Science Fiction and Fantasy.

NEW AND UPCOMING TITLES
Each month we feature our new titles and reader favorites.

AUTHOR INFO
Author bios, bibliographies and links to personal websites.

CONTESTS AND OTHER FUN STUFF
Advance galley giveaways, autographed copies, and more.

THE ASPECT BUZZ
What's new, hot and upcoming from Warner Aspect: awards news, bestsellers, movie tie-in information . . .